ASKING
FOR IT

Also by Louise O'Neill

Only Ever Yours

LOUISE O'NEILL

ASKING FOR IT

Quercus

First published in Great Britain in 2015 by

Quercus Publishing Ltd
Carmelite House
50 Victoria Embankment
London EC4Y 0DZ

An Hachette UK company

A CIP catalogue record for this book is available from the British Library

HARDBACK ISBN 978 1 78429 586 8
TPB ISBN 978 1 84866 417 3
EBOOK ISBN 978 1 84866 820 1

10 9 8 7 6 5 4

Typeset in Perpetua by Nigel Hazle
Printed and bound in Great Britain by Clays Ltd, St Ives plc

For my beautiful sister, Michelle.

Last year

Thursday

My mother's face appears in the mirror beside my own, bright red lips on powdered skin.

Her hair is still in its neat bob despite the sticky heat. She gets it done every Saturday. 'I deserve a treat,' she says as she leaves the house. 'I don't care how expensive it is.'

Karen Hennessy gets her hair blow-dried three times a week. She never mentions the cost.

I'm flushed, patches of red breaking out on my cheeks, the greying vest top I wore to bed sticking to me. I look from her face to mine.

You're so like your mother, people always say. You're the image of her.

'Morning,' she says. 'What are you doing, just staring at yourself in the mirror?' She frowns at my chest, at where the nipples are outlined through the sweat-stained fabric.

'Nothing,' I say as I wrap my arms over them. 'What do you want?'

'Just checking you were awake.'

I point at my desk, my open laptop, the folder full of notes, a copy of *Fiche Bliain ag Fás* and an Irish–English dictionary next to it. 'I've been awake since five,' I say. 'O'Leary is giving us an oral test today.'

Jamie will get full marks, of course. O'Leary will close his eyes as she speaks, leaning back in his chair. He always looks surprised when he looks up again and remembers who is talking. He can never quite believe that the best Irish he has ever heard from a student is coming from someone who looks like Jamie.

'Oh, never mind Diarmuid O'Leary.' She half smirks. 'Does he know you're *my* daughter?' I don't answer.

'I brought you your vitamin tablet,' she says. 'You're supposed to have it before your morning meal.'

'I'll take it later.'

'Emmie, come on. The Health Hut had to order these in especially for you.'

'I know that, Mam.' Her lips go a little thin, so I make myself smile at her. 'And I really appreciate it.'

'I'll leave it here, shall I?' She places the tablet and

a glass of water down on my bedside locker, next to my iPhone and a collection of mismatched earrings.

She stands behind me again, placing one hand on my left hip, the other at the base of my spine, and tucks my pelvis in. 'You need to watch your posture, pet.' She smells of flour and cinnamon, undercut with the same floral perfume she has used for years. I can still picture her sitting at the vanity table in her dressing area, a silver silk dress spilling over her body, a slash of bright lipstick, her pale brown hair twisted into a chignon. Her hair was longer then. Dad would call up the stairs, 'We're going to be late, Nora,' and she would reply 'I'm coming, dear,' using that special voice she used with him, with all men. (And I would wonder why she never used that voice with me.) The last thing she would do was take her perfume, unscrewing the gold top, and spray some on to her wrists. I'd sit at the top of the stairs, watching her hips move under the silk as she walked down towards Dad, waiting for her. His eyes never left hers, not even when I started to cry as they left, arms flailing as the babysitter restrained me.

Her fingers rest on my stomach. 'Do you have your period?' she says. 'You look a little bloated.'

I push her hand off me. 'You don't need to worry, Mam. I'm not pregnant.'

I walk away from her and check my phone. Ali has texted. Again. Even though I still haven't replied to her last two messages.

'Please don't speak to me like that.'

'Like what?'

'With that *tone*.'

'There was no tone.'

Her shoulders are tense, and I know that she's ready to go downstairs and tell Dad, tell him that I've been disrespectful and rude. He will sigh and tell me that he is disappointed in me. He won't listen to me, no matter what I tell him, no matter how hard I try to explain. *There are no 'sides'*, he'll say. *Please treat your mother with more respect.*

There is only one side in this and it's never mine.

'Sorry, Mam.'

She pauses. 'Take that vitamin,' she says, 'and then come downstairs to join Daddy and me for breakfast. He wants to see you before he goes to work.' She turns at the door to look at me, her gaze working up my body, lingering on my face. And I know exactly what she is going to say to me.

'You look beautiful this morning, Emmie. As always.'

The door closes behind her and the air in my room turns to soup. I wade through it, pushing up my sash window in search of relief, and I can taste the tang of sea salt on the breeze. There are six other houses curving around the bay like a wishbone, all painted in the same canary yellow with black window frames and doors; sensible, boxy cars lining the glistening tarmac drives, Toyotas and Volvos and Hondas in black or silver, as if any other colour would attract too much attention. Nina Kelleher from two doors down is herding her daughters, Lily and Ava, into the back of a station wagon, a slice of toast between gritted teeth as she slams the door behind Lily, waving at Helen O'Shea who is on bended knees in the next driveway, retying her son's shoelaces. 'God, the state of the place,' Jamie had said last year when we drove past a council housing estate on the outskirts of Ballinatoom, the neat houses crammed together, carefully tended flower baskets on the windowsills, gangs of snot-nosed children playing red rover in the small patch of green in the centre of the houses. Maggie had just gotten her driving licence then, and the four of us had piled into her parents' Volvo, giddy with the sense of freedom, that we could go anywhere or do anything we wanted, although we never went much further than Kilgavan. We drove around Ballinatoom, through the roundabout, up Main Street, past the church, left at the garage at the edge of town, past the playground, down the bypass, and then we were at the roundabout again. We went around

7

and around and then around again, eating penny sweets and watching out for boys we knew in other cars, Maggie insisting we turn down the music as we passed O'Brien's funeral home, a thin line of people queuing up outside to pay their respects. 'It's just so *yellow,*' Jamie said, turning to look out the back window as we drove past the estate. 'Is there some sort of rule that says every housing estate built in this country has to be painted in bright yellow?' Out of the corner of my eye I could see Ali, sitting next to her in the back, elbowing her, jerking her head at me.

'Here,' I said, turning around and handing Jamie the iPod. 'Choose something else to put on, I'm sick of this playlist.' And I could hear Ali breathing a sigh of relief that there hadn't been any fighting, not this time.

Jamie wouldn't say that now. She would be happy to live in our estate now.

'For fuck's sake, Mags,' I say when I open the passenger door, shoving empty Tayto packets, a hockey ball, her mouth guard, a leaking red pen and about twenty balled-up pieces of paper out of the way.

'Sorry.'

'You say that every morning. And yet it's *still* the same.' I take a book out of my bag to sit on to protect my skirt from the red ink. 'It's roasting in here. Are all of the windows opened?'

'Yes,' Jamie says from the back seat. 'Such a pity you're not allowed to use the Volvo any more, Mags. That has air con, doesn't it?'

'I brought some of Mam's muffins,' I say. I don't want to talk about the Volvo. I reach into the bag and hand one to Maggie.

'They're still warm. God, your mom is amazing,' she says, steering with one hand as she takes a bite.

'Yeah,' I say, looking out the window. 'She's the best.'

I turn around to offer the sandwich bag to Ali and Jamie. Ali pushes her blonde hair extensions back off her face. 'No, I shouldn't.' She takes a sip of coffee from her Nespresso travel mug. 'Mom has signed us up for this paleo food challenge thing.' She bites her lip. 'Emma?'

'Yeah?'

'Are we OK?'

'What?'

'You never texted me back earlier. I was just wondering if you were mad at me or something.'

She's wearing too much eyeliner, black gloop crusting in the corners of her eyes. Her dad bought her a Mac beauty case a few months ago, like one a professional make-up artist would have, filled to the brim with products and brushes. 'Just because,' Ali had told us with a shrug. Maggie had squealed with excitement, grabbing a liquid eyeliner to practise on Jamie. 'Cool,' I said. My fingers gripped a highlighting cream I had wanted for ages, but Mam said was too expensive. 'Although I always think the Mac girls look like trannies.'

'God, Ali,' I sigh. 'Get a grip, will you?'

I hold out the muffins to Jamie. It doesn't register, so I wave the bag at her. 'Hello. Earth to Jamie.'

She hesitates, looking at the bag and then at me again. She pulls a muffin out and takes a huge bite, almost swallowing it whole.

'Take it easy,' I say. 'Even Maggie didn't eat hers that fast.'

'Shut up,' Maggie says. 'I had swim club at 6 a.m. I think I can have a muffin if I want one.'

'I don't know how you get up that early,' I say. 'I got out of bed, like, ten minutes before you arrived. I'm a disaster.'

Jamie crumples the muffin case in her hand. 'I was up earlier than that, Mags,' she says. 'I had to study for the Irish exam we have today.'

'Oh shit,' I say. 'I totally forgot about that. I am so screwed.'

'Didn't you forget to study for physics last week as well?' Jamie narrows her eyes at me. 'What a coincidence.'

I got seventy-eight per cent in that test, Mr O'Flynn placing the booklet on my desk with a wink and a murmured 'Well done'. I left it on my desk so everyone could see it. 'And then in first place,' he continued, 'congratulations, Jamie.' Jamie took the booklet from him, '93%' scrawled across the front in red marker. Her expression didn't change as she shoved it into her school bag. I looked at my own again, and it was as if the number drifted off the page, rising towards me, searing itself into my eyes. I wanted to rip it into fifty thousand pieces.

'Well done, J.' I smiled at her, in case anyone thought I was jealous. 'God, I wish I had actually studied now.'

'Did you get new sunglasses?' Maggie asks when Ali reaches into the yellow Céline backpack her mother bought her in Paris to grab a pair of tortoiseshell Ray-Bans. 'What happened to the Warby Parkers your dad got you?'

'It's weird,' she says, and I make my face stay very still. 'I can't find them anywhere.'

'Ah, no,' Maggie says as she turns into the car park.

'Can't you just get a new pair?' I ask, and my voice sounds normal. She can afford it.

'You can only get that style in the US. I told you that.'

'Oh yeah, I think I remember them.' I hang my backpack off one shoulder and start rooting through it to find my Irish textbook. 'They were a bit big for your face anyway, hun.'

St Brigid's Secondary School lies ahead of us, a grey concrete building with square windows glinting in the sunlight, squat prefabs lined up beside it. The gym, tennis courts and car park are to the front; steep grass fields at the back, cows mooing frantically whenever students sneak behind the gym to smoke. The nuns had sold the land to fund a new convent at the other side of Ballinatoom, the remaining five rattling around the cavernous building, just waiting to die. I look around me at the hundreds of girls getting out of cars, flushed and uncomfortable. The dark grey pleated woollen skirts, grey knee-high socks and dark grey blazers are not suited to this heat, but Mr Griffin, the principal, made an announcement over the intercom yesterday that 'the uniform must be worn in its entirety, girls, no matter what the weather. There are no exceptions to that rule.'

All the students walk forward, laughing and linking arms and rifling through backpacks and yelling out at each other to wait up. I nod at the girls passing who call my name, say hello, ask me where I got my sunglasses, or what lip gloss I'm wearing, or how I'm feeling about our Irish exam today. I smile, telling them, 'Thanks, you're such a pet,' and doling out compliments in return. I imagine them whispering to themselves once I'm out of earshot about how nice I am, how genuine, how I always seem to have time for everybody, how it's amazing that I can still be so down to earth when I look the way I do.

By the time the final bell rings, I am exhausted. I have to smile and be nice and look like I care about other people's problems or else I'll get called a bitch. People don't understand how tiring it is to have to put on this performance all day.

Ali:	Where are you now?
Ali:	Did you get my last text, hun? I'm not sure if it delivered.
Ali:	Hey, just checking if you got those last 2 texts I sent you. Where will I meet you guys after class? I'm waiting over by the Home Ec rooms.

'Hey.' Ali is lying on the concrete by the Fiesta, using her blazer as a blanket, her skirt rolled up and shirt open to catch as much of the sun as she can. 'Did you get my text messages?'

'No.'

I check the time on my phone, putting my hand above my eyes as I squint back at the school.

'For God's sake,' I say, 'where is she? I don't have any suncream. I'm going to start burning if she doesn't get here soon.'

'Shit,' Ali says. 'I didn't bring any with me. I'm so sorry. I should have thought.'

'You *know* how delicate my skin is,' I say, holding my blazer over my head as a shield. 'And remember what Karen said about sun damage, she said those UV—'

'Yeah, if I wanted a lecture from my mother, I'd ask her for one myself.'

'Emma!' I wince when I hear that squeaky voice. 'Hi!'

'Hi, Chloe.'

It's Chloe Hegarty, her hair standing up in a halo of frizz at her hairline, breakouts all around her jaw and chin, one patch of acne crusted over with yellow pus. I wish she would go and see a dermatologist. I turn away, pretending I need to get something from my bag.

'Ouch,' Ali says as Chloe slinks off.

'Whatever,' I say. 'Oh, thank Christ, there they are.' I see the girls coming out from the prefab nearest to the gym. Maggie's head is bent over her iPhone already, her fingers keying furiously, Jamie trailing behind her. 'Hurry on,' I call out to them.

'Sorry,' Maggie says when she reaches us. Her blazer is wrapped around the straps of her bag and she fumbles underneath it for her keys without looking up from her phone. It beeps again, and she lets the satchel fall on the ground, her face softening as she reads the new text.

'Mags,' I say. 'For fuck's sake, I'm roasting. Can you at least open the door first?'

'Sorry,' she says again. 'Eli says he's going to be in the park at five with the lads if we want to meet him there.' She puts the phone on the bonnet of the car, placing the bag next to it as she searches through it. She pulls out three tattered copybooks, old tissues, a leopard-print headscarf, an iPod, Tic Tacs, a leaking lunch box and an A4 pad. 'They're definitely in here somewhere,' she mutters, using a tissue to wipe away the oily residue of her tuna sandwich from her fingers. 'Wait! Here they be.' She opens her own door first, recoiling as a blast of hot air hits her in the face. She crawls into the car, opening the other doors from the inside.

'Jesus,' Jamie says as we get in, cranking all the windows open. 'When are you getting your new car again, Ali?'

'Only three months to my birthday!' Ali takes out her iPhone and swipes through her camera roll. She holds up a photo of a brand-new Mini Cooper in baby blue, and Jamie and Maggie 'ooh' in appreciation.

'I feel like you see Mini Coopers everywhere these days,' I hear myself saying. 'They're so popular now.'

Ali's hand drops to her lap, the photo still open on her iPhone.

'Slow down,' I tell Maggie as we drive through the narrow main street of Ballinatoom, with its skittle-coloured buildings on either side, pubs and butcher shops and greengrocers all crammed in. A group of lads from St Michael's are clogging up the footpaths, ignoring an elderly man trying to navigate his way past them with his walking stick. Their navy V-neck sweaters are tied around their waists, showing off sunburnt arms, sweat patches on unbuttoned white shirts, and blue-and-yellow striped ties hanging loosely around their necks, brown bags of penny sweets and cans of Coke clutched in their hands. There's a large banner strung between two buildings, in black and gold, announcing a country and western music festival. It's the same every year, hundreds of middle-aged fans from all over the country arriving in Ballinatoom wearing cowboy boots and Stetsons, humming Nathan Carter songs under their breath. 'Aren't you lucky to live here?' they ask us, breathing in the country air. Why? I want to ask them. Why are we lucky to live here? But I know the answer that I'll get.

It's so beautiful here, they'll say. There's such a sense of community. People look out for each other.

It's true, I guess.

Within minutes we're at Connolly Gardens. There is a square of grass with a narrow ribbon of concrete path looping around it, and a marble fountain in the middle. A curved terrace of large Georgian houses surrounds the square, all painted pastel shades. We park outside Maggie's house, a pale azure colour with cream window frames, a black cast-iron knocker in the shape of a lion's head on the cream door.

'Aren't you going to come in?' Maggie asks as she pushes the front door open and only Jamie follows her. Ali sneaks a look at me, waiting until I shake my head before saying, 'No, I'm good, Mags. I'll wait here with Em.'

'And will you get suncream?' I call after them. I don't want to have to talk to Maggie's mother. The last time I called, she disappeared into her 'client space' to get a 'book that I think will really speak to you, Emma'. Hannah had caused quite a stir when the Bennetts moved here from North Cork five years ago. She was heavily pregnant with Maggie's baby sister, Alice Eve, her bump bulging underneath tight T-shirts, and she didn't seem to care that old ladies tutted and averted their eyes when they saw a flash of swollen belly. Everyone whispered about the new arrivals, about how the mother was 'a play-therapist, whatever that means', and the father was 'an accountant, and must be doing well for himself if they can afford that house – you should have seen the price of it', and that the other daughter was twelve or thirteen, and really pretty. I had been worried when I heard that until I saw Maggie and realized that, yes, she was pretty. But she wasn't prettier than me.

'I hear the wife is very attractive,' Mam said to Dad the night they arrived, passing him the mashed potatoes at dinner. 'And I do think it's brave of her to allow herself to go grey so early.'

'Ready?' Maggie says when she opens the front door again.

'Oh, you look so cool,' Ali says. Maggie is wearing that men's checked shirt she bought in a charity shop as a dress and her metallic silver Doc Martens. She has a paisley scarf holding her curls back, wrapped twice around her head and tied in an oversized bow on top, almost the size of her head, and multiple silver rings on her fingers.

'Jesus,' I say. 'You look like you're Amish or something.'

Maggie takes a look at herself in the oval mirror hanging above the spindly-legged hall table. I hate that stupid mirror, with the affirmation 'You are beautiful on the inside' scored into it in silver cursive script. I always want to scratch it out.

'Savage,' she says happily. 'I love the Amish look.'

Connolly Gardens is quiet at this time of day. There are three women sitting on a bench at the other side of the green, all wearing black Lycra leggings, skintight vest tops and Birkenstocks, rolled up yoga mats and brown paper bags from the Health Hut at their feet. Another woman in cropped combat trousers and a baggy T-shirt is chasing after two toddlers, holding out suncream and wide-brimmed hats; some older children in swimming togs are running around the fountain, barefoot and shrieking.

'Hey, sexy.' A boy in a baseball cap leans out of the window of a car parked at the entrance to the gardens, his friend in the passenger seat throwing his head back in laughter. We keep walking, pretending we didn't hear. I look back over my shoulder, and of course he's pointing at me.

'What's wrong?' he calls.

'Nothing's wrong.'

'Then smile a little. I bet you're even more beautiful when you smile.'

'Christ,' I say, when there is enough distance between us. 'Why is it always me?'

'Maybe because you were the only one who looked back and made eye contact with them?' Jamie says, and Maggie starts laughing.

'Come on, J, don't be so hard on her. Maybe she fancies one of them.' Maggie presses her lips together to stop herself from giggling. 'The guy in the white tracksuit was a total ride. Just your type, right, Em?'

'Ha ha,' I say as she and Jamie laugh. 'Very funny.'

Ali doesn't join in, turning her face away from us. 'It's so hard being your friend,' she told me at one of Dylan Walsh's parties last year. She was wasted, slumped over the toilet bowl. 'It's like I don't exist when you're around.' She retched again, and I checked my phone to see if anyone had texted me. She wiped her mouth with the back of her hand. 'And sometimes –' she took a deep breath – 'I think that's why you like being my friend.'

I told her not to be silly. I told her she was wrong.

'To be honest, Al, I'm sick of being harassed,' I told her.

'Yeah,' she said, 'it must be *so* difficult being told you're gorgeous all the time.'

'It's superficial,' I said, because that's what you're

supposed to say when people tell you you're beautiful. 'It doesn't mean anything.'

Ali stops suddenly, Jamie slamming into the back of her. 'Shit.'

'Jesus, Ali. Watch it, will you?' Jamie says, taking a step back.

'Shhh,' Ali says, then lowers her voice. 'Look who's over there.'

Sean Casey and Jack Dineen are in a corner of the park, hidden behind the fountain. They've taken their shirts off and are throwing a rugby ball between them, their bodies lean and tight.

'Sean is gorgeous,' Ali sighs.

'Sean needs some suncream,' I say.

He looks up at this, his face going even redder when he sees me.

'Hey, Emma.' He waves at me, and I wiggle my fingers at him in return.

'You shouldn't encourage Sean,' Maggie told me on Skype last week. 'You know how Ali feels about him.'

'I'm not encouraging him,' I answered in exasperation, 'but what am I supposed to do? Ignore him? I don't want to hurt his feelings.'

(I don't want him to think I'm a bitch.)

'I'll check us in on Facebook,' Ali says when we find

an empty bench. I sit at one end, Jamie next to me, both of us using the shade of a small oak tree behind us to block out the sun. Ali takes off her blazer to use as a blanket on the grass, Maggie borrowing mine to do the same. She gives me the fair-trade, fragrance-free, chemical-free suncream Hannah uses, and I pour some between my palms, rubbing it into my legs. I look up to see if Jack Dineen has noticed, but he's tackling Sean to the ground, trying to wrestle the ball off him.

'Eh, I think that's rubbed in at this stage, Emma.'

'What?'

Jamie squirts some suncream on to her legs and starts to massage it into her skin. 'Oh yes, yes, yes,' she says. 'That feels *so good*.'

'Oh, shut up,' I say. I close my eyes, the world around me fading into sound. I can hear the cars driving past, a horn blasting. 'Do you think he likes me?' Ali asks Maggie. 'Has Eli ever said anything to you? Did he say if Sean ever mentions me?' Maggie's reply in soothing tones, breaking off mid-sentence every time her phone beeps, a fly buzzing near me that I'm too lazy to swat away, one of the mothers calling, 'Fionn, come here right now, it's time to go home.' I'm only half listening as Ali tells a story about some girl in the States who had her webcam hacked while she was touching herself and she took an overdose.

'Ugh,' I say, screwing my nose up. 'That is so gross.'

'Hannah says that masturbation is a normal thing for people to do, men and women,' Maggie says as she checks her phone again.

'What, so you do it, do you?' I wink at her. 'When I rang you last night and you said you were "in the shower" you were actually rubbing one out?'

'No!' Maggie's face is turning red. 'Of course not.'

'Hmm-mmm.'

'I don't,' Maggie says. 'I *don't*. Hello, I have Eli, don't I?'

'*Anyway*, back to the story,' Ali says. She hates it when we interrupt her like this. 'The hacker sent this girl the video of herself and told her if she didn't, I don't know, give him a blow job or something, he'd post the video on Twitter and send a link to everyone at her school. So she killed herself.'

'How did she do it?' Jamie asks, leaning forward on the bench until her belly touches her thighs, but Ali just shrugs.

'It's a pity it wasn't Sarah Swallows.' I stretch my arms out over my head. 'She would have been only too delighted to help, the dirty slut.'

'Who's a dirty slut?' a boy's voice asks. It's Eli, Conor and Fitzy behind him.

23

'Hi, Eli.' I push my sunglasses back into my hair and smile at him. 'How are you?'

'I'm good—' he begins, but Maggie screams as if she hasn't seen him in years, and jumps up into his arms, wrapping her legs around his waist. He manages to sit down with her still like that, murmuring hello to her through kisses. He doesn't finish his sentence to me. Conor sits beside me, of course.

'Hey, Emmie,' he says. I raise an eyebrow at him. 'Emma, I mean.'

'Hey.' I lower my voice so none of the others can hear me. 'How's your mam?'

'She's fine. Still very tired, but I guess that's to be expected. Thanks though.'

'For what?'

'For asking.' He looks at me intently, his left shoulder grazing off mine.

'Lads, would ye get a room?' Fitzy says to Maggie and Eli as he sits next to Jamie.

'Sorry.' Maggie breaks away, but only barely, their faces inches away from one another. She brushes a hand over Eli's tightly cropped Afro. 'I can't resist him.'

My phone beeps. Ali has checked us in again, this time including the boys. I roll my eyes and stretch out my legs, only half listening as the heat melts through my bones.

'It's roasting, isn't it . . .'

'Suncream . . . factor fifty . . . fair trade . . .'

'Fair what?'

Laughter. A patch of sun breaking through the trees, the sky moving. The buzzing fly is back, landing on my legs, tickling my skin.

'. . . and I can't get the exact right shade of blue. I want it to look exactly like . . .'

'. . . yes, I *loved* that piece, even though Mr Shanahan said he thinks the Turner Prize is worthless these days.'

'Mr Shanahan is basically mentally unstable.'

Fitzy and Maggie have become really good friends since Fitzy had to get a special dispensation to come to St Brigid's so he could take art for his Leaving Cert. 'She's cool,' he told me at his last birthday party. 'She's pretty, but she's still smart *and* funny. Let's face it, you can't say that about too many girls in Ballinatoom, can you?' I couldn't think of a response for a second, and he looked triumphant. 'Maggie's the best,' I said at last. 'Although I'm surprised to hear you think she's pretty. I didn't think you were into . . .' He stopped, fear freezing his features, and I felt a grubby joy. 'Never mind.' I smiled, and took another slice of birthday cake. 'You don't mind if I have some more, do you?' I looked around at the nearly empty room. 'I'm sure there's plenty left.'

There is a screech of brakes, tyres against concrete. A blast of heavy metal music, a girl's voice screaming over it, 'I'm warning you, if you . . .' A car door slamming, a horn blaring. 'Fuck off, you stupid cunt,' a boy's voice yells as the car speeds off.

'Dylan and Julie?' Ali says, without even sitting up to check.

'Yup.'

'God,' Maggie sighs, reaching to give Eli a kiss on the neck. 'I'm so glad we're not like that, baby, aren't you?'

'Aw, baby,' Fitzy does a perfect imitation of Maggie's voice before a rugby ball whizzes past his face, almost hitting him. He fumbles over Conor's outstretched legs, Jamie snapping, 'Hey, watch it,' as he falls against her. He apologizes, shaking his hair out of his eyes, and gets to his feet, brushing grass off his rolled-up chinos.

Dylan runs towards us, Jack and Sean close behind him. He rescues the ball, tossing it from one hand to the other. He doesn't even look at me, just stares at Jamie.

'Hey, Jamie,' he says. 'How're things with you?'

She ignores him, slumping down in her seat, tucking her chin into her chest.

'I said, "Hello, Jamie,"' he says again. 'No need to be ignorant about it.'

'Take it easy, Dylan.' Maggie pushes her round John Lennon glasses up into that mane of unruly hair and squints at him.

'Who asked you?'

Eli stands up, his six-foot-four frame dwarfing Dylan. Eli used to get into a lot of fights before, whenever some kid decided that calling him the N-word seemed like a good idea, but he promised Maggie that he'd learn to control his temper. 'He says that he'd do anything for me, that he's never felt like this about anyone else before,' she told us when they first started hooking up, almost three years ago now. I wanted to tell her that boys always say that, in the beginning.

Eli starts to say something to Dylan when his phone beeps. He looks at the screen and frowns.

'Who is it?' Maggie asks.

'Mum. She can see all of us out here.' He turns towards a primrose-coloured house in Connolly Gardens, three doors down from Maggie's, and waves at a shadowy figure in the front window. 'I have to go home. Dad's on nights this week and she needs me to mind Priscilla and Isaac.'

'Do you want me to come with you?'

Eli helps her stand up, untangling her sunglasses from her hair and gently placing them back on her face. It falls silent once they've left, and I try and think of something to say. *Emma O'Donovan is hot,* I overheard a boy in my year say when we were fourteen and had just started going to the Attic Disco, *but she's as boring as fuck.*

'How are you guys feeling about the match tomorrow night?' I direct the question at Jack, still standing at the edge of the group. His dark hair is spiky with gel, despite the heat, his navy T-shirt clinging to his torso. He's a bit short for a boy, about five foot eight, but he's built. 'My dad told me there's a rumour that a Cork selector is going to be at it.'

'Well, he's Ciarán O'Brien's brother, so he'd be at the match anyway.' Jack shrugs.

'Still an opportunity though,' Sean butts in. He comes closer to me, smelling of sweat and grass, and sits by my feet. 'We had a team meeting about it yesterday.

'Speaking of the match,' he continues, 'I'm going to have a party afterwards. My parents will be out of town.' Ali sits up, but Sean's eyes never leave mine. 'What do you say, Emma? Are you up for it?'

I've told him that I'm not interested in him like that, that I'm never going to be interested, because Ali likes him. 'But I don't like Ali,' he said that night when he cornered me outside Reilly's pub. 'I like you.' I pushed him away. 'I would, Sean. You know I would,' I said. 'But Ali's one of my best friends. I couldn't do that to her.'

'It had better be a good show,' Dylan says. 'Especially after my last party. Am I right, Emma?'

'Yeah, it was good.'

'Just good?' He raises an eyebrow at me. 'That's not what Kevin Brennan said.'

(Kevin, throwing me against a wall at the party, his teeth sharp.)

'Why?' I say. 'What exactly did Kevin say?'

(. . . he is dragging me into a dimly lit bedroom that smells of Play-Doh. Tripping over a headless Barbie. A candy-pink duvet, people laughing outside. *Let's get back to the party*, I kept saying.)

'Oh –' Dylan smirks – 'just that you had fun.'

(Kevin's hands on my shoulders, pushing me down, saying, *Go on, come on, Emma.* It seemed easiest to go along with it. Everyone is always saying how cute he is anyway.)

'What kind of fun?' My voice is tight.

(Afterwards I made him *swear* he wouldn't tell anyone.)

'Well, I don't know what Kevin said, but nothing happened,' I say.

'That's not what he told us.' Dylan looks to Jack for confirmation.

'Then he's a fucking liar.' I stop. 'Look, whatever,' I say, making myself sound calm. 'If he has to invent stories to make himself feel like more of a man, that's not my problem.'

'Girls are all the same,' Dylan says, rolling his eyes. 'Get wasted and get a bit slutty, then in the morning try and pretend it never happened because you regret it.' He directs this at Jamie and I laugh, a little too loudly.

'I have to go,' Jamie says, grabbing her school bag. A notebook and a tin pencil case fall out and Ali jumps up to help her, but Jamie waves her off, shoving the stuff back into her bag. 'I have to get to work.'

'OK, hun,' Ali says, sitting back down. 'Call me later?' Jamie doesn't reply, just walks away alone. Dylan stares after her.

'Come on,' he says to Sean and Jack when she's out of sight. 'Let's get out of here.' And they leave, throwing the rugby ball between them. None of them looks back at me.

'I think I'm going to head,' I say. 'Wait . . . *shit*. Maggie said she'd drop me home.'

'Mom texted me ten minutes ago. She's in town,' Ali says. 'We can go meet her in Mannequin? She'll drive you home once she's finished.'

'Maybe.'

It's always the same when we meet Karen there. Pushing open the black door, hit by the cool air and the vanilla-scented candles; our school shoes sinking into the plush cream carpet, expensive clothes draped off black jewelled hangers. The manager looks up, the ready smile on her face dimming when she sees the grey uniform. 'Yes, girls?' she'll say, her voice clipped, until Ali comes closer and she sees who it is. 'Oh, Ali,' she'll coo. 'You should see what your mother is trying on. It's *divine*.' Karen will push back the heavy cream curtain of the dressing room, wearing yet another dress, or coat, or a T-shirt that she *literally has to have*. She'll force Ali into a dressing room then, handing her a pair of jeans to try on, and you can see she's trying not to wince when she looks at the size. Then she'll turn to me, and insist I try something on too, and my head will swim when I see the price tags (*That's obscene,* I can almost hear my mother say, *and with people starving in the world*), but Karen will tell me not to think about that, just to pick whatever I want. There'll be a dress that looks like nothing on the hanger, but when I try it on it moulds to my body like a second skin, and Karen's jaw drops when I come out of the dressing room. 'You look stunning. You could be a model,' she'll say as she stands behind me, and the two of us look so good together in the reflection that I can pretend for a moment that it's really us who are mother and daughter. 'You have to have it. Will you let me buy it for you?' she'll ask, and I'll want to say yes. I will want her to buy me one of everything in the shop. She can afford it. But I won't. I can't.

'I can give Emma a lift,' Conor says, and I nod at him.

'See you later, guys,' Ali calls as we walk away. My phone beeps.

Ali:	Are you going to score Conor?
Me:	Ugh, no.
Ali:	But he looooooves you.
Me:	Fuck off.

'Emmie.' Conor clears his throat to get my attention. 'Sorry, *Emma*. We're just here.'

'It's very . . . clean,' I say as we get into his car.

He flicks the Lisa Simpson-shaped air freshener with a finger. 'Is that annoying you? I can take it down if it is. I know perfumes can make you——'

'I'm fine.'

He reaches into the glove compartment to get his glasses, then reverses the car, his hand on the back of my headrest as he turns to check behind him.

I stare out the window as the closely packed houses

of the town centre melt away into a narrow road, curved trees on the right hanging over us, clinging to the ditch. The tide is out, turning the bay on the left to marsh, patchy with green weeds.

'It's good to see you,' he says, turning the radio down.

'Yeah.'

'I feel like I never see you any more.'

'I know. I've just been busy, you know, schoolwork, blah blah.'

'I meant what I said earlier.' His hands tighten on the steering wheel. 'About being grateful to you.'

(The O'Callaghan house. A smell of disinfectant. Dymphna smiling as I give her the paisley headscarf I had bought in Dunnes for her.)

'It was nothing, Conor.'

(Sitting on his bed, staring at the Anchorman poster on the wall. He started to cry. I didn't know what to do. *Be a big boy*, my dad used to tell Bryan. *Stop that.* Wrapping my arms around Conor, heads pressed together.)

'It wasn't nothing to me,' he says. (His head turning slightly then, his breath on my cheek. And I could feel something melting inside me, something that I needed to keep under control.) 'I want you to—'

'Yeah, cool,' I interrupt as the car pulls into our estate. I look through the Kellehers' window, Nina and her husband Niall thrown on the couch, each with a glass of wine in hand. They're clinging to either side as if they're afraid they might accidentally touch. One of the kids runs in. A hand sneaks down, a ruffle of her curly hair, eye contact with the television never breaking. My gaze drifts across all the houses in the estate, a similar scene playing out in each one, chairs and faces focused on their TVs.

Conor parks next to his dad's Merc, and I have the car door open before he has a chance to pull up the handbrake. He reaches across me, grabbing my wrist. 'You shouldn't have laughed.'

'What are you on about?'

'Earlier. When Dylan said that about Jamie. You shouldn't have laughed.'

I can see my mother through the window, a neat lace-trimmed pink apron on, waiting for my father to come home.

You're just like your mother, you know.

'Oh, for fuck's sake, Conor,' I say. 'It was just a joke. Lighten up, will you?'

(Jamie's face in the park, stricken.)

(Jamie coming to my house after it happened last year, crying and crying. *What'll I do, Emma? What am I supposed to do now?*)

And I wish I could go back to that moment. I would

tell Dylan to fuck off and leave Jamie alone. I would stand up for her. I would be better.

'What do you mean?' I lean back in my seat, knowing my unbuttoned shirt is revealing the edges of my black lace bra. Conor glances down, and then looks up again just as quickly.

'I mean, I'm just, I mean . . .'

'Yes?' My voice is soft. I shift forward, a strand of hair falling in front of my face. He puts his hand up to brush it out of place, then jerks back.

'Thanks for the lift, Conor.' And I get out of the car.

My bedroom is immaculate again. The oak four-poster bed has been remade, the lilac patchwork quilt neatly tucked in and turned down. The magazines have been stacked at the base of my bed, the tops of my make-up bottles put back on and organized on my vanity table, any streaks of foundation on the white wood washed off. Even my earrings and necklaces have been tidied away. I open the doors of my wardrobe and find everything has been neatly folded or hung properly on the good, wooden hangers. Mam has been at work.

A good daughter would feel grateful. (I didn't say she could come into my room.)

It was a nice thing of her to do. (But I never asked her.)

(I won't be able to find anything, she'll have put stuff away in the wrong places, like she always does.)

I wish . . . I don't know what I wish.

I lie on my bed, staring at the constellation of glow-in-the-dark stickers on the ceiling, the back of my legs sticky against the damp material. The heat is oppressive, almost like it's pressing down on me, like it might make an indentation in my skin. I turn on to my front, then my back again, then curl on my side, but nothing helps.

I lie there for hours.

Friday

After school, the four of us are in Maggie's car again, rolling down the windows to let the hot air escape, Jamie and Maggie bickering over whether to listen to Kate Bush or Taylor Swift. We drive through Ballinatoom, and around, and up Main Street again, and around again, over and over. I watch the sunlight on the bare skin of my forearm resting on the open window, anticipation licking my stomach. Maybe this will be the weekend something, *anything*, happens.

Ali grins at me. 'Wait, I totally forgot to ask you about Conor O'Callaghan.'

'What about Conor?'

'Did anything happen when he dropped you home last night?' I groan out loud as she waggles her tongue at me.

'Ugh, no. As much as he wanted to, obviously.'

'Oh, *obviously*, but of course, *mais oui*,' Maggie teases. 'The menfolk can't resist your charms, you sorcerer, you.'

'Whatever.'

'Seriously though —' Maggie glances at me in her rear-view mirror — 'Conor's a good guy. You could do a lot worse.'

'You *have* done a lot worse,' Jamie mutters under her breath.

'Keep your eyes on the road, please, Mags,' I say. 'And yeah, Conor's cool and everything, but I'd never actually *be* with him.'

'I thought you had scored with him already?' Jamie asks, jabbing at the volume control on the radio.

'Conor? No, we've never been together. What made you think that?'

'Oh, I don't know.' She shrugs. 'You've been with everyone else. It's hard to keep track.' She laughs, like it's only a joke. She pulls down the sun visor and watches me in the mirror to see my reaction. I laugh too. (*Fucking bitch.*)

'I'd better get home,' I say, looking at my phone.

'I thought we were all going to the match together?' Ali says. 'I thought we'd agreed.' She leans forward so her head is between the two front seats. 'You two are still coming, right?'

'I don't know,' Jamie says. 'I promised my mother I would give her a hand with Christopher. He's being really clingy at the moment.' She looks at me in the mirror again. 'And I have a shitload of homework to do as well. Not all of us are so lucky that we can just "forget" to study and still come out with A's.'

'What's that supposed—'

'Why don't we go back to my house?' Ali says quickly. 'Come on. Just the four of us.'

'I'm in,' Maggie says. 'I want to see the new swimming pool.'

'I don't have togs with me,' I say.

'Don't worry about that,' Ali says, 'we have loads of spares.'

I can't think of any other excuse, so I nod, ignoring Ali's squeal of delight. We drive almost five miles away from the town centre until we get to Ali's house, the Old Rectory. It's surrounded by high brick walls, and she leans out of the window to key in the code on a silver flat-screen set into the wrought-iron front gates. There is a gravel drive, almost a mile long, surrounded by acres of empty fields. Her parents keep buying up more and more of the land around them. You could fit my entire estate in here.

Maggie parks beside the porch. The three-storey

red-brick house has huge windows with white latticed frames covered in climbing wisteria and roses. *Did you see the price of the place the Hennessys bought?* my mother asked my father, waving the property supplement at him. He took it from her, putting on his reading glasses so he could see. It was all anyone could talk about for months afterwards. *You're rich,* the other kids would say to Ali in school. *My mam says your dad is a millionaire.* She would get flustered, drop her school books or her bag or her lunch box, her face aflame.

Being wealthy is wasted on someone like Ali.

We pass the sculpture of a naked woman draped against one of the stone pillars on the porch, her belly bloated and full. Apparently it's of Karen when she was pregnant, something Ali denies, of course.

'I still can't believe you have your own swimming pool,' Maggie says as Ali opens the front door.

'Mom's idea,' Ali says, leading us through the reception area. It looks like a lobby in a posh hotel, with the Waterford crystal chandelier and what Karen informed us is a Persian rug on the stripped wooden floorboards. *It was embarrassingly expensive, girls,* she told us, *but I just had to have it.*

I close the door of the bathroom behind me, the swimming togs Ali has given me in my hands. It's in its packaging, Melissa Obadash scrawled across the front, the price tag still attached.

More money than sense, my mother's voice says in my head.

I run my hand over the wallpaper, embossed magnolia with gold flowers etched on it. There's a freestanding bath with gold claw feet, the toilet paper folded into a point by Magda, the housekeeper, Aveda hand wash and hand cream by the deep cream sink, the taps plated in gold. There's an antique dresser painted in cream, a selection of perfume bottles on top. Coco Mademoiselle perfume. I've wanted that one for ages, *But you'll have to wait until Christmas*, Mam told me, *or save up your own money for it, Emma.*

I spray a little on my wrists.

(They won't even notice.)

I open my school bag.

(It's not like they can't afford it.)

And I stuff it in so quickly I barely even notice myself doing it, so it's like I didn't do anything at all. I stand up straight, staring at myself in the mirror. I am beautiful. I mouth the words at my reflection. That is something Ali's money can't buy.

We walk through the new sauna, Ali opening a wooden door into a long, narrow gazebo, closed in on all sides with frosted glass. 'What the . . .' She steps back, ignoring my hiss as she crushes my toes beneath her feet.

Inside there's a photographer standing on a step going down into the pool, up to his calves in water, his camera clicking as Karen swims towards him. He backs up the steps, almost knocking over a skeletal woman with peroxide-blonde hair who is sorting through a rail of bikinis, each one smaller than the next. Karen, never breaking eye contact with the camera, emerges from the water, her chestnut hair slicked back off her angular, fine-boned face. She is completely naked.

'*Mom*,' Ali screams, and the spell is broken, everyone turning to stare at us.

'Oh my God, Ali, you scared me. What's wrong with you?'

'You're . . . You're not wearing any clothes.'

'Calm, darling,' Karen drawls. A mousy-looking girl in shorts and white Converse darts out from behind the rail of clothes and hands Karen a fluffy white towel. 'I have a bikini on.' She pulls at the fabric. 'See, it's just flesh-coloured.'

'Mom,' Ali's lip starts quivering, 'what are you doing? I thought we——'

'Oh, sweetie,' Karen says, 'don't be like that. This shoot is for a different magazine.' She gestures at the assistant to get her something to drink. The girl rushes over to the desk running the length of the clothes rail, laden down with snacks and bottles, and brings Karen a Diet Coke with a straw in it, holding it out for her to sip from.

'Hi, girls!' Karen disappears behind a free-standing room divider, slapping the wet nude bikini over the top as the stylist hands her a silver suit. She steps out from behind the screen, her perfect body barely covered by the one-piece. The stylist moves around her, with a mouthful of clamps, adjusting the material to make sure the fit is right. 'Jamie, how *is* Lien?'

'She's fine.'

'We haven't seen her at Yogalates in ages, I was——'

'My mother is fine, Mrs Hennessy,' Jamie says, 'but I'll pass on your regards.'

With that she stalks out of the gazebo, Ali hurrying after her, calling her name.

'Oh God, I've said the wrong thing, haven't I?' Karen says, looking after them. 'Ali will probably kill me later.' She bites her lip. 'I'm always saying the wrong thing. I really didn't mean to offend her.'

'Why would she be offended?' the photographer says, looking up from his laptop.

Karen lowers her voice. 'There's a lot of drama going

on for poor Jamie at home. Her father's Christy Murphy.' He looks at her blankly. '*Christy Murphy,*' she repeats. 'Don't you ever watch the news? He was in property, building, hotels, the whole lot. Lost everything in the crash.' Both he and the stylist give a dramatic intake of breath. 'I know. God, can you even imagine? And Ali told me that Jamie has to work part-time now to help out, you know, financially. The whole thing is so awful. And it's awkward – I don't know if Lien even *wants* to see me. If it was me I'd be too mortified to face anyone, you know?'

'Maybe the daughter could do some modelling?' the stylist offers.

'What?' Karen looks surprised. 'Jamie?'

'Why not?' the stylist says. 'She's tall enough, and Asian girls are so on trend this season.'

I wait for Karen to say, *No, not Jamie. If anyone is going to be a model it should be Emma,* but she shrugs, and lies down on a striped sunlounger, pouting at the camera.

'Come on,' I say to Maggie. 'Let's go.'

'So,' Maggie says as the door to the swimming pool slams behind us and we go to find the others, 'do you think Jamie would want to be a model?'

'Jamie?'

'You heard what the stylist said.'

'I doubt it. I mean, being a model is a bit desperate, isn't it? You'd want to really love yourself, like.'

'Do you think?'

'Jesus, I thought you'd be totally against it, as a feminist. Isn't it just more patriarchal bullshit?'

'All right, all right.' Maggie holds her hands up in a gesture of surrender. 'Calm, girl.' There's a pause, and she has the same expression on her face Hannah does when she's about to ask you a personal question. 'Are you OK?'

'I'm fine,' I say. 'Totally fine.'

'You can't park there.' A sunburnt man in a high-vis jacket, shorts, socks and sandals barks at us as Maggie pulls her car up as near to the entrance to the GAA pitch as she possibly can. 'That's reserved.'

We look at Ali, but she stays quiet. She hasn't said much since we left her house.

'Hey.' I nudge her, then tilt my head at the man. 'He says we can't park here.'

'Oh, sorry.' She shakes herself out of her daze, reaching into her handbag and pulling out a neon-pink piece of cardboard. 'My dad gave me this?' She hands it to him, and his eyes narrow as he looks over it.

'And who exactly is your dad?' he asks.

'James Hennessy?' Ali mumbles, and he splutters an apology, waving us through.

The pitch is nestled in a valley, surrounded by sloping hills on three sides, the grass yellow and parched. *I don't understand how in a country that gets as much rain as this one does, we can be having a drought, have you ever heard the like of it?* the old people keep saying to each other as they pay for their groceries in Spar, their Calvita cheese, cooked ham and white sliced pan in their hands, ignoring the queue of customers behind them, talking too long to the bored shop girl who just wants them to leave so she can go back to reading her magazine. We walk past a group of sixth years from St Michael's, all wearing the blue-and-yellow Ballinatoom jersey with 'Hennessy's Pharmacies' stitched on the front in red, nudging each other as I pass.

We climb halfway up the hill on the left and settle in front of the clubhouse. A soft cashmere blanket from Avoca is pulled out of Ali's wicker carrier basket. (*Be careful*, I could imagine Mam saying if that was ours. *Don't get any stains on it. It's for good use.*) 'One for you, one for me,' she says as she hands me a bottle of factor-fifty suncream, keeping the SPF6 oil.

'Ah, the old skin cancer in a bottle.'

'And one for you, one for me.' She ignores me again,

giving us a packet of Haribo Tangfastics, grabbing the medjool dates for herself.

'I can't eat these,' I say.

'Why not?' Jamie sighs.

'Eh, because of the gelatine?'

'Oh my God, are you still pretending to be a vegetarian?'

'How is it pretending when I—'

'I have popcorn,' Ali says. 'That'll be OK, won't it?'

I take the bag off her. (I should smile. I should say thank you.) 'Fine,' I say.

We lie down, propping ourselves up on our elbows, and pretend to watch the match. The ball goes back and forth, players taken off and brought on, the crowd baying for blood, then proclaiming them gods for our time.

'They're not playing very well, are they?' Ali says as the old man next to her, wearing dark tweed trousers and a matching jacket despite the heat, starts screaming obscenities at the *stupid cunting ref* and, *Will ya look, Campbell, will ya just fucking open your eyes and look around ya?*

Campbell's mother, standing two metres away from us, winces at that but she doesn't comment. 'They'd better get their shit together for the County,' I say. 'I want to go to the Winner's Gala ball again.'

'You were so lucky to get to go last year,' Maggie says. Sean Casey asked me, and I told him I'd have to talk to Ali first. I could tell she didn't want me to, but I knew Ali would never say no to me. *Fine*, she said, her shoulders slumping. *Go if you want to.*

'Sure what's the point of bringing the Dineen lad on at this stage?' the old man grumbles as one of the Ballinatoom players limps towards the dugout, moving sluggishly in the hazy heat. I sit up at the mention of his name. 'I didn't think much of him at the friendly against Nemo, but if Ciarán O'Brien, in all of his fucking wisdom, thinks Dineen will make such a difference . . .' The rest of his sentence is drowned out by the crowd's screaming, and I snap my head back to see Jack weaving around the exhausted backs, the ref blowing the whistle pretty much as the ball hits the back of the net.

'That Dineen lad is brilliant . . .' I hear people saying as they start walking towards the clubhouse.

'. . . there's talk that the young Dineen lad is going to make the Cork team . . .'

'. . . he has to, doesn't he?'

'I haven't seen footballing like that in years.'

I beckon my girls together, waiting until we're in a close-knit circle.

'I'm going to score with Jack Dineen tomorrow night.'

'Oh my God, like,' Jamie says. 'Does he even stand a chance?'

I wait a beat. 'Nope,' I say. 'Not a chance.'

And we all crack up laughing, Jamie too, and for a second it feels like nothing has changed.

There's a sudden ear-splitting scream. It's Dylan Walsh in front of the clubhouse, with Julie Clancy thrown over his shoulder. She's banging on his back telling him to, *Leave me down*, but she's laughing so hard she can barely get the words out. He drops her a little and she wraps her legs around his waist, his hands holding her up by the ass as they kiss.

'Dylan Walsh is so gross.' Maggie's face is screwed up in a grimace. 'No offence, J, but I don't know what you were at.'

They move ahead of us, chatting loudly about the outfits they're going to wear tomorrow, Maggie telling Ali she's thinking 'lots of checks, you know?' Jamie has stopped dead, dozens of other supporters milling around her.

'Come on,' I say, reaching out to grab her hand. 'We agreed it was best not to—'

'Fuck off,' she says, pulling away from me. I check quickly to make sure the others haven't heard, but they're at the entrance gates, chatting to my dad. He's still wearing his pinstriped business suit, but has taken off the jacket. He has patches of sweat around his armpits. You should buy him special deodorant, I told Mam last summer. You can get this stuff that, like, means you never sweat. I'm sure I read that causes cancer, she had replied, as if that had anything to do with the conversation.

'There's my princess.' He puts his arm around my waist and gives me a kiss on the cheek.

'How are you, Jamie?' Dad asks. 'Did you enjoy the match?' She murmurs yes. 'That Dineen lad is in your class, isn't he?'

'You don't say "class" any more, Daddy. We're not in national school.'

'Sorry. Your year then.' I nod. 'He's a handy player for someone so young.' Dad grabs a handkerchief from his pocket and dabs at his brow.

'Sean Casey is in our year too,' Ali pipes up.

'Yeah, but sure he's only a sub,' I say.

Dad's eyes drift over my shoulder, and he breaks into a huge smile. 'And here's the man himself!'

I spin on my heel, but it's just Ciarán O'Brien, his shock of hair suspiciously dark for someone of his age.

'Ciarán, congratulations! Great game. Your lad played well.'

'Ah, we were grand. Still a bit weak in the forwards,' Ciarán says. 'No chance of Bryan coming back for us?'

'Ah,' Dad looks embarrassed. 'He says the UL team is enough for him at the moment.'

'Hmm,' Ciarán grunts. He looks at each of us in our turn, smiling extra widely when he sees Ali, enquiring after her dad.

'And is one of these lovely ladies your own daughter?' he asks, and Dad gives me another squeeze around the waist, saying, 'This is our youngest, Emma.'

Ciarán looks me up and down. I probably shouldn't have worn such a low-cut top.

'Well, well, well.' He winks at Dad. 'You have a heartbreaker on your hands there, Denis. I'd say you must be bating them off with a stick.' He tilts his head in a hello to a passer-by, shaking a couple of outreached hands, then makes a drinking gesture at Dad. 'Pint?'

'God, did you see the way Ciarán O'Brien was checking me out?' I shudder as we watch them leave.

'Well, what do you expect, princess?' Jamie says. 'You're about to take someone's eye out.'

(Jamie and I getting ready in my bathroom. She fidgets nervously with her dress. *Do you think it's too short?* she says, spinning around to see herself from the back. *Don't be stupid*, I say, handing her another drink. *With your legs?*)

51

'You really are your dad's pet, aren't you?' Ali says, a little wistfully. 'All those hugs and kisses. My dad is so not a hugger.'

'I wouldn't mind if he was,' I say. Ali's dad, James, is an absolute ride. She groans in disgust and shoves me as hard as she can, cackling with laughter when I stumble against a girl walking past me.

'Eh, *excuse* me.' It's Susan Twomey, surrounded by ten of her friends, all slim and tanned, with long hair spilling over their shoulders in various shades of blonde. All of them are wearing what looks like the children's version of the Ballinatoom jersey, minuscule shorts and wedge sandals.

'Susan,' one of the WAGs mutters under her breath, 'Paul's coming.'

He runs up to us and grabs Susan around the waist, although how he can pick her out of this line-up is beyond me, and gives her a massive kiss, ruffling her hair and saying 'We won, we won!' as if the rest of us hadn't been at the match.

'How come you didn't go to the clubhouse?' He turns to one of the others. 'Ben was looking for you too.' The girl looks guilty, her eyes darting to Susan and then to the ground.

'Ugh, baby,' Susan says. 'It's so gross in there – that

rag they use to dry the glasses looks like it hasn't been washed in twenty years.'

He smiles at her, then glances at the rest of us, doing a barely perceptible double take when he sees me. He looks me up and down, just like his father did, running a hand across his brown buzz cut. Susan grits her teeth.

'Emily, isn't it?' she says, walking towards me.

'It's Emma, actually.'

'You must be *freezing*, Emily.' She gives a sympathetic shiver, standing so close to me I can smell the biscuit tang of her fake tan. She unwraps my cardigan from around my waist and places it around my shoulders, hoiking up my crop top to cover my cleavage. Her friends snicker, and my ears start to burn.

'Thanks for your concern, *Sharon*,' I say. I take off the cardigan again, wrapping it around the strap of my bag, and pull the top even further down. 'But I'm not cold at all.' I direct this at Paul with a smile. And as I walk away, my legs tremble with an adrenalin rush so strong I almost feel sick from it.

'There you are,' Mam says. She's sitting at the kitchen table, tapping at the iPad. 'I'm trying to watch something on playback and it keeps freezing. What's wrong with this thing at all?'

'Did you ask Bryan? He's better at stuff like that than I am.'

'He's not feeling well. Food poisoning.'

'Food poisoning?' I say as I go into the TV room after I tried in vain to help Mam fix RTÉ Player. 'I did that already,' she snapped when I suggested turning it off and back on again. 'And put a jumper on yourself.' She handed me Bryan's UL hoodie. 'You'll embarrass your brother if you go in to him like that.'

Bryan is thrown down on the black leather sofa, a blue plastic basin next to him and one of Mam's patchwork quilts in red gingham pulled up to his neck. His skin is tinged with grey, his dark curly hair coated with sweat and sticking to his head. 'Looks like someone had fun last night.'

'Tesco value vodka,' he croaks. 'May as well have been drinking lighter fluid.'

I nudge his feet off the sofa so I can sit next to him, yanking some of the quilt away from him.

'Ah, the poor Bryany.' I pat him on the head. He grunts, turning his attention back to the TV. 'You look very skinny. Maybe I should come visit you again, feed you up.'

'And give me food poisoning for real? No, thanks.' He pulls the quilt off me, looking a bit more awake. 'And anyway, you're not allowed back to UL, not after your visit at midterm.'

'Are your roommates still pining after me?'

'They're managing to survive, somehow.'

Ali: Today was fun, wasn't it?

Ali: I'm so bored.

Ali: Anyone want to Skype?

I tell Bryan to turn up the volume as Graham Norton flips an unfortunate-looking girl off the Big Red Chair.

'The state of her,' I say. 'You think she'd have got her hair done or something if she knew she was going to be on TV.'

My phone beeps again. Ali has tagged me in a photo on Instagram, a selfie of the four of us at the match captioned 'Me and my girls, fresh as fuck.'

I look at the photo closely. I'm definitely the prettiest out of the four of us.

(It's just because Jamie is tall. Models need to be tall.)

(It's just because Asian girls are on trend this season.)

I turn my phone on silent and put it face down on the armrest.

'How's Jen?' I ask.

'You can ask her yourself tomorrow night. She's staying over.'

'What, like a sleepover?' I joke, but he doesn't laugh. 'Wait, are you serious? Do Mam and Dad know?'

'Of course.'

'That is so unfair. As if they would ever let me have anyone to stay.'

'That's different, Emmie,' he says. 'Anyway, they won't be here. I got them a deal for a night's stay in a four-star down in Killarney. It was Jen's idea – she and Sean and Laura got the same one for their folks because it's John Junior's anniversary this weekend.'

'Oh yeah, Sean did mention something about that at the park,' I say, turning my mouth down. 'Won't it seem a bit random though? You just buying Mam and Dad a hotel voucher?'

'Hardly random.' He presses mute on the TV. 'It was for their wedding anniversary.'

'What? When was that?'

'Today, you moron. They're thirty-five years married.'

'Oh shit.' I try and think of what I'm going to do. 'Can I go in on yours? Ah, please, Bryan. I'll sign the card and I'll give you the money later.' He raises an eyebrow at me. He's forever slipping me cash and I tend to 'forget' to pay him back.

'It's too late, Emmie. I've already given it to them.'

I'm about to argue with him when Mam comes into

the room, her mobile phone tucked between her cheek and her shoulder, a large tray with three cups of tea and a plate of biscuits in her hands.

'Oh, I know, Bernadette, it's ridiculous.' She places the tray on the coffee table in front of us, straightens up and takes her phone in her hand. 'OK, I'd better go here. Bryan's back from UL for the weekend, he's so good. I know . . . I know . . . Yes . . . Yes . . . OK, bye bye bye bye bye.' She hangs up and places her hand on Bryan's forehead. 'Are you comfortable? Do you want more water?'

'I'm grand, Mam.'

'Well, I made your favourite biscuits.' She points at the tray. 'Oatmeal and raisin.'

I hate raisins, I want to say. I haven't eaten raisins in about ten years.

'Did you get it sorted?' I ask her.

'What?'

'RTÉ Player.'

'Oh no, I'm going to wait till your father gets home.' She frowns at me. 'Emmie, give your brother some room, he's not feeling well.' She flops into the leather recliner next to the sofa as Bryan starts demolishing the cookies, his appetite miraculously returned.

'Where's Dad?' he asks.

'He's gone for a drink with Ciarán O'Brien.'

57

'Ciarán O'Brien, is it? Or Ciarán, King of Ballinatoom, to give him his official title.'

'Ah, stop that now.' Mam takes one of the cups from the tray and throws two cubes of sugar in it.

'Mam,' Bryan looks at her incredulously, 'how can you say that, after what happened with Eoin Sayers and—'

'Well.' Her lips tighten. 'You weren't exactly innocent in that little escapade yourself now, were you? And you would have been expelled too if Ciarán hadn't intervened on your behalf.'

'Oh yeah, I'm sure he did that out of the goodness of his heart. Nothing to do with the fact that we had the college's All-Ireland and—'

'Well, if Eoin had played football, I'm sure Ciarán would have spoken up for him as well.'

'Jesus, Mam, that's the point—'

'Bryan.' Her voice is razor sharp and we both start. Mam never gets cross with Bryan. 'Ciarán O'Brien does a lot for this town, and he's very well respected. You were lucky that he stepped in when he did.'

She gestures at Bryan for the remote control, stretching across to get it from him, and changes the channel, ignoring our protests.

'No talking,' she says, 'not while *The Late Late* is on.'

58

We fall silent. 'Isn't this nice?' she says. 'I can't remember the last time we all sat in together on a Friday night; it must have been last year some time. You two are always so busy these days. Why I—'

'Shhh,' I say. '*The Late Late* is on.'

Saturday

Ali: What you wearing tonight?

Ali: Oh my god, you look so hot in that. I
          love it.

Ali: Can I come over earlier? My mom is
          driving me insane.

It's nearly 8 p.m. I'm lying on my bed, clicking through photos of Jack on Facebook. I take a swig of my drink, wincing as the sharp taste of vodka hits my throat, burning a hole in my empty stomach.

'Is that all you're going to eat?' Bryan asked me earlier when I chopped up half a banana into a small bowl of natural yogurt. 'Mam left dinner for us.'

'Eating is cheating,' I said, and he laughed.

My parents left for Killarney before lunchtime, Mam phoning Sheila Heffernan to boast about what a generous son she has, *Yes, a four-star hotel, can you believe it, Sheila? Not many boys his age would be so thoughtful.* 'And what are your plans for tonight?' she asked me as Dad put their overnight case in the boot, her voice a little cooler, and I wonder if Dad or Bryan ever notice that, notice how different she sounds when she's talking to me, or if it's just my imagination. I tried to act casual. 'Oh, nothing much. Probably going to go to Maggie's, watch a DVD or something.' (I'm eighteen, I'm an adult, what does it matter to you what I do?) 'Well . . .' She looked reluctant, but not even she could argue with watching a DVD on a Saturday night. 'Be back by midnight. I expect you to phone me from the house phone as soon as you're home.'

That's not going to happen, but I'll just tell her tomorrow that it kept going to voicemail, that her reception must have been weak down in Killarney. 'Will there be boys there?' Jesus. 'Yes, Mam. Eli will be there.' 'The African lad?' Dad had interjected. 'Dad, he's not African.' 'Sure, of course he's African.' Dad laughed. 'His father is the man up in CUH, isn't he?' I nod. 'He's as black as the ace of spades.' 'Yeah, but his mam is Irish,' I said slowly. 'And Eli's lived in Ballinatoom all his life. And Conor and Fitzy will probably be there too,' I lied, and Dad visibly relaxed. 'I just don't know if I feel comfortable—' Mam began, but Dad interrupted her, saying that he trusted me to be responsible. Bryan and I watched as the car pulled out the drive. *Freedom.*

I yank at the thin straps of my dress, pulling the material away from my clammy body. The heat is curling in through the open window, wrapping around my limbs. I can hear the sound of the kids on the estate shouting 'Red rover, red rover . . .' I sit on the windowsill and see the two Mannix boys playing with a little girl I don't know. The girl and the older boy are on the swing set, ignoring the other boy whining that he wants a go, *s'not fair*, and it could almost be me and Conor when we were kids, Fitzy insisting every game that I suggested was 'stupid', until I burst into tears. 'Don't cry,' Conor would plead with me, telling Fitzy to leave me alone. He promised that I could choose whatever game I wanted. 'I hate it when you cry, Emmie,' he said.

Maggie:	Hey hun, we're nearly there. I hope you don't mind but I said to Eli about tonight and he's coming too. xx
Me:	K.
Maggie:	Are you annoyed?
Me:	No, of course not.

(Yes. Yes, I am. But not surprised.)

| Maggie: | Yay, thanks babe. Oh, and don't kill me but |

Fitzy is here too, he offered us a lift and I felt bad so asked him along. SORRY!!!!!! xxx See you in 2 mins.

I grit my teeth. Now I'm going to have to text Conor as well.

Me: Few of us hanging in my place tonight. Nothing major. You can come if you're not up to anything else.

He texts back with indecent haste.

Conor: Hey Emmie! I'd love to come, thanks for asking me. See you soon. X

I stare at the X for a few seconds. I wish he wouldn't do that.

'Bryan?' I knock, pushing the door open when I hear him grunt. A musty smell of unwashed socks and Abercrombie Fierce hits me. He's sitting on his bed, lifting weights. There is a plate with bits of dried lasagne stuck to it and a mug of tea half hidden under the bed. (*Emmie, what have I told you about eating in your bedroom? Do you want to have an infestation of mice, is that what you want?*) The green-and-navy tartan curtains are closed, the exposed bulb hanging from the ceiling giving the room a blank glare.

'Right, so a few more people are coming tonight.'

'How many is a few more?' His face contorts as he raises the weight.

'Just Eli Boahen, Ethan Fitzpatrick and Conor from next door.'

'Grand.' He drops the weight on the bed and grabs one of the good hand towels, peach with white bows on it, and starts wiping his face. I want to tell him that Mam will kill him for doing that. But we both know she won't. 'You're not wearing that, are you?' he says.

I smooth down my new dress. It's black, cut down to the navel, and very, very short. 'What's wrong with what I'm wearing?'

'I don't know, Em.' Bryan takes a gulp from his water bottle. 'It's a bit slutty, isn't it?'

I stare pointedly at the FHM poster Blu-Tacked on to the wall opposite the bed, of some topless model, one finger in her mouth, the other hand reaching into her knickers.

'That's different.'

The doorbell rings so I just roll my eyes at him.

'You look fab,' Maggie says when I answer the door, giving me a kiss on the cheek, Ali doing the same. Eli nods hello, a case of beer under one arm, walking into the kitchen with Fitzy. I lean in to give Jamie a kiss as well, feeling her stiffen as I do so. I can smell a hint of vomit underneath her perfume.

'You all look gorgeous,' I say. Jamie and Ali are both

wearing short dresses, except Jamie is wearing hers with Converse and an oversized knit jumper. Maggie is wearing skinny jeans tucked into black ankle boots, a sheer white tank gaping so much at the armpits you can see the black lace triangle bra underneath it; her hair is slicked up into a high topknot, dark burgundy lipstick her only make-up.

'Did you see Ali's shoes?' Jamie says. 'Aren't they just amazing?'

Is that a hint of a red sole? (*You want what for Christmas? And how much would they cost? I am not spending that kind of money on a pair of shoes, Emmie.*) 'Very nice,' I say, feeling sick. 'Very . . . high.'

'My mother always wears shoes this high,' Ali says, 'and she's even taller than I am.'

'They're fab,' Maggie says.

Ali looks at me again, almost pleadingly. I clear my throat. 'Did you bring the cough syrup?'

'Yup,' Ali says, holding up a large red-and-white shopping bag with 'Hennessy's' emblazoned across the front. She had been reluctant when I asked her earlier to swipe it from her dad's pharmacy. *I'll get in trouble, Emma,* she said. I wrapped an arm around her waist, resting my head on her shoulder. *Please, Ali. Come on. It'll be fun. Please?* And I could feel her melt.

'Cool,' I say as the doorbell rings again. I point them

through to the kitchen. 'There's 7 Up and Jolly Ranchers on the kitchen table.'

'Wow.' Conor's standing on the front porch, a paper-wrapped bottle in his hands. 'You look . . .' He trails off. Neither of us moves; we just stare at each other.

'Sorry.' He thrusts the bottle into my hands, and I'm glad to have something else to look at.

'There was no need, Conor.'

'Ah, it's just some wine from the fridge.'

'Conor,' Jamie shouts as we walk into the kitchen.

She thrusts a red cup full of purple liquid at me and then one at Conor. 'Drink up.' I take mine, but Conor refuses, handing it back to Jamie, who drains it. She points a finger at Ali and barks, 'Cigarette. Now,' at her. She shoves open the stiff patio door, and Ali follows, rummaging in her Chanel bag for her own packet of fags.

Maggie hops up on the counter next to the fridge, her skinny legs dangling about a foot from the ground. She leans back against the apple-patterned wall tiles and yawns. 'The heat is making me sleepy.' Eli walks towards us. I smile at him but he doesn't see me, I guess, as he stands between Maggie's legs, nudging her knees apart so he can get closer.

I hear Jamie scream from outside, Ali shushing her nervously.

'Jesus,' I say, 'how is she drunk already?'

'She was tipsy when we picked her up,' Maggie says. 'I think her parents had another fight, they—'

'Yeah, well, we all have problems,' I say. Jamie screams again, and my jaw clenches. 'Seriously, the neighbours are going to complain if she doesn't shut the fuck up.'

'Do you think she's OK?' Conor asks. 'Should I go out and check on her?'

'She's fine,' I say. 'She's just looking for attention. Ignore her.'

'You girls are such bitches to each other,' Eli chuckles, and Maggie elbows him in the ribs.

'Come on, Em, be nice,' she says. 'Jamie's just nervous about tonight, with both Dylan and Julie being there.'

'She shouldn't have fucked him then,' Eli says. 'Shit, she was *wasted* that night though.'

I look away, staring at my reflection in the night-black glass of the patio door.

Ali grabs her iPhone from the marble counter and hands it to Eli, instructing him to take a photo of us.

'Oh, wait, Fitzy and Conor, get in it too,' she insists. She thinks it'll look cooler if we have boys in the photos, to prove that she has male friends. She stands between them, a thrilled expression on her face. Immediately after it's taken, Maggie jumps down off the counter and she and Ali crowd around the phone.

'Aren't you going to look at the photo too?' Eli sounds amused.

'No.' I hold eye contact with him for a second longer than is strictly necessary. 'I don't need to.' Eli shifts from one foot to the other, then looks away.

'I look like shit in this picture.'

'No, you don't,' Maggie says. 'You look fab.'

'Fat, more like.'

'Ali . . .' Maggie sighs. 'Shut up. You don't look fat.'

Ali insists on taking another photo, then another, until they're finally happy with the perfect one to upload to Facebook. Maggie starts swiping through Ali's old photos, showing a few to Eli, going pink as he tells her how pretty she looks. She gives a sudden snort of laughter.

'This is hilarious!' she says. 'Why didn't you send these to me too, Em?'

'Send what to you?' I say. Ali lunges for the camera but it's too late, I'm looking at a series of photos of me, taken with FatBooth, my face as bloated as Chloe Hegarty's. I hand Ali back her phone. 'I didn't take these. Guess Ali had some free time on her hands.'

'It was just a joke,' she mumbles.

The doorbell rings again.

'Em.' Ali follows me as I walk away. 'Em, please. It was a joke.'

'Hilarious.'

'I'm sorry. Please don't be cross with me. I'm sorry, OK? Are you fighting with me?'

I don't answer for a moment, a knife edge of satisfaction cutting through me when I see her forehead pinch with anxiety. I can almost taste her fear that she's annoyed me, that she's gone too far.

'No,' I say finally.

'Are you sure? You still seem mad at me.'

'Jesus, Ali.' I shake her hand off me and gesture at her to go back into the kitchen. 'I have to answer the door.'

Bryan comes bounding down the stairs, two steps at a time. He's freshly showered and barefoot, wearing a Beatles T-shirt and jeans.

'Hey.' He opens the door and reaches out to Jen, drawing her close to kiss her.

'Ew,' I say, and they break apart, smiling at each other.

'Hi, Emma,' Jen says, hugging me hello. She's the same height as Bryan, and seems to be made up of points and sharp edges from her teeth to her elbows, but there's something luminescent about her, her skin so pale it almost glows. 'You looking forward to tonight?'

'Yeah, should be fun.'

'Tell Sean he'd better have the place cleaned up when I get home. I'm not doing it for him.' I nod. 'I love your dress, by the way,' she says. 'Zara, right?'

'Yeah,' I say, smirking at Bryan. 'On sale. Fifteen euro.'

'Ah, feck it, I bought the same one for full price months ago.' She turns to Bryan. 'Remember? I wore it for your birthday party? You loved it.'

I try not to laugh. 'OK, I'll let ye at it.'

The kitchen is empty when I return. The sliding door is wide open, tiny black midges buzzing around the recessed light bulbs in the ceiling, like constellations of black stars. I pour myself another drink from the pitcher, throwing it back, and refill the cup again before grabbing Precious from the counter, wiping away the dusting of ginger hairs she's left, and follow the rest of them outside.

Maggie is doing somersaults on the trampoline to show off her years of gymnastic training. Ali is bouncing half-heartedly beside her, her hands holding the hem of her skirt down. Jamie is standing at the edge, watching them, draining what's left in her red cup. She should take it easy. She should know what happens when you drink too much.

'That is seriously cool.' Conor claps Fitzy on the back, Eli raising a can of beer to him. The three of them are sitting on the garden chairs, the case of beer open on the table.

'What's cool?' I say.

Conor sits up straight. 'Ethan got accepted into the Rhode Island School of Design.'

'It's one of the most prestigious art colleges in the States,' Eli says when I look confused. 'It's a huge deal.'

'That's amazing, Fitzy,' I say, but he doesn't look up from his phone. There's an awkward pause.

'Who was at the door?' Conor asks.

'Jen Casey. She and Bryan are watching a movie.'

'Bryan's home?' Conor grins. 'Are they in the living room or the TV room?'

'TV room,' I say.

'Fitz, you coming to say hello?'

He looks up from his phone. 'What?'

'You coming to say hello? Bryan's here.'

'Yeah, cool,' Fitzy says. 'You know I'm always happy to see Bryan.'

I smile at him, as if that didn't hurt. Leaving my phone and cup on the table next to the beer, warning Eli to be careful of it, I heave myself on to the trampoline with the girls. We jump and jump, higher and higher, until I want to reach into the inky black sky and swallow the stars.

'J, wait,' Ali calls after her as Jamie walks into the

kitchen. 'I'd better go after her, check if she's OK.' She gets down from the trampoline, yanking her dress down her thighs. I turn to Maggie, reaching my hands out to her instead, but she points at my chest. I look down, and the top of my dress has fallen out of place, exposing my boobs. I laugh, expecting her to join in, but she's staring at Eli. She picks up her red cup on her way back into the kitchen and throws whatever is left in it down her throat, ignoring Eli's protests that he 'wasn't looking, not really'.

Was Eli looking? (I want him to have been looking.)

I lie on the trampoline, staring up at the sky. I visited my aunt Beth in London last summer, and at night-time we sat in the tiny honeysuckled garden of her Hammersmith townhouse, eating salads that she had picked up at Whole Foods Market, drinking glasses of Pimms, and all I could think about was that you couldn't see the stars, blurred behind smog clouds and the glare of city lights. *You can have all of this*, Beth told me. *It'll be easy for you, with the way you look. And you can hold a conversation too, which always helps. The world is your oyster, Emmie. But you need to leave Ballinatoom, you need to get out of there like I did. Is that really all you want for your life?* London. The echoing bang-bang as her neighbours stomped up their wooden staircases, the heat rising from the concrete, the sweat-stained armpits on the tube, the grubby beggar who touched my feet and asked for spare change, the constant requests to repeat myself because my accent was too thick, the eyes that skimmed over my skinny jeans and ballet pumps. 'How did you get on?' Ali asked me when I got home. 'Was it amazing?' Maggie said. And I told them about Beth's shabby-chic home, the forest-green wallpaper and velvet couch, the Union Jack cushions, and her Proenza Schouler bag, her daily Bikram yoga classes, and her office with a view of Big Ben, and the shopping spree she treated me to at Topshop. I told them I loved it. I told them it was the best week of my life.

Is it possible to want everything to change and nothing to change, all at the same time?

I close my eyes, the wobbles undulating in waves through me, swirling in my throat and filling my eyes and my brain, making everything go soft. I can hear the patio door swish open, then close again, the sound of footsteps, an exhaled breath as someone drags their body on to the trampoline, the material sagging as they lie down next to me.

'Are you asleep?'

It's Conor.

I wait for a few moments before answering. 'No.' I open one eye, and he's on his side, watching me.

'I need another drink,' I say, trying to sit up, but he stops me, placing one hand on my shoulder.

'Wait. That shit is strong, Emmie. Just give it some time before your next one. Unless you want a repeat of what happened at Dylan's.'

'Shut up.'

'You were such a mess.' He shakes his head.

'Sound out for bringing me home.'

I never thanked him properly.

'No problem. Of course it took longer than I had expected, what with you refusing to get off the footpath on to the road because it wasn't a road, it was a black lagoon.'

'Stop it.'

'A black lagoon with sharks in it.'

'Those trips were strong,' I protest, but I lie back down.

I had woken up the next day in his single bed, Conor asleep on the ground next to me. I looked around his neat, clean bedroom for something I couldn't even name. A photograph of the two of us from when we were kids, maybe? Whatever it was I was searching for, it wasn't there. I pushed back the duvet cover as quietly as I could and tiptoed out of his room without saying goodbye.

We lie in silence for a few moments. I curl my legs

74

into my stomach, running my hands down the smooth skin of my shins, and he reaches out, and very, very gently touches my little finger with his, his arm pressing against mine. He drops his hand slowly, barely touching the side of my waist, and for some reason I don't move away. I turn my head towards him, and he does the same. His eyes darken, his fingers pressing into my skin as he starts to make circles at my waist, agonizingly slow. I wonder, just for a second, what it would be like to pull that T-shirt over his head and to kiss him, to see what that would do to him. His fingers drop a little lower, they're on my hip bone now and my breath turns jagged.

'I must get another drink.' I clamber off the trampoline and walk away without looking back.

'Would you mind bringing us to the front door?' Ali asks as Fitzy stops the car at the bottom of the drive up to the Caseys' farmhouse.

'Sorry, Ali,' he exhales, the breath coming out of his nose, halfway between a snort and a sigh. 'But I'd never get out of that mess.' He points at the haphazard queue of cars.

The windows of the house are rattling, as if the music is beating against the glass. There is a group of people outside the front door, red pinpricks of cigarette ends burning in the dark. The air is heavy with the smell of cow shit. Ali and I struggle to walk over the cattle grid, our heels getting stuck in the gaps between the metal bars, Maggie and Jamie looking on and laughing with the boys. Conor is the only one who comes back to help, wrapping his arm around my waist and lifting me on to the concrete at the other side.

'Thanks,' I say as he places me down. He turns back to help Ali, but she's managed to make it across.

'Oh, Ali,' I say, pointing at her feet. 'Your shoes.'

'It doesn't matter,' Ali says, bending down to wipe the dirt off them.

They probably cost five hundred euros, and it doesn't matter that they're ruined after one wear. I smile tightly at her.

Outside the back door there's a small outhouse, overalls hanging off hooks on the concrete wall, a row of mucky wellies lined up underneath. We open the back door and walk into a poky kitchen. The door to the living room is closed, as is the window, and the small room is foggy with sweet-smelling smoke.

'Shit.' Maggie coughs, waving her hand in front of her face as she drags Eli into the living room, the others following.

'For fuck's sake.' A pallid-faced guy whose name I

can never remember steps in front of me to shut the door behind them.

'Blowback?' He (Oisin? Eddie?) asks, waving a joint at me.

I nod and he turns the joint around in his mouth and carefully places it between his lips, waiting until I come closer, opening my mouth to suck in the smoke. I hold it in for a few seconds, then breathe it out, clouds rushing through my brain as I try not to cough.

In the living room, the main lights are switched off, a couple of small lamps on, some boys gathered around an iPod docking station hooked up to a boom box. They seem to be arguing with a stumbling girl, their mouths moving, but I can't hear them over the music. All the furniture has been pushed out to the edges of the room, and there are couples on the chairs and a large three-seater sofa, grinding up on each other. Three girls in tight bandage dresses are in the empty space in the middle, their arms flailing as they dance. Fitzy, Ali, Jamie, Maggie and Eli are standing by a table covered in a hand-crocheted tablecloth, now destroyed with beer stains and fag burns. Maggie is pouring what's left in the 7 Up bottle into chipped enamel mugs, Eli passing cans of beer to Fitzy and Conor.

'Emmie, do you want a—' Conor starts, but the door to the hall crashes open, hitting him on the back.

77

'Shit, sorry, man,' Dylan says, giving him a punch on the shoulder. 'I didn't know you were there.' Then he sees her and his face lights up. 'Hey, Jamie, how are you?' He sidles up to her. Her fingers tighten around the enamel mug and she gulps her drink back, staring away from him.

'Jamie,' he tries again. 'Did you hear me? How are things?'

'Dylan.' It's Julie Clancy, Sarah Swallows hovering behind her. She's wearing heavy eyeliner, multiple piercings in her ears, nose and eyebrow. 'What are you doing?'

'Nothing,' he replies, stepping away from Jamie. 'Just talking.'

'To that slut?' Julie squares up to her, prodding Jamie's collarbone with her finger. 'What is your problem? It's not enough that you fucked my boyfriend once – now you want to do it again?'

'Jules,' Dylan warns her. 'Come on, be cool. I said—'

'As if I would sleep with him. *As if,*' Jamie says.

'Oh, please.' Dylan narrows his eyes at her. 'You loved it.'

Eli laughs, shutting up when Maggie glares at him. Julie swallows a sob and rushes across the room, falling to her knees to search under an armchair, ignoring the yelps of protest from the couple she's disturbing. Unearthing her bag and coat, she runs through the door to the kitchen, Sarah Swallows calling after her, the two of them engulfed by smoke before the door closes again.

'Dylan, come on,' Conor says. 'How is she going to get home?'

'She has her car.'

'She can't drive — you saw the state she was in.'

Dylan looks like he might go after her, then he just shrugs. 'Whatever. It's not my problem.'

Ali wraps an arm around Jamie's waist, squeezing it, whispering into her ear. (I need to get away from this. From her.)

In the hall there is a small wooden table and chair, a plug-in house phone, notepad and pen, and the pieces of a broken vase on top. To the left a staircase goes upstairs, the front door leading to the garden is on the right, and a short narrow corridor straight ahead, with two doors on either side, photos and ugly oil paintings in gilt frames hanging on the walls.

'There you are.' Sean emerges from the TV room opposite the bathroom.

'Hey, you,' I say, as if he was the very person I'd been looking for. 'Did you know there's a broken vase in your hall?'

He groans. 'Mam is going to kill me. I told Laura to—'

'Laura's here?'

He slouches against the wall next to a photograph of him and Jen in the bath together. I press my lips together to stop myself from smiling, but he follows my gaze, his face turning red when he sees what I'm looking at. 'I told her she could stay for the party if she kept her mouth shut and didn't tell the parents about it,' he says, moving to block the photo, 'and then she invited some of her friends . . .' He pushes himself off the wall. 'Sorry. I know it's not cool, having your fifteen-year-old sister at a party, but—'

'Casey.' Matt Reynolds falls out of the TV room. He's covered in a film of sweat, a few whiskers of hair glistening on his upper lip. I peer past him to see if Jack Dineen is in there, but all I can see are the backs of three boys, none of them Jack, watching another two lads playing Grand Theft Auto. Where is he? It's going to be such a waste of this outfit if he doesn't show; I won't be able to wear it again for ages because everyone here will have seen it. Matt pulls up his top to wipe his face, and I almost heave when I see his doughy tummy.

'Are you apologizing for your sister?' Matt shakes his head. 'Don't apologize. She's fucking hot. And her friend . . .' He tries to focus his eyes. 'Not the fat one, the other one, the little one.' He holds his hand out to about three feet tall.

'Mia,' Sean supplies.

'Mia!' Matt starts chanting, 'Mia, Mia, Mia . . .' breaking away from Sean to throw his hands in the air. 'She's a fucking ride.' Sean looks at me, and I don't want to seem boring so I smile to show that I'm cool.

'Anyway,' I say, once Matt has staggered off into the kitchen to get another drink, 'who else from the football team is here tonight?'

'I don't know.' Sean pulls me towards him. 'Does it matter?'

'Sorry, Sean.' I gently push him away. 'I have to go find the girls.'

'Where have you been?' Maggie leans back to grab a beer from the case behind her and hands it to me. She's still perched on the edge of the table, her legs wrapped around Eli, who is standing with his back to her. Fitzy, Jamie and Ali are dancing in the middle of the room.

'Shit, J is wasted,' I say as I watch her fall down, clutching at Fitzy, who drags her back up to standing. I haven't seen her this drunk since . . . Well, it's been a long time.

'Hey,' I say. Maggie is resting her head on Eli's shoulder, one arm wrapped around his chest as he runs his fingers up and down her forearm. 'Where's Conor?'

'He's chatting up Mia Deasy.' Maggie points to where the iPod station is and I have to squint to see in the darkness. Laura Casey, Jen and Sean's youngest sister, is talking to a chubby girl with frizzy red hair, the two of them sipping their beers self-consciously. Conor has to lean down to talk to Mia, tiny even in high heels, her oversized eyelashes and round eyes making her look like a human Bratz doll.

Conor throws his head back as if she's said something really funny, and my stomach clenches. I reach behind Maggie and grab another can of beer. 'I'm going to give this to Conor. I think he's all out.

'Hey,' I say, resting my hand on the small of Conor's back and handing him the can. 'I thought you might need a top-up.

'Mia.' I brush against Conor's chest as I lean over to give her a kiss on the cheek. 'How are you? I've been meaning to talk to you for ages. How's first year going? Are you settling in to the convent?'

'I'm in third year,' Mia says quickly when Conor almost spits out his beer in shock. 'I'm in the same year as Laura. I'm nearly sixteen.'

'Sorry. It's because you're so tiny, I guess. It's adorable. You're like a child.' I try not to smile as Conor shifts away from her. 'I'm jealous.'

'Oh my God, why would you be jealous of me?' Mia's eyes widen. 'You're gorgeous. And I love your outfit.'

'Oh, thanks,' I say. 'I wasn't sure of it earlier. Come on, Conor, your honest opinion – what do you think of this dress?'

'Dress? Is that what they're calling T-shirts these days?'

'Stop it!' I swat him on the arm. 'You sound like Bryan. He told me it looked slutty.'

'Your brother Bryan?'

'Yeah.'

'Bryan has never met an FHM poster he didn't like.'

'Exactly!' I say. I move in front of Mia and hold his gaze. 'See, I knew you would get it. Do you remember when Mam found all that porn on his computer and wanted to know what BBW stood for?'

The two of us convulse with laughter and he doesn't even seem to notice Mia leaving. We chat for another ten or fifteen minutes, until I forget why I even came over here in the first place. I'm actually enjoying myself, I realize. I never enjoy myself at parties, not really.

'*Dineen.*'

The music has stopped so I hear his name clearly.

'And remember when—'

83

'No, sorry,' I interrupt Conor, just in time to see Jack Dineen, tanned in a loose white wife-beater, walk through the kitchen door, shouting over his shoulder to someone behind him, and Laura and Mia and their friend in the corner start whispering loudly *'Oh my God . . .' '. . . no way . . .' '. . . is that actually . . .' '. . . yes, it is,'* and then Paul O'Brien walks in. It's like someone famous has arrived – a moment of silence, then whispers, elbow nudging, stifled giggles.

I don't get the fuss; he's nowhere near as cute as Jack. Everyone is obsessed with him because he's 'Paul O'Brien'. He's what I call a Reputation Boy. They might have been cute years ago, but no one seems to have noticed that the appeal has faded, that he's 'gone off', as Mam would say. Sean sprints into the dining room, barely looking in my direction, and slaps both of them on the back. Paul makes a drinking gesture with his hand. His eyes fall on Laura and her friends, lingering on Mia, looking her up and down. He raises his eyebrows, turning to Jack, and says something, Jack snorting with laughter, turning to stare at Mia as well.

'Hey.' Conor takes hold of my elbow. 'Do you want to go outside for some fresh air? It's really hot in here.'

I step away from him. 'No, I'm OK, thanks. I'm going to get another beer.'

Tossing my hair back, I walk towards Eli and Maggie, making sure I'm in Paul and Jack's eyeline.

'Hey.' I put my hand on Maggie's shoulder and pull her face away from Eli's. 'Where have Jamie and Ali gone?'

'They were dancing.'

'They're not here any more.'

'They could be in the living room. Or maybe outside?' she says, her lipstick smudged.

'Oh, you two.' I lean in to pick a piece of lint off Eli's shoulder, ignoring Maggie frowning at me. I wouldn't do anything with Eli, of course not. He's my best friend's boyfriend. But it's always nice to see if I *could*. 'You should get a room.' I say this as slowly as I can. 'There's plenty available.

'Sorry,' I murmur, stepping between Jack and Paul to grab another can of beer from the case on the dining table.

'Hey, Emma,' Jack says, and I half smile at him.

'Yes, hello, Emma,' Paul says, and I tip my can in his direction. 'I have to say, you're looking particularly lovely this evening.'

'Thanks.' I turn on my heel and walk away before he can say anything else.

There's no sign of Jamie and Ali in the garden, just some lads sitting around a rickety wooden table between two tall monkey-puzzle trees, playing poker. There's a couple pressed up against the wall, the boy looking like he's trying to mould her body into the pebble-dashed wall. Two blonde girls are smoking, wearing denim hotpants so short I can see their ass cheeks.

It takes my eyes a few seconds to adjust to the gloom in the TV room, but the girls aren't in here either. I have to breathe through my mouth because of the mixture of Lynx, smoke and sweat.

'Are you cold, Emma?' Matt Reynolds pipes up from the two-seater chair opposite me.

'What?'

'I was just asking if you were cold?'

'Not especially, Matt. It's, like, thirty degrees outside.'

He leans forward, his legs splayed apart, and rests his elbows on his knees, crouching down. 'Are you sure? Because it looks like you're pretty cold to me.'

The others burst into raucous laughter, the guy next to Matt giving him a high five, and I feel like getting up and slapping him across his stupid face.

'Very funny,' I say. 'So mature.'

'What's funny?' Jack opens the door. (I knew he would come looking for me.)

'Oh, nothing,' I say. 'Poor Matt here is just overawed at the sight of my nipples. It must be tough being a virgin at such an advanced age.' I take a sip of my beer and pull a sympathetic face. 'Like a bull tied to a gate, I'd imagine.'

He splutters, 'Fuck you, Emma. You're not that fucking hot, you know,' and starts listing the girls he's shagged. '. . . and then there was Lauren, and Saoirse, and . . .' the others laughing even harder this time, hitting the armrests, stamping their feet, and jeering, 'Virgin, virgin, virgin . . .' at him.

'Can I sit there?'

I take another sip of my beer before I look up. 'But I'm sitting here.'

'There's room for one more, I think.'

'I don't know.' I lean back in the chair. 'I'm pretty comfortable.'

Jack rolls his eyes at me and sits on the armrest, pretending to watch the two lads playing the Xbox.

'I need some health. This mission is killing me,' one of them says, clicking furiously at the controls.

'Just fuck a hooker, that'll help,' Matt Reynolds says, and they laugh.

'So,' Jack says to me, 'were you at the match yesterday?'

'Yeah,' I say, giving an exaggerated yawn. 'But I left, like, ten minutes before the end.'

'Ah,' he says, 'then you missed the best part. I scored the winning goal.'

'You scored a goal? Oh, well done *you*.'

I tap his knee when I say this and he grabs my hand. I try and pull away but he won't let me. He swirls his thumb gently on my palm, a dimple forming in his left cheek, and I feel myself go liquid.

'Maybe you'll come to the next match.'

'Maybe I will.'

'And maybe you should stay until the end this time.'

'Maybe I should.'

Our voices are getting lower, our heads moving closer to each other, inch by inch, wondering which one of us is going to crack and be the first to lean in so afterwards we can say that the other person instigated things. I'm getting so turned on I almost feel queasy, but this is the bit I enjoy the most, I think. The build-up, that moment just before you finally kiss, that's always better than the actual sex. During sex I'm thinking about what I look like, trying to make sure the other person is having a better time with me than they did with the last girl. And, of course, even before they come I'm wondering how I'm going to make them keep their mouth shut about what we did or didn't do.

'Emma.' It's Ali, tapping my shoulder.

'What is it?'

'I'm sorry, OK,' she says, 'but I really need your help.'

I press my lips together tightly, but I don't want to seem like a shitty friend in front of Jack, so I follow her out the room.

'Jesus, Ali, what could be so important—'

'Oh my God, are you still angry with me because of what happened earlier?'

'What?'

'About what happened earlier.' She lowers her voice. 'The FatBooth thing.'

'Oh, for fuck's sake, Ali, I haven't thought about that since. I was about to score with Jack when you—'

'I know, and I'm sorry,' she cuts in. 'But I didn't know what to do.' She opens the door into the dated bathroom, the bath, toilet and sink a matching avocado colour, a scuzzy wool mat on the white lino.

'Jesus,' I say when I see Jamie collapsed over the toilet seat, heaving, but there's nothing left to throw up, only a trickle of bile dribbling through her lips.

'I know,' Ali says. 'What should we do? Should I call her parents?'

'No,' I say quickly. Jamie's mam will have a nervous breakdown if she sees Jamie like this. 'What happened to her? She was fine the last time I saw ye.'

'She scored with Colin Daly.'

'So?'

Ali turns her head towards me and says out of the side of her mouth, 'He tried to have sex with her, and when she said she didn't want to, he said that he had heard from Dylan Walsh that she was a sure bet.' Jamie moans when she hears Dylan's name, dry-heaving into the toilet again.

There's a knock on the door.

'There's someone in here,' I call out but they knock again, more urgently.

'We said, *just a minute*,' Ali snaps, and Sean Casey answers uncertainly, 'Is everything OK in there?'

'Shit.' Ali steps over Jamie's legs to get to the mirror, pulling her make-up bag out of the navy quilted handbag. 'Do I look all right?' She applies more bronzer to her overly tanned face, smooths down some flyaway hairs at her centre parting.

'Sorry, Sean,' she calls out, and I step in front of her.

'You are not leaving me alone to deal with this, Ali.'

'Please, Em. I'm begging you. Please do this for me. It's Sean.'

'And I was with Jack.'

'I never ask you to do anything for me,' she says, and we both know it's the truth. 'But I'm asking you now. Please?' She hesitates. 'I really, really like him, Em.'

He doesn't like you, I want to tell her. He wants to be with me.

'*Fine*,' I say, and she squeals, gives me a massive hug and rushes out. I bolt the door after her and sit on the edge of the bathtub. Ali had the presence of mind to tie Jamie's hair into a ponytail, so at least I don't have to hold it back. I check my phone, sending Maggie a Snapchat, taking a selfie and posting it on Instagram, snorting when Matt Reynolds comments on the photo asking for a tit pic. After one violent retch that sounds like it might burst the lining of her stomach, Jamie wipes her mouth, then gets to her feet unsteadily, holding on to the toilet for balance.

'Do you need help?'

She bends over the sink, splashing her face with water. Standing up straight, she looks at me in the mirror. Her face is blotchy, her eyeliner smeared halfway down her cheeks.

'What do you care?'

'Jamie—'

'You said it would be better.'

'Jamie, I—'

'It's not better, Emma. It's not better.' Her breath is rasping in her throat. 'You said, you said . . .' She can barely get the words out through her tears. She looks such a mess, and there must be something wrong with me, because I know I should feel sorry for her, but all I feel is disgust. *Look at yourself*, I want to tell her. *You're ruining your make-up. Do you even care?* I try to shush her, telling her to 'Come on, J, you need to calm down, this isn't the right place for this', but she ignores me, sitting on the toilet seat, her head in between her knees so all I can hear through her wails is '. . . you said . . . you said that if I . . . Dylan . . . you told me to . . .'

'Come on. Stop it.'

'But you *told* me—'

'It's happened to loads of people. It happens all the time. You wake up the next morning, and you regret it or you don't remember what happened exactly, but it's easier not to make a fuss—'

'But that's not how it happened.' She stares up at me. 'I *told* you what happened.'

'But I wasn't there with you, was I? How do I know what really—'

'But *I told you*. I didn't want . . . I didn't want to.'

'You didn't say no.' I crouch down in front of her, placing my hands on her shoulders. 'You told me you didn't say no.'

'But –' she shrugs my hands off her and looks at me with such despair that my skin crawls – 'I didn't say yes either.'

A phone call last Halloween. Jamie. (I look at the

screen in surprise. Jamie never calls me.) *Do you want to go to Dylan's party?* Maggie had hockey training. Ali was in the Bahamas. Just the two of us. (It was never just the two of us. We were too competitive for that, always needing one of the other girls there to act as a buffer.) Drinking. Another shot, another one, another one. Jamie in her Sailor Moon costume. Getting a lot of attention. *You're so hot, Jamie*, they kept saying. I didn't like it. I stroked her hair, kissed her, my tongue in her mouth, the boys crowing. (Her skin was so soft against mine.) She fell. I laughed. Zach's hands on my waist then, replacing hers, hot breath on my neck, and then we were kissing, and folding on to a bed, and clothes were coming off. The next morning, too many missed calls. (Come to my house, her voice message said in a trembling tone.) Keying in the passcode at the reinforced gates to Jamie's home. Her mother calling me a bad influence. Jamie, sitting on the bed, crying and crying and crying. (I felt uncomfortable.) (I felt weirdly excited by the drama.) *Be careful*, I warned her. (Dylan is a dick, but he isn't *that*, he wouldn't do *that*.) *You can't just say stuff like that. When you say that word, you can't take it back.* She kept asking, *What will I do? What will I do, what will I do, what will I do, what will I do, what will I do?*

It would change everything.

I didn't want anything to change.

Let's just pretend it didn't happen, I told her. *It's easier that way. Easier for you.*

'Jamie, come on. We talked it through and we agreed, didn't we? We agreed it would be easier not to make a big deal of it, especially when everyone there was underage and there'd be so much shit if it got out. It would just mean that people would be pissed off with you for getting them in trouble, and you'd miss out on all of the parties because Dylan's friends wouldn't want you there any more . . .' I trail off. I hope no one outside can hear us. 'Listen,' I say after a few minutes, checking my phone, 'I think you should go home.' She doesn't respond, just turns away from me, trying to get her breathing back under control. I text Danny the Taxi, asking him to come collect her as soon as he can.

'Emmie? Is everything OK in there?' It's Conor, his voice concerned. 'Ali said you might need some help.'

'Grand,' I say as I open the door to him. 'J's not feeling well. I've ordered a taxi to bring her home.'

Conor helps me get Jamie to her feet, wrapping his arm around her shoulder.

'What taxi is it?' he asks, propping her up as her knees buckle.

'Danny.'

'I can't afford a taxi,' Jamie slurs up at Conor. 'Me.

Jamie Murphy. I can't even afford a fucking taxi any more.'

'We could ask Fitzy to drive her?' Conor suggests, but I shake my head. I don't want to have to ask Fitzy for a favour. I grab my clutch bag from the side of the bathtub and start scrambling through make-up and cotton buds and a tiny hip flask of vodka, looking for cash.

'I'll take care of it,' Conor says.

'Really?' I ask, and he nods.

'Oh, thank you.' I lean in and kiss him on the cheek. 'That is so great of you. I was going to bring her home myself, but if you're going anyway . . .' I walk away so I don't have to see his face fall. 'You know where she lives, right?'

I push open the door into the TV room. 'Hey, sorry—'

I shut up. Mia is sitting on Jack's lap, irritatingly tiny and doll-like, half-heartedly pushing his hand away as he tries to inch it further up her thighs.

'I didn't realize you were into children, Jack,' I say before I can stop myself, raising my voice so I can be heard over the tinny sounds from the Xbox. He opens one eye, sees it's me, and then he actually *shrugs*, and closes his eyes again, as if he's decided that *Mia* is the one he wants to be with.

'Replaced by a younger model already, O'Donovan?'

'Shut up, Matt,' I say, my teeth gritting as Mia lets out a tiny moan.

I open my bag and grab the small hip flask, swallowing what's left in it, feeling it burn my throat.

'Seriously, man, it must have been like an oven on that pitch yesterday.'

'Yeah, you were amazing. Is it true there was a selector from the Cork team there?'

'Do you think he'll choose you for the senior panel?'

'He'll have to.'

Paul O'Brien must have followed Jack in here, slouching in a low-slung chair opposite. He's surrounded by three lads from fifth year, all leaning towards him eagerly, asking if he needs another beer, or a fag, or a toke of their joint. His eyes are dark, watching me. He leans forward to place his can by his feet.

'Here,' he interrupts the guy sitting on his armrest. 'Do you mind getting me another one? I'm out.'

The guy smiles at me on his way past. Pulling my hair over one shoulder, so the tips of it are almost touching my hip bone, I weave my way through his devoted audience and sit on the empty armrest of his chair.

'Sorry,' I say. 'But I need to rest. My feet are sore.' I reach down to rub my toes, and his eyes trail down my legs.

'O'Brien,' Ben Coughlan, the goalie for the football

team, says from the open door frame. He's in his late twenties as well, about five foot ten, his dark red hair cropped close to his skull. 'I'm leaving.' He twirls a set of car keys around his fingers.

'Are you driving?' I ask him.

'Obviously.'

'What if you get stopped by the cops?' I try again. 'Aren't you nervous?'

He rolls his eyes to heaven and I feel as if I'm ten years old. 'I think I'm safe enough there, don't you?'

'Paul, did you hear me?' Ben tries again. 'I'm leaving now.'

'Cool,' Paul says, but he's looking at me. 'I think I'm going to stay.'

'The girls are in Reilly's and they're waiting for us. Aine said Susan is going mental. Have you checked your phone?' Paul shrugs, and Ben can't help but smile. 'Your funeral. Do you have the—'

'Yeah.' Paul pushes himself out of the low chair and hands Ben something from his pocket. Ben gives him a mock salute, looks over his shoulder at where I'm sitting, murmuring something under his breath that makes Paul punch him on the shoulder.

'What was that you gave him?' I ask Paul as he settles back into the chair.

'Nothing for an innocent girl like you to be concerned with.'

'Who said I was innocent?' I raise an eyebrow at him. 'What was it?'

'Why? Do you want some?' he says, waiting for me to back down like we're playing chicken. I hesitate, and he laughs.

I am sick of people thinking they know me. I am Emma fucking O'Donovan. No one knows what I'm capable of.

'Yes.' I lean over to whisper in his ear, knowing that the top of my dress will fall open. 'I want it.' His breathing is getting heavier, and it's because of me, I am making him feel this way. (My mother yanking my shoulders back. *Stand up straight, Emma, look confident, look like you know where you're going.*) 'Come on, Paul. Sharing is caring.'

He runs his tongue across his teeth and sneaks a look around the room to make sure no one is watching. The others have gone back to the Xbox, shouting instructions at the two lads playing FIFA. He reaches into the pocket of his jeans and pulls out a clear plastic baggie. Inside it, there is what looks like the firecrackers we used to play with as kids, tiny balls of white paper, twisted at the end. He turns his body to shield me, pulling one out. I pop it into my mouth. (I hope Jack saw me do that, I hope he knows that I'm not who he thinks I am.) Paul puts his hand out, as if he's looking for money.

'Oh, I don't pay for things,' I say, and he smiles, then places a finger over his lips as if to silence me, and says, 'Don't tell anyone, OK?'

'Wouldn't look good, I guess. The captain of the football team, the future Cork player. Shouldn't you be setting a good example?'

'We haven't got a match for another three weeks.' He makes a face at me. 'Just keep it quiet, got it?'

He doesn't need to worry. I'm used to keeping secrets.

'Are you going to have some?' I ask him.

'I had one earlier.'

'Really?'

'I have a strong tolerance.' He pulls me off the armrest until I'm sitting on his lap.

'Isn't that Paul O'Brien?' I hear a girl say as the door to the TV room opens, and I sit up straighter when I see the jealousy that flashes on her face. I look at Paul again. He looks more handsome somehow, as if their envy is a flattering Instagram filter. 'I thought he had a girlfriend.'

'Don't worry about that now,' he says to me, and I want to tell him I'm not worried. Boys with girlfriends are my favourite. You don't have to worry that they're going to tell tales afterwards. 'Susan and I have an arrangement.'

His hand trails up my thigh, but Jack doesn't see it, too busy sticking his tongue down Mia's throat.

'Sorry – what?' I realize Paul is waiting for me to reply.

'I asked you if you were at the match earlier?'

'Yeah, of course.'

'Did you see how slow we were at the start?' He shakes his head. 'Fucking hell. Everyone just expects that we'll win the county again, but how are we supposed to do that when lads like your brother are quitting the team because of college and half the others are off in Australia or Canada?' He pulls his iPhone out of his pocket and opens Facebook. 'I mean, take Cian Healy for example.' He holds out the photo so that I can see. 'He was the best midfielder on the team because he was so tall.' Cian looks *amazing*. He's so tanned, and seems to have given up wearing shirts entirely. 'And who do we have now? Kelly is grand, but he's too short. But last time I was talking to Cian, he said that he was having too much fun to come home, that the surf was too good to leave. The fucking surf.' He scrolls through some more photos, showing me one of a dilapidated wooden-framed house, a group of about twenty-five people squashed together to fit into the frame, their faces familiar from matches and Saturday nights drinking in Casement Quay and hungover heads at Sunday Mass.

He puts his phone back in his pocket. 'No wonder Cian doesn't want to come back. Ballinatoom is such a hole. It's the same old shit, every Saturday night. Nothing ever happens here.'

'Why don't you go too then?' I say.

'Go where?'

'Australia.'

He stiffens. 'I can't just *leave*. This is the year that I'm going to be chosen for the Cork senior team, I know it. I've worked too hard for this.'

(Or waited too long for his uncle to finally be made a selector.)

'Sorry. I just thought it sounded like you wanted to travel.'

'I have travelled. I was in Arizona last year, which was really incredible, you know? Have you ever been?'

'To Arizona?'

'Yeah.'

'No, not Arizona. I've been to Orlando though. And San Francisco.'

'That's not the *real* America.' He frowns at me. 'Arizona is where the real American people live, not some jumped-up city dickheads.' He talks for a few more minutes about the beauty of Arizona, the people, the food.

'Wow,' I say when he pauses to catch his breath. 'How long were you there for?'

'Just over three and a half weeks. Best month of my life.'

A shiver ripples over my skin, like the tiniest chip of a pebble hitting a pool of water. It starts swirling in my feet, and creeps slowly up my legs, bleeding from one cell into the next, and it feels so good, it feels so good, *it feels so good* that I can't help but quiver with it, stretching my feet and my toes out like my body might break open.

'Well, well.' Paul looks amused. 'That didn't take long. Enjoying yourself?'

My lips spread in a smile, my eyelids flickering. He leans in to whisper in my ear. 'I saw you at the GAA gala last year, you know. You were the hottest girl there.' His words seep through my chest, expanding in my lungs like helium.

And for a moment it's almost too much for me, the smell of his woody aftershave, the velvet softness of his T-shirt brushing against my arm. I stretch again, my spine lengthening so much I feel as if it might tear out of my back and shoot for the ceiling like a firework.

'Come on.' He nudges me off his knee until I'm standing. I drop my head, my breath feeling like the beginning of something that I can't name. 'Let's go find more beers.'

He pulls me along with him, but I don't want to go, I want to lie down somewhere quiet by myself so I can feel this sherbet dissolving through my veins. In the dining room, I hide my face in his shoulder while he cracks open his can, but the music wraps around me, pulling me into the centre of the room. I feel it invade me, take over, filling my empty bones.

'Are you OK?' It's Maggie. I hug her, trying to melt into her so that our hearts can touch, *beat, beat, beat,* against each other.

I hold her head in my hands and press my nose against hers so I can look her in the eye as closely as possible.

'You're sweating,' Maggie says, pulling away. 'Have you . . . *taken* something?'

I let her go and she fades away, thawing into the shadows.

'. . . She's a mess . . .'

I bend backwards.

'What are we going to do?'

I can hear my heart beat and 'Should we call her parents?' and *nothingness to fall through* 'Has she taken anything?' *blurring* 'But where would she . . . ? She's probably just drunk' *all I am made of is soft* 'It's not like her though, you know what a control freak she is,' *I run my hands over his shoulders, so broad, so solid, and he loves her (he's a great kisser, she giggles, and I need to know, I need to know) I press my lips to his and he doesn't move away, and* 'Jesus Christ, what are you doing?' *what?* 'Emma.' *what?* 'Emma. Emma. Emma. What the fuck do you think you're doing? Emma. Emma.' *Higher. Higher. Higher.* 'For fuck's sake, she's a mess' *inside me* 'Emma. Emma.'

'*Emma.*'

'Hey.' It's Paul, and the mist begins to rise again and I can feel the music trickling out of my feet. (I can feel my feet.) (My feet are on the floor.)

'Take it easy, all right?' he says. 'You're being really obvious.'

Conor has reappeared with a glass of water. He leads me over to the table and sits me on a stool.

'Jamie got home OK,' he tells Maggie (*Jamie, I love you, Jamie, I am sorry, I will make it better, I will make it better for you*), but Maggie isn't listening to us, she's yelling at Eli. Conor is so nice (so much nicer than me, but for once I don't hate him for that) and I wrap my arms around him, and press our hearts together too. I kiss him. I pull back.

Something flashes across his face, but I tilt my head back as the mist descends again.

'Finally,' Paul says when my eyes refocus. I hadn't realized he was still standing beside me. I smile at him, but he doesn't smile back, and then over his shoulder I can see them, holding hands by the boom box. Jack is talking to a guy I don't know, while Mia stares at me. Maggie is mouthing at Eli furiously while he throws his hands up in defence. Jack nods at something his friend has said, and his gaze sweeps across the room until he sees me. He tilts his head at me, his hand nestled in the small of Mia's back, and I need him to . . . I need him to *see* me.

I take Paul's hand in mine.

'Well, you didn't look like you were trying very hard to stop her, Eli,' I hear Maggie say as Conor steps in front of Paul and me.

'I don't think this is such a good idea.'

'Who are you, her dad?'

'She's in no state to—'

'Seriously,' Paul says, 'fuck off.'

'I think you should come home with me, Emmie.' Conor tries to grab my wrist but no, no. He's not enough. (No one will be impressed by Conor.) I shake his hand off me, and I lead Paul into the hall, down the corridor past Sean and a red-eyed Ali. I push open the second door on the right, ignoring Sean calling after me, 'Not in there, lads, that's my parents' room, like,' and pull Paul in, locking the door behind us.

'Hey.'

'Hey.'

John and Deirdre Casey's bedroom is pristine, a large double bed taking up most of it, the bedclothes white with oversized pink roses splattered across them, the curtains and carpet matching. The far wall is a white fitted wardrobe, bedside lockers on either side of the bed. On the locker nearest to the door, there is a photo frame, a tube of hand cream and a box of tissues. The other locker is empty except for a plastic alarm clock, '01.35' gleaming in red. Paul puts his can of beer down, grabs me by the waist and pushes me on to the bed, lying on top of me as he kisses me.

I need water. I am so thirsty.

His belt buckle is cutting into my hip. I feel like the breath is being squeezed out of my lungs and I can't fill them back up again. He pulls his T-shirt over his head. His chest is broad, covered in dark, coarse hair. He unbuckles his belt, kicks off his flip-flops and stands there in his boxers, coming for me, pushing my dress down my body. He turns me around and kisses my neck from behind, running his hands all over my body, whispering to me what he's going to do to me, and what he wants me to do to him.

'Stick . . .' (*Emmie, why would a boy buy the cow when he can have the milk for free?*) '. . . in there . . . now.' (*It's different for boys and girls.*)

'. . . I like that . . .' (*Be more ladylike.*)

'. . . You like that, don't you? . . .' (*Cover yourself up, Emmie, for goodness sake.*) '. . . Dirty little . . .'

(I don't like that word . . .)

Don't use that word, wait. No.

(. . . but I don't say anything.)

A rush comes upon me again, a stuttering, fading one, shimmering through me as he pushes my face into the centre of the rose-print on the duvet, and I feel like the flower is eating my face. I try to get up.

'What?' he says. 'What's wrong with you?'

'Maybe we should . . .' I try and swallow, but my mouth is too dry. 'Paul, maybe we should go back to the party.'

'Don't be silly,' he says. (I brought him in here. This was my idea.) 'Don't be a fucking cock-tease.'

'Wait,' I try and say. 'Wait, I don't feel . . .'

But he pushes me back down, yanking my underwear aside, and he's inside me, and I'm not ready and it hurts and I don't feel well, and I don't think he's using a condom, and I should stop him, I should stop him and tell him to get one. I have one in my wallet. But he'll think I'm a slut if I say that, but they say in magazines to always have condoms, but it's too late now, and I don't feel well, and I don't know, I don't know, I don't know if there's any point in stopping him now. And it's too late now anyway.

(It doesn't matter, it doesn't matter, it's no big deal, and who cares, who cares anyway?)

He's wrapped some of my hair around his fist, wrenching my head back. I can see the photo on the bedside locker is of John Junior. He is like a toddler version of Sean, his red-blond hair in messy curls, his short dungarees showing off knees scuffed with dirt. I wonder what he must have been like, all those years ago, eaten alive by the slurry pit, yelling for someone to save him, but he couldn't breathe, he couldn't breathe with his mouth crammed full of shit. Paul bites my shoulder, hard, and it hurts, *and it hurts*, and I want to tell him to stop but I can tell he thinks this is what I want, that this is something I should enjoy (would other girls like it?) so I moan, they always like that, that'll make it end quicker, and he leans over me again, biting my ear, telling me I'm a slut, and he knows I want it, *you know you want it, Emma*, thrusting harder and harder, slamming his body into mine. I just want it to be over. And finally, it is, his fingertips gouging into my hip bones, and he pulls out, giving a long, desperate groan while a wet heat splatters across my lower back. He collapses to the side of me, his breath coming fast and heavy.

I hold myself very still, lying on my stomach, my head turned away from him. There are people laughing outside, muttered conversations, a moment of silence when someone changes a song on the iPod, then a low drone of music again.

'Fuck, that was amazing,' he says after a few moments. 'Did you come?'

'Yes, of course.'

He pats the back of my head. 'You'd better clean yourself up.'

The en-suite toilet is cramped; there's only room for a toilet and a basin. I pull on my knickers and take a rolled-up washcloth from a pink-and-white checked basket on the cistern, hold it under the running water and rub the drying stickiness off myself. I look in the bathroom cabinet above the sink, rummaging through toothpaste, haemorrhoid cream, KY Jelly, mouthwash and bottles of pills until I find a hair scrunchie. I tie up my hair into a high bun, tucking the matted ends under. My tongue feels swollen with thirst, and I turn the tap on and stick my head under it. When I straighten up, I wipe my mouth in the mirror. I look different somehow, like the bones of my face have shifted. My jaw is jutting at an odd angle, my pupils so large that my eyes look completely black, but I'm still me, *Emma O'Donovan, my name is Emma O'Donovan, I am Emma, Emma, Emma*. A wave of dizziness hits, and I lean my face against the cold glass.

'Jesus, Susan.' Paul's voice, angry and harsh. I wait until there is silence before I open the door. He is lying on the bed, all of his clothes back on.

'Girlfriend problems?' I close the door behind me, then lean against it, showing myself to him.

'You could say that,' he says, patting the bed next to him.

'Bitches be crazy,' I say, aligning my body with his, and he runs his hands all over me, as if he's trying to claim me for himself. It's as if he wants to own me. 'What's her problem?'

'She wants to get married,' he says, his hands stilling.

'But you're only, like, what? Twenty-eight?'

'Aine and Ben are nearly there. Ben's even gone shopping for a ring.' He continues as if I haven't said anything. 'And a few of the other lads on the team as well. Susan and me have been together for six years now. She says it's "time to take the next step". Fucking women.'

'I never want to get married,' I say. 'Gross.'

'Of course you don't.' He pulls my body closer,

wrapping one of his legs over mine. 'You're not like other girls, are you?'

His phone starts to ring, and he switches it to silent, throwing it next to the framed photo of John Junior. We kiss, his tongue heavy in my mouth. The phone rings again, vibrating against the wood. He breaks away from me, cursing, and cuts the call dead.

'Here,' he says, 'what's your number?'

'What's the point? This is only a one-night type of thing.' I always say that when boys ask me for my number.

'Come on.' He doesn't look me in the face, just runs his hands up and down my body. 'Susan is away a lot,' he says, and I laugh.

'Come on,' he says again. 'I would very much like to fuck you again.'

I must have been good; he must have enjoyed it if he wants to see me again.

I call out my number to him and he phones me immediately, my phone lighting up, then cutting out, and he says, 'And now you have my number too.'

'Look at what we have here, then.'

I scream, jumping off the bed and yanking the covers around me, Paul getting to his feet as well. Laura and her friend are walking past, and they gasp when they see me, naked except for my knickers and crouched down on the floor, the duvet wrapped around me, searching under the bed for my dress. Dylan and Paul just stand there, watching me.

'Close the fucking door, will you?' I pull my dress back on.

'Lads.' Sean stumbles in, wrapping an arm around Paul and Dylan's necks. He hiccups. 'Did you have fun?' He looks at me, and he tries to smile. 'Did you, Emma?'

'Will you *please* close the door?' I plead. 'How did you even get in? I thought I locked it.'

Paul makes an 'oops' face and says, 'Ah, you're too hot not to show you off.' He grabs my arm and pulls me up to standing. 'Look at her.'

This is the price of my beauty, and I am willing to pay it. I am willing.

Dylan snorts (but who cares – he likes Jamie; some guys have a thing for Asian chicks, it doesn't mean anything).

I smile, although my arm hurts where Paul pulled me. I sit on the bed. 'So. What's the story?'

'Not much,' Dylan says, taking a swig out of his plastic Coke bottle before passing it to Paul. He tilts his head at me. 'Where's Jamie?' He tries and fails to look casual. 'Did she go home?'

'It's never going to happen, Dylan. She's not interested.'

'Did I say I was fucking interested in her?' He looks away. 'I was just asking a question.' He grabs the Coke bottle back off Paul and takes a swig. 'Listen, I've heard there's another party happening in town. You guys up for it?' He holds out the Coke bottle to Paul, but Sean goes to grab it off him, knocking it out of his hands.

'Shit.'

'Casey.' Dylan throws his hands up in disgust. 'I don't have any more drink left.'

He turns to leave, his hand on the door handle, when Sean yells after him, 'Wait. Wait. I just remembered. My mam has some stuff.'

'What kind of "stuff"?'

Sean brushes the edge of the photo frame. He puts the picture facing down and opens the drawer to the bedside locker, rifling through it until he pulls out a cream cotton washbag. He unzips it, and there are about five different bottles filled with pills.

'Well, well, well.' Paul stands up and goes to lock the door again. He takes the washbag off Sean, muttering under his breath as he looks through it. Dylan holds his hand out, swallowing down a little blue pill as soon as Paul gives it to him.

'Here.' Paul holds one out for me. 'For you, my darling.'

I don't know if I want to.

'Come on,' he says when I hesitate. 'Let's just take these before we go.'

Dylan cackles, as if he knows that Emma O'Donovan would never take pills, even prescription ones. He thinks that he knows me. He thinks that I am boring, and traditional, and a good girl, and I am going to study hard for my Leaving Cert and go to university, and get a good job, and marry someone sensible (*All this talk of romantic love*, Mam sighs. *What's important is that you have similar values and beliefs, that you come from similar cultures, that you're the same rather than different. That's what makes for a successful relationship*) and he thinks I will have children, and turn into my mother. I am going to be just like my mother.

I'm so sick of everyone in this stupid fucking town thinking they know what I would or wouldn't do.

I reach out and take the tablet and swallow it down, gagging at its acrid taste without water.

'So –' I smirk at Dylan – 'did someone say something about another party?'

Sunday

'Emmie. *Emmie!*'

I don't want to get up for school, Mam. I don't feel well. I try to get up, but tiredness is holding my head underwater. Desperate for air. I am . . .

Air.

'Denis, help me. Will you *help me*, for God's sake. We need to get her inside.'

A pinch under my arm, squeezing tight. Too tight.

You're hurting me.

'Emma, you're making a holy show of yourself. Get up. *Get up*, I said.'

Her voice is too loud.

She touches my face, whispering angrily, *wake up, Emma, wake up wake up wake up.* I try and open my eyelids, but I can't, the skin scraping as it folds against itself.

'She's burning up. Look at those blisters.' My mother's voice is panicked. 'Feel her forehead, Denis. *Denis, I said, feel her forehead.* Her skin will be ruined.'

Daddy? Daddy, help me, I want to say, but my tongue has been cut out of my mouth with the pain.

He is silent. I hear the front door open, squeaking on its frame, and she tells him to run and get the thermometer. There are hands around my waist, dragging me off the ground, the material of my dress chafing the raw skin, and I almost scream. I see the open door, the hallway, then the roof of the porch before it dissolves into red flesh again, and the earth moves, it moves, and I move with it, falling to my hands and knees, feeling the concrete tear at me. I stretch my hands out before me, watching as the white scuffed skin fills with stripes of blood, carving lines into my palms, dripping on to the concrete below me.

'Denis. Would you stop just standing there like an eejit and *help me.*'

Dad reappears, and he has a strange look on his face. Words gargle at the back of my throat, coming out in a clotted mess. He takes a step away from me.

'Denis, pick her up. For God's sake, will you move?'

He scoops me up in his arms, carrying me over the threshold; Mam telling him to *mind the rug.* Once inside the hall, I lie down on the wooden floor, tasting vomit in my breath.

'What the . . . ?'

Bryan on the stairs, his eyes bleary with sleep. Jen is standing behind him, wearing his old Ballinatoom jersey, her long legs bare. Her jaw drops in horror, and I know something must be very, very wrong.

'Please, cover yourself up, Jennifer,' Mam hisses.

'Don't speak to her like that,' Bryan says, taking a step back up the stairs to hide Jen from view. 'Why are you even home so early?'

'It's four o clock in the afternoon.' Mam is standing at the bottom of the stairs, her hand gripping the banister, the knuckles whitening.

'I thought you said you weren't going to be back until this evening.'

I close my eyes again.

'Yes, I can see that's what you thought.' She's almost shouting now. 'I gave you one job. *One* job. To mind your sister.' I can hear her shoes squeak against the wooden floor as she turns on her heel towards me. 'And look at her. Just look at the state of her.'

'She's eighteen, Mam.'

'I don't care what age she is. This is a *respectable* house and I expect you to follow my rules under my roof.

I suppose you didn't even go to Mass?' Bryan snorts at this – unwisely, I think – and she screams at him: 'Don't you *dare* laugh at me.'

Please be quiet, please be quiet, please be quiet.

'Denis! Are you just going to let him talk to me like that?' Dad mumbles something, shifting from one foot to the other. 'Do you really think this is funny?' Mam continues. I feel like I'm going to be sick.

Don't get sick, don't get sick, don't get sick, don't get sick.

'You were supposed to be taking care of her and we arrive home and find her lying on the porch. I thought she was dead – dead, do you hear me?' I try to sit up and the room spins like I'm on a merry-go-round. 'We left you in charge.' Oh shit, I can feel it coming, boiling up inside me, crawling up my throat, and I try and stop it, but when I get on to my hands and knees to stand up (I need to get to the toilet, someone help me get to the toilet) the walls and the floor melt into one, and I'm falling through it, *down, down, down . . .*

'I thought we could *trust* you, Bryan, I thought—'

And my body heaves, bile spurting out of my mouth and splashing against her low court sandals, and it's on the rug too, and I didn't mean it and I'm sorry. I'm so sorry.

There is noise and there is blackness, and I fall into both.

Monday

My eyes are sinking into my head as if they're dissolving in quicksand. It is too bright. (What day is it?) The curtains are open, sunlight blasting through the windows, drilling holes into my brain. Dust is shimmering through the air. My skin feels tight, wrapping around my bones like cling film. I claw my way up to sitting, waves of static turning in my head. (What time is it?)

I fall back down.

'You've been a silly girl, haven't you?' Dr Fitzpatrick's face flashes before me, a more lined version of Fitzy's, except for his flat nose, broken and reset too many times over years of rugby matches. Mam is there too, trying to smile at the other patients in the waiting room at SouthDoc.

'Just a touch of sunstroke, I reckon,' Mam told Mrs

Ryan, an elderly woman with hairs growing out of a mole on her chin, her fingers gnarled with arthritis. 'She fell asleep outside. In *this* weather.' Mam threw her eyes to heaven in a 'kids today' type of way. 'Oh, I know, it's terrible close,' Mrs Ryan agreed. 'Still, we shouldn't complain, I suppose. We get enough rain.' I was swaying in my seat, Mam holding me up, barely touching me with the tips of her fingers. Dr Fitzpatrick called me into the surgery, and I can see myself getting up and moving towards him, my knees buckling beneath me as I fall to the ground again. Chairs scraping back on tiles — *give her room, get back and give her room to breathe* — and then there is nothing.

The front of my body is painted in sunburn, curving around my arms and legs until it fades into my normal alabaster white. I place a hand on my chest, then both hands on my cheeks, my skin almost sizzling hot to the touch. I swing my legs out of bed, cursing as I knock a glass of water over, grabbing my iPhone to make sure it doesn't get wet. One new message.

Bryan: Seriously, Emma. FUCK YOU.

I put the phone down, a lump of nausea squirming in my throat like a worm. Maybe if I don't look at it, it will go away.

I pick up the phone.

Bryan: Mam and Dad are raging with me because
           of you. They've cut my weekly money and
           have taken the car off me for two months.
           You need to get your fucking act together.

I read the message again. The words feel wrong, somehow, like the position of the letters doesn't make any sense.

The other messages were sent by me to the girls last night. There are vowels missing, and words spelled entirely wrong, there are repeated messages to Jamie, all of which are blank. But there is no response to any of them.

Why haven't they replied? Are they fighting with me?

There are dozens of notifications but I don't open them up. I don't have the energy.

Why haven't the girls replied to any of my text messages?

I try to remember. I fumble through my memories of Saturday night, but they run away from me.

It doesn't mean anything. I just drank too much. *How did I get home?* I shouldn't have drunk so much. *Why am I so sunburnt?* And it was stupid taking that wrap off Paul; why did I do that? *Why can't I remember anything?* I see a bag of pills, blue ones, and yellow ones, and pink ones, no, wait, what? It's as if my dreams are swirling through my memories, making them sticky, and I can't pull them apart to see which are which.

Voices. Laughing. Hands grabbing at me, pushing through the black felt of the night, no bodies, no faces, just hands, white as chalk against the darkness. *What happened?*

'Ah sure, look who it is.' Sheila Heffernan is sitting at the kitchen counter, her short, bright red hair gelled into solid spikes. The two of them are sipping tea out of china cups, a half-eaten loaf of Mam's Madeira cake between them. Sheila holds her powdered cheek out for me to kiss, but I can't move any closer to her, the smell of her perfume ramming into my nostrils.

'Why are you still in your pyjamas?' Mam asks.

'I don't feel well.'

'Yes, your mother was just telling me about your trip to SouthDoc.' Sheila shakes her head, the misshapen beaded earrings she made in her jewellery design class banging against her neck. 'What on *earth* were you doing?'

'I told you, Sheila,' Mam says. 'She was doing a bit of sunbathing and fell asleep outside.' She gestures at the cake. 'Have some, Emma. Freshly baked this morning.'

I turn away, breathing deeply. Mam will never speak to me again if I vomit on the kitchen floor in front of

Sheila. 'Or there's your granola in the Cath Kidston tin.' She smiles at Sheila. 'Home-made, of course.'

'I'm not hungry.'

'Now, now, Emma.' Sheila wags a finger at me. 'Breakfast is the most important meal of the day. I know all you young girls are watching your figures, although *thankfully* I don't have that problem with my Caroline, she has always been as thin as a whippet, takes after—'

'Oh, Emma has never had any problems with her weight,' Mam interrupts, looking in my direction, although her gaze seems to be focused an inch above my head. 'She's naturally slim, like the rest of us, thank God.' Sheila, another forkful of cake halfway to her mouth, pauses, and slowly drops it back on the plate.

'We should be leaving, Nora,' she says pulling at her turquoise tunic. 'The class starts in twenty minutes, and I'm so sick of Bernadette Quirke hogging the front row. And – did I tell you? – when I rang her last week to say I didn't have time to do the church flowers, she was very sour with me. And after me explaining about Aidan's flu. I was run off my feet.'

'I know, Sheila, you've been so busy.'

'I don't think I can go to school,' I say. 'I really don't feel well.'

'You're going to school,' Mam says, her left eye

starting to quiver almost imperceptibly. 'Where's Maggie? She should be here by now.'

I check my phone again, but there's nothing. I step away, standing in the kitchen doorway with my back to the room. I try Maggie, then Ali, then, as a last resort, Jamie. I try Maggie again, Ali, and then Maggie again, and again, and again, but there is still no answer.

'Is there a problem?' Sheila has crept up right behind me.

'I think there's something wrong with the phone network,' I lie, taking a step back from her.

'Oh.' She peers at her ancient Nokia. 'I have all five bars.'

'Mam –' I turn to her – 'please. I don't feel well. Can I stay at home?'

'Why are we still having this conversation?' Her lips have gotten so thin it looks like she's swallowed them. She forces a smile at Sheila, gesturing at her to walk ahead of us into the corridor. 'The car door should be open, we'll be there in a second.' Mam waits until she's out of sight before hissing at me, 'And where is Maggie, I'd like to know?'

'She's not answering her phone.'

'She's probably disgusted with you for your behaviour on Saturday night, and I wouldn't blame her.'

'Please, Mam, I'm begging you, I really don't feel—'

'You have two minutes to change into your school uniform and get in the car. Now, Emma.'

There's a collective intake of breath when I open the door into my Irish class. There are three rows of tables on each side of the room, a narrow gap in between so the teacher can walk around and keep an eye on us, and every girl on every row is staring at me. I put my hands out, laughing, and say, 'Hey, third-degree burns are so hot right now,' holding my sunburnt face in my hands like I'm on the cover of *Vogue*, but no one laughs. Aisling Leahy nudges Catherine Whyte, sticking her tongue against the inside of her mouth as if she's giving a blow job, and the two of them start snickering.

'*Bi ciuin!*' Mr O'Leary snaps at them. I stare at the worn-out carpet, waiting for my punishment.

'And what time do you call this?' O'Leary sits back in his chair, peering over his half-moon glasses. He looks pointedly at the clock hanging above the whiteboard.

'Sorry, Mr O'Leary, I—'

'I don't have time for excuses. Report for detention at big lunch.'

'But—'

'Arguing is an excellent way to find yourself with

125

after-school detention as well, Miss Ní Dhonnabháin.' He snaps his fingers at the rows of seats. '*Suigh síos.*'

Ali, Maggie and Jamie are sitting in the back left-hand row, where we always sit for Irish class, but the seat nearest to the window, *my* seat, isn't empty. Chloe Hegarty is sitting there, staring out the window at the sun bouncing off the artificial green of the AstroTurf pitch.

'Are you deaf, Emma?' Mr O'Leary heaves himself up from his seat and stands far too close for comfort to me, broken veins running like threadworms across his cheeks and nose. 'I thought I told you to sit down.'

'My seat is taken,' I say, staring at the girls.

'I don't care.' He draws the words out slowly.

'But——'

'*Sit down.* You are wasting precious *scrudu* time.'

'Test?' *Shit, shit, shit, shit.* 'What test?'

'You are, eh, *testing* my last nerve, Miss Ní Dhonnabháin. You have a grammar test today. It will count as thirty-five per cent of your mark for your summer exams. I believe I told you this on Friday, did I not? Now. Take. A. Seat.'

There's only one seat left, in the front row, next to Josephine Hurley, who everyone knows is a total lesbian because she watches the rest of us as we get changed for PE. Chloe was forced to share a room with her when we went on our school tour to Rome last year, and she told me that Josephine kept walking in on her while she was in the shower and claiming it was an 'accident'. I sit down with an exaggerated sigh, something that would usually generate a laugh, but there's nothing, and even Josephine shuffles her chair away from me, murmuring something to Lisa Keane on her other side. I can hear my name whispered, and the two of them stifling giggles. I stare at a poster of Ireland on the wall, all the rivers and mountain ranges and lakes picked out in different colours, trying to steady my breathing.

I am Emma O'Donovan.

I am Emma O'Donovan.

I am Emma O'Donovan.

I am Emma O'Donovan.

The bell rings, and I have to hand in an empty exam booklet.

'Remember, Miss Ní Dhonnabháin,' O'Leary says as he's gathering up his board markers and books, 'detention at big lunch. And please, never arrive late to my class again. *A dhéanann tú a thuiscint?*'

'Yes, Mr O'Leary, I understand.' He frowns at me to speak in Irish too. 'Sorry. I meant . . . *Tuigim.*'

He leaves; a few girls who are in lower-level English following him to go to their next class. The door slams shut behind them. I get to my feet, knocking over Josephine's pencil case as I do so, ignoring her squeak of protest. She can pick it up herself, the stupid bitch.

'Hey.' I stand in front of the girls in the back row. 'Where were you this morning? I tried ringing all of you about a million times.'

Maggie drops her chin, but Jamie stares at me. Ali still hasn't looked up.

'I suppose you rang Eli too, did you?' Jamie says.

'Eli? Why would I ring Eli?'

'You seemed pretty friendly with him on Saturday night.'

'Jamie.' Maggie's head snaps back up. 'Just forget it.'

'Forget it?' Jamie says. 'You want us to forget that your so-called best friend kissed your boyfriend?'

Kissed? I kissed Eli? *Fuuuuuck.*

'I didn't . . . I didn't . . .' (Did I? I can't remember.) 'For God's sake, J, we were all just messing around. It was only a bit of banter. Maggie knows that. Don't you, Mags?'

She looks at me wearily. 'I do, Em. It was nothing. I'd barely even call it a kiss.'

'Maggie!' Jamie looks at her in horror. 'It was still your *boyfriend.* She kissed your boyfriend.'

I fold my arms across my chest. 'Why are you assuming that *I* kissed *him*? Maybe Eli made a move on me.'

'Emma.' A note of steel enters Maggie's voice. 'Don't do that. Eli does not fancy you.'

(What?)

(Why not?)

'I know that,' I say. 'I never said that he did.'

'Everyone *has* to fancy you, don't they, Emma?' Jamie mutters. 'One boy just isn't enough for you any more.' Someone in the row in front of us giggles at this.

'Why are you making such a big deal about this?' I ask her. 'Maggie doesn't care, so why should you?'

'As if you don't know,' Jamie says through gritted teeth. *'As if*, Emma.'

'I don't know,' I say, and then I catch myself, reminding myself that *I am Emma O'Donovan*, and that Emma O'Donovan does not cower before bitches like Jamie Murphy. I stand up straight. 'Look, J, I don't know what your problem is, but I've had a really shit couple of days, and I don't appreciate you being such a bitch to me. Like, do you have any idea what's going on for me at home? My parents—'

'I don't give a shit about your fucking parents.' Maggie places a hand on her forearm to calm her down, but Jamie jerks it off.

'No, Maggie. Stop trying to make this better. It's not like this is the first time she's fucked you over. Like, hello?

The fucking Volvo? She never even apologized for that, did she?'

'That had nothing to do with you. And I *did* apologize to Maggie.' All the girls in our class are staring at us now, open-mouthed. 'I did, didn't I?'

'You did, I guess.' Maggie bites her lip. 'But I got in a lot of trouble, Em, and you kind of treated the whole thing like it was a joke. I would never have gone out in that weather if you hadn't asked me to pick you up.'

'I didn't *force* you, did I? I was stuck out in Aaron's house, and no taxi would come out because of the flooding, and Mam kept phoning me. What else was I supposed to do?'

Ali finally lifts her head and looks me straight in the eye. 'Well, maybe, Emma, you could try to be less of a whore. Just a thought.'

Her words are like fists, driving into my stomach, leaving me winded. 'What?' My head is spinning. Did Ali just say that to me? *Ali?* 'I told you, I didn't sleep with Aaron that time, no matter what he said afterwards. We only—'

'Oh, stop lying.' Ali bangs her fist on the table, and both Maggie and Jamie start. 'That's all you ever do,' she says, '*lie, lie, lie, lie.*'

'Why are you being like this?' The words come out of

my mouth in a plaintive whimper. 'What have I done that is so terrible, Ali?'

'Oh, I don't know. How about the time you told me you didn't want to lend me that red top from River Island because you were afraid I would stretch it? How about the time you went on for an hour about how beautiful my mom was, and then ten minutes later casually dropped it into the conversation what a pity it was I didn't look like her? What about the time you told Maggie that Eli kept coming on to you and they nearly broke up? What about the time—'

'OK,' I say, feeling pressure building up behind my eyes, 'I get it. I'm a fucking bitch. I'm the worst friend in the whole entire world. Why are you making such a big deal out of it this time?'

'You slept with him,' Ali whispers, and she blinks away tears.

'Aaron?' I'm confused. 'Oh, wait, *Paul O'Brien*? What do you care?'

'Not *Paul*. Although I suppose the fact that he has a *girlfriend* is irrelevant. Emma O'Donovan always has to get whatever it is she wants.' Her voice trembles. 'I can't believe you had sex with Sean.'

'Sean?' I almost laugh in her face. 'Sean Casey? What are you on about?'

'Oh, shut up, Emma.' She stares out the window for a moment to compose herself, then looks at me again, and it's like I'm looking at a stranger. 'You are absolutely disgusting, do you know that? Four guys in one night? Do you have any fucking self-respect, Emma?' I just stand there. I am waiting for someone to defend me. But no one does. They look gleeful, like they have been waiting for this for the last eighteen years and it hasn't come a minute too soon. 'Like Paul wasn't enough for you,' Ali continues. 'You had to ride Sean too, and fucking *Dylan Walsh* – like, what is wrong with you, Emma? You're sick. You're actually *sick*.'

'Julie is going to kick your ass,' Sarah Swallows adds helpfully from the row in front of us. 'Just so you know.'

'I don't know what the fuck *any* of you are talking about.' I grip on to the edge of the desk with my fingertips.

'Maggie.' My voice cracks, and I hate myself for it. 'Maggie. Please.'

She puts her hand out to cover mine. 'Emma.' She waits until I look up at her, my eyes pricking with tears, but I can't cry, not in front of all these people. 'Listen to me – were you taking stuff at the party?'

'Of course she was.' Jamie rolls her eyes. 'Did you not see her? She was chewing the face off herself.'

'J,' Maggie warns her, then squeezes my fingers. 'Emma, come on, just tell me – did you take anything?'

'No, of course I—'

'Please, Emma.' She pulls her hand away and starts to massage her temples. 'Please. Just tell me the truth. Is that why you did this? Because you were off your face?'

'But I didn't. I don't know what you're talking about. This is—'

'There's no point in denying it.' Maggie is getting exasperated. (She is sick of me.) (They are all sick of me.) 'Eli told me. You're just making things worse by lying.'

'But I'm not lying. I admit I slept with Paul, but—'

'Stop it. He has a girlfriend. And besides that, you knew how Ali felt about Sean. She doesn't deserve this.'

'But I *didn't* have sex with him. And it's not my fault that he doesn't fancy her. I mean, I told him that she . . .' I stop myself just in time.

'Told him what?' Ali's face is stricken. 'Told Sean what, Emma? What did you tell him about me?' I look away. 'You told him I liked him, is that it?' she says. I don't deny it and she looks like she wants to kill me.

'Well, maybe I should tell him to get an STI test as quickly as possible,' she says. 'Chlamydia is *so* easy to treat these days, isn't it?'

As soon as she says it, I think I see regret in her eyes,

but then it's gone. Maybe it was never there in the first place.

'Fuck you,' I hiss, as the classroom gasps in delight. I can hear people fumbling in bags for phones, the clicking of keys as people text. Lisa Keane has taken out her iPhone and is pointing it at us. 'If you're filming this, I will literally cut you.' I make a lunge at her, but she just laughs at me. Lisa Keane is laughing at *me*.

'Easy Emma,' Jamie says, then smiles in delight. 'Yes, Easy Emma. I do like a bit of alliteration. It's nearly as good as Sarah Swallows.'

'Hey,' Sarah says. 'Don't drag me into this mess.'

I take a deep breath. 'I don't think name-calling is helping here,' I say, trying to channel Hannah in therapist mode. 'Can't we go somewhere private and talk this out?'

'No.' I've never seen Ali so resolute, and suddenly I feel very afraid. 'You *knew* how I felt about Sean, but it didn't matter. Whatever Emma O'Donovan wants, Emma O'Donovan gets, right?'

'But I *didn't*—'

'It's not enough that everybody else *always* prefers you.' Her lip starts to quiver, and Jamie wraps a hand around her waist. 'You just had to prove that Sean liked you best too.'

134

I crouch down until I'm eye level with her. 'Ali—'

'Fuck off and leave us alone,' Jamie says.

'But I—'

'Emma.' Maggie's voice is firm. 'I think it's probably best if you just leave now.'

'Oh, whatever,' I say as I stand up, moving towards my new seat at the front of the class. 'I don't give a fuck anyway. It's not my fault Sean doesn't like you. He's probably not into *giants*.'

No one laughs. They always laugh at my jokes.

'I'm relieved he doesn't like me,' Ali says. 'Since he's probably riddled now anyway.'

'I told you,' I say. (Who is she? Ali would never say things like this, especially not to me. Ali is good and kind and loyal.) 'I didn't . . . I don't even fucking remember what happened on Saturday night, but I definitely didn't—'

'What are you trying to say, Emma?' Jamie narrows her eyes at me.

The room goes quiet, muffled, like when you wake up in the morning and you can somehow sense that it's snowed the night before.

I don't know. I don't know what I'm trying to say.

'That's right,' Jamie says. 'Best not to say anything. No one likes a girl who makes a fuss, do they?'

*

10.00 a.m.

I wait for what feels like hours, then sneak a peek at the clock on the wall again.

10.04 a.m.

At small break, the bell rings and Maggie and Jamie form a protective circle around a red-eyed Ali. She is the victim.

'You know you're not allowed to stay in the classroom during break,' Ms O'Regan calls at me from the open doorway. 'Out you get.'

I walk to the ref alone. Why did I forget my phone, I need to text Sean and Dylan, I need to ask them what they've been saying, why are they saying things that aren't true. (But I don't remember, I don't remember.) The ref is a large, dark room, the old-fashioned brown lino and oak-panelled walls swallowing any light. There are round Formica tables filling the middle of the room, a glass-plated hot-food counter at the top, about a hundred girls in there, chatting, laughing, arguing.

I join the queue for food, the two second years in front of me turning to look at me, smothering smiles. They nudge another friend, a plump girl with box braids. 'What?' she says, her eyes widening as they jerk their heads back towards me. I pick up an apple from the basket next to the stack of trays at the front and walk to the cash desk. Mr O'Flynn is on duty and I hand him a euro coin without comment.

'Got a little bit of sun over the weekend, I see?' he teases as he hands me back my change.

'Hmmm.' I'm not in the mood for flirting today.

I stand facing down the long hall, all the tables seeming to be full of gaping mouths and pointed fingers and whispers behind cupped hands. Ali, Maggie and Jamie are the only ones not looking at me.

'Hey.' I sit at the nearest table, throwing my bag at my feet and cleaning my apple on the folds of my skirt. 'God, I am so dead in that Irish exam. I can't believe I forgot about it—'

'You can't sit here,' Chloe Hegarty says, her moon-shaped face screwed up as if she's smelled something rotten.

'What?'

Chloe Hegarty phones me at least three times a week, and believes me when I tell her that I must have 'just missed' her because I was in the shower. Chloe Hegarty gave me a present for my eighteenth birthday even though I didn't even invite her to my party. Chloe Hegarty bakes a batch of mini apple pies for me every Christmas because she knows I hate mince pies. Chloe Hegarty told me once that she considers me to be her best friend.

'Sorry,' she says, 'but you can't sit here.'

I don't know how I do it, but I get to my feet and I walk away.

I am Emma O'Donovan, I tell myself over and over and over again, as I sit on the toilet seat in a bathroom cubicle, trying to eat my apple, waiting for the bell to ring.

The day crawls on. During class I can focus on the teacher, and everyone is quiet, people can't whisper *slut, liar, skank, bitch, whore,* when they're here.

But then the teachers leave.

The moments when we're waiting for the next teacher to fill their place, or we have to travel in the halls to another room, shoulder after shoulder banging up against mine, my books knocked off my desk . . . Whispers. All I can hear are whispers.

Slut, liar, skank, bitch, whore . . .

We're waiting for the geography teacher to arrive. It's the last class of the day. I can go home after this. I can curl up in bed, cover my head with my pillow to block out the world outside. I can fall asleep and forget this day ever happened. Everything will have gone back to normal tomorrow. Sean and Dylan will admit that they were lying, and Eli will tell Maggie, and she'll phone me to apologize and she'll make Ali and Jamie apologize too, and everyone will be sorry. I pretend to look over the essay on climate change that we had to write for today's class. Where is Miss Coughlan? Would she ever just get here? If she was here they would all be quiet and stop whispering and I wouldn't have to ignore the waves of voices around me, rising and falling, the peals of laughter, all melting away into one split second of silence in which I hear my name. *Emma O'Donovan?* A gasp, breaths held, heads turning in my direction to see my reaction, then fits of nervous giggles.

Laughing at me.

They are all laughing at me.

And I'm getting to my feet and I run, run, run; run away from them all, from the chatter and laughter and noise, I run down the corridor, *Emma O'Donovan? Emma O'Donovan? Emma O'Donovan?* beating in my bones. I sit on the toilet, heels of my palms digging into my eyes, trying to remember how to breathe.

Trying to remember. (I can't remember, I can't remember.)

Emma O'Donovan? Emma O'Donovan? Emma O'Donovan?

She's waiting for me when I swing the door of the toilet cubicle open, her brassy red hair scraped back off her face in an unflattering ponytail.

'Julie—'

'Save it.' She comes closer to me, nudging me

backwards into the cubicle, giving me one hard push so I land heavily on the toilet seat. She bends over, her face inches away from mine. 'Dylan told me what happened.'

'But I'm telling you, I didn't—'

'You're fucking finished, do you hear me? Finished.' She places both her hands on my shoulders and squeezes hard, digging her fingernails into me. I try and get up, but she shoves me back down, spitting, 'Did I fucking say that we were finished talking?'

'You . . . you . . . you can't speak to me like that.' I'm breathless with the shock of it, but she laughs in my face.

'Or what? What are you going to do about it?'

If this had happened last week, the girls would be here with me, they would have pulled Julie off me and told her to cop on. If this had happened last week, I wouldn't be alone.

'Julie, I don't know what Dylan told you, but it's not—'

'Oh, shut the fuck up.' She loses her cool. 'Don't fucking lie to me. I saw the Snapchat—'

'Is there a problem here?' Miss Coughlan pops her head around the door, her lips pursed at us.

'No, miss,' Julie says. 'Emma ran out of class because she was feeling sick. I thought I should make sure she was all right.'

'And that required screaming at her, did it?' Miss Coughlan gives Julie a dubious look. 'Is everything OK, Emma?'

'Yes, Miss Coughlan.' I try to smile at her. 'I'm fine.'

After school, I stand on the footpath watching as Maggie's Fiesta veers out of the car park, black smoke farting from the exhaust pipe. I practise in my head what I would say to anyone if they asked why Maggie didn't give me a lift. *I just felt like the walk*, I'd say. *I needed fresh air.*

But no one asks me.

I walk towards the exit, weaving my way through the throngs of younger girls, their hands clutching on to the straps of brightly coloured backpacks, threatening to fall backwards with the weight of their books. I wait for them to say hello, to ask advice on their hair, or how I get my skin so clear, or to tell me that I *should be a model, you're so beautiful*. But there is none of that today, only miles of dead space around me.

I hear my name called from a passing car. I see it as it comes towards me, like a missile, and yet I do not step out of the way. I wait for it, the heaviness of it slamming against me like a broken promise. The unopened can of Coke falls to the ground. Julie Clancy leans out of Sarah's dark green Yaris, her middle finger held up as the car screeches away.

'And what time do you call this? You should have been home an hour ago. I've been phoning you and phoning you. Why haven't you been answering your mobile?' Mam says when I trudge through the front door. She's sitting on the bottom step of the stairs waiting for me.

'I forgot my phone.'

'I don't care. I specifically told you to come straight home after school.' I'm staring at the mat, and the new patch of yellow discoloration on the cream shagpile. She gasps as I straighten up. 'What happened to your face?'

'I walked into an open locker. It was an accident.'

'And why are your clothes damp?'

'It's raining.' I open the door to show her, the haze of drizzle making everything past our porch blurry. 'See?'

A car pulls up the driveway next to us, Conor's mam waving as she rushes into the house, a newspaper over her head.

'The good weather finally broke, Dymphna,' Mam calls out, smiling at her until she closes the door behind her. 'And how exactly did you get so wet going from Maggie's car to the porch? I'm not a fool, Emma. You obviously went to Connolly Gardens after school when I told you that you were to come straight home.' She waits for me to say something, then grabs hold of my arm. 'Well?'

Her fingers tear into my sunburnt skin and I shake her off. 'I walked.'

'All the way from school?' Her eyebrows nearly disappear into her hairline. 'But why would you walk all that way in this weather? Emma, I just don't understand what has gotten into you; this is so unlike you. I can't tell you how disappointed I am in your . . .'

I climb the stairs slowly as she yells after me to *come back here this instant, young lady, I'm still talking to you.*

I peel off the sodden uniform squelching against my skin and dump it into the Hello Kitty laundry basket Ali brought me as a joke present from her trip to Japan. It lands on top of the dress I wore on Saturday night. I take it out. It's destroyed, vomit all over it. I throw it in the bin beside my bed. I never want to wear it again. I close the door to my en-suite behind me, and I stand naked in front of the full-length mirror on the wall beside the shower. The front of my body is so burnt it's almost purple, bubbles of blisters forming around my hairline and my hands. I peer closer at the mirror. Beneath the sunburn, there's shadowing, bruises blossoming around my neck and hips. I sit on the toilet, wincing as I pee. It still stings, maybe even worse today than it did yesterday. When I'm finished, I angle my lower body closer to the mirror, ducking down to stare at the reflection. It's chafed, red raw, the same pattern of bruising dotted on my inner thighs.

Paul must have liked it rough.

The water beats down on my tight skin. I shampoo my hair, trying to massage out the pressure building around my skull. I breathe in the coconut smell, blinking water out of my eyes.

I had sex with Paul.

I open my mouth, rivulets running down my tongue.

Why can't I remember? Just fucking remember, Emma.

Strands of ice across my eyeballs. Fizzing through me. Hands pushing my bones into the centre of my body, as if they're trying to make me smaller. *Lads, I don't know if this is a good idea.* Laughter, something wet splaying across my skin.

My phone rings as I get out of the shower.

'Hello?' I say, touching the screen of my iPhone and putting it on loudspeaker as I sit on the bed and towel-dry my hair.

'What the fuck do you think you're doing, Emma?'

'Bryan?' I dry my hands on the towel, turn off the speakerphone, and press it to my ear. 'Is that you?'

'Yeah, of course it's me. I presume my number came up.'

'Hey.' My eyes feel scratchy, and I blink hard. 'What

is your problem? I told Mam and Dad that you didn't have anything to do with me going to the party, that I said I was going for a sleepover at Ali's.'

'I don't give a fuck about that. Have you checked your Facebook?'

'No. I left my—'

'Go on it. Now.' I think he's hung up but then he says, 'I've never been so ashamed in my life.'

The phone goes dead, and I let it fall from my trembling fingers, watching as it slips off the quilt and lands on the floor with a thud. I get to my feet, the towel dropping away. I sit at my desk, and open my laptop.

630 notifications. I can hear my breath coming in and out, and in and out, until the whole room shrinks and dissolves into my breathing, in, out, in, out, in, out, in, out, and that's all there is. *In. Out. In. Out.*

It's a page that I've never seen before, but it has a photo of me as the profile picture. It was taken at the GAA gala last year and was used for the cover of the *Ballinatoom Opinion,* a huge billboard of it at the entrance to the town for an entire week in January. I look beautiful. (*I prefer your hair down though, Emma,* Mam had frowned. *Your ears stick out a little.*)

The page has hundreds of likes, and five little stars lined up under the name. 'Easy Emma.' I'm tagged in all of the photos.

My ribcage feels as if it's caving in to my stomach. Another like, and another, and another appears on one of the photos. 234 likes on just one picture. I've never gotten so many likes before, not even that time I uploaded a photo of myself in my bikini in Côte d'Azur. Maggie had shared it on her page, saying, 'Can we all just take a moment to appreciate The Body that is Emma O'Donovan?' Eli had liked that comment. (And I couldn't help wondering what that meant.)

345 likes.

I click on the photo.

Pale limbs, long hair, head lolling back on to the pillow. The photos start at the head, work down the body, lingering on the naked flesh spread across the rose-covered sheets.

It's not me.

Dylan on top of that girl (*me, me, that can't be me, that's not me*) his hands over the (*my – no, her*) face, as if to cover her up. She has no face. She is just a body, a life-size doll to play with.

She is an It. She is a thing. (*me, me, me, me, me*)

I don't remember. I . . .

Now Dylan has two thumbs up to the camera. In the next photos his fingers are inside the body, the girl (*me, me, oh God I'm going to be sick*) but she doesn't move. Her head and shoulders have fallen off the edge of the bed. He spreads her legs, gesturing for the camera to come closer, the next few photos of pink flesh, and I think of the hundreds of likes, of all the people who have seen this, who have seen her like this.

Me.

My breath is coming faster and faster.

Who's taking the photos?

Fitzy, I thought you were . . . Standing at the edge of the room, his face queasy (*why has he got a can in his hand, he was driving?*). Paul lifts the girl's legs, holding them up in the air, while Dylan puts his head in between them. In the next photo he is staring at the camera, grimacing like the girl, *like I, it's me (it can't be me)*, smells bad, and as I read the comments under that photo, I feel shame ripping through me, breaking me apart.

Then it's Sean. (*Here, I made you a Valentine's Day card*, he told me shyly, his front two teeth missing, his hair standing up in a cowlick. We are only eight but he has told me he wants to marry me when he's bigger, and Conor is fighting with him because he wants to marry me too. And my mother hugs me, and tells me that I am *going to be a heartbreaker and that all the boys will be after me*. She tells me that she loves me.) Sean falls, one photo of him tripping, the next of him lying on the ground, the next photo again of him getting to his feet, clutching the rose-print bedspread, a bleary-eyed smile on his face. And then he climbs on the bed and he . . .

No. No. Turn it off, Emma. Turn it off.

I feel like someone has taken a blade to my insides, scraping away at them.

A photo of Sean, his face twisting in a grimace, then another, puke gushing out of his mouth on to my face, and it's in my hair, and they are all laughing. In the next photo he has rolled off me, and is on all fours beside the bed, still vomiting. Fitzy walks towards the camera, the next photo of him with his hand reaching out, the one after that is a close-up of his sweater. Then there's another photo of Sean passed out, face down, Paul and Dylan bent over with laughter beside him.

Matt Reynolds has commented under the photo: 'Looks like Nirvana's Rape Me is the song of the night.' Twenty people have liked it. I scroll through the names. And I know all of them. Screenshots of Snapchats, one after the other.

A photo of them leaving, the Caseys' farmhouse in the background, the air a pale blue as dawn begins to break.

The girl is on the ground in the next photo. She lies there. Another photo. Dylan is standing above her, his dick in his hand, a thin yellow stream flowing from him on to her head.

Someone has commented under the photo: 'Some people deserve to get pissed on.' Five people have liked it. Six. No, ten, twelve, fifteen. Twenty. Twenty-five.

'Emmie?' A woman's voice, calling me from outside my bedroom, jolts me out of this cataleptic state and I slam the laptop shut as she turns the doorknob. 'Why is your door locked?'

'I'm getting dressed after my shower.' My voice sounds so normal. I sound like nothing has changed.

'Well, come downstairs quickly. Dinner is ready.'

'I'm not hungry.'

Mam sighs, but she doesn't argue. 'Fine.'

I wait until I hear her light footsteps on the stairs, then her heels clicking against the wooden floor of the hall.

I curl up into a ball and try to think of ways to make it stop.

Tuesday

'Ugh, I look like shit today.'

'You don't, hun, honestly, if—'

'Oh my *God*, you don't have to lie to me, I know I look like—'

'If anyone looks like shit, it's me. If these spots don't clear—'

'I swear I could see Lucy looking at me earlier and I was like, OK, Lucy, I know I look wrecked today, I couldn't sleep last night, and she was all like, What are you talking about, I wasn't even looking at you, but it was *so* obvious she was. I wouldn't mind, but it's not like she can talk or anything. Did you see the fucking state of—'

'Hey.' A third voice. The sound of footsteps, the cubicle door next to mine opening, the low hiss of pee hitting water. Velcro ripping as she opens her bag, rustling

150

as she looks through it, a muttered curse. 'Does anyone have a tampon? My period came early.'

'Better early than late.'

'Don't even joke about that. I'd be on the first boat to England, like.'

One of the girls from the sinks approaches, hesitating outside my cubicle. I can see her short grey socks and Dubarry shoes. I curl my legs up, pressing my feet against the chipboard door, covering over a cartoon penis in pink marker, my lunch box cradled in my lap. 'Which toilet are you in?'

'Here.' A thud. 'I'm sticking my foot out.'

'Cool. There you go.'

The toilet flushes a couple of minutes later, the cubicle door opens, the water tap running again.

'What's the craic?'

'Not much,' the first voice says, raising her voice to be heard over the roar of the hand dryer. 'Just talking about Lucy Dineen's new haircut.' Laughter. 'Stunning, isn't it?'

'As if anyone is going to be looking at her hair, with those tits. They're like the size of her head.'

'If I had boobs like that, I'd wear a burka or something. Did you *see* that top she was wearing on Saturday night?'

'I know.' A snort. 'I was like, OK, Lucy, we're not fifteen and going to the Attic Disco any more.'

'None of the guys could keep their eyes off her though.'

'Whatever. What a slut.'

'Speaking of sluts,' the first voice says, 'you're friends with that Emma O'Donovan in fifth year, aren't you?' My heartbeat slows to a heavy thud. Should I flush the toilet? Should I walk out and wash my hands, pretend I didn't hear them mention my name? But then they'll know that I was eating my lunch in the toilet by myself. No one else will sit with me.

(You can't sit with us.)

'I wouldn't say we're friends,' the new voice says. 'Our mams are best friends.' And I know why she sounded familiar. It's Caroline Heffernan, Sheila's daughter. We used to play together when our mothers were having coffee and bitching about Bernadette Quirke. I'd abandon Conor as soon as she arrived, thrilled to have another girl to play Barbies with. Then she went into first year and started hanging out with her new friends at the bank corner in town, and I was still in sixth class, and it wasn't cool for her to be seen with a kid in primary school.

'Have you seen the photos?' the second girl asks.

'Bitch, please,' the first girl says. '*Everyone* has seen those photos.'

I bend over, burying my face in my hands. *This is not happening, this is not happening, this is not happening, this is not happening, this is not happening.* I repeat the words over and over again, trying to make them true.

'What a whore.'

'I *know*. It's actually disgusting, like. Who does that? Who actually does shit like that? And lets them *video* it?'

'Apparently she was off her face,' the first girl says. 'Olivia was talking about it last night and she said Emma O'Donovan was all over Paul O'Brien at that party, that he kept telling her that he had a girlfriend but that she, like, basically *forced* him to score with her anyway. God, she thinks she's so fucking gorgeous. Do you remember the GAA gala last year? Like, as if it wasn't bad enough that a fucking *fourth year* got invited, she had to come on to every guy there.'

'Well, she *is* pretty, you have to give her that.'

'Yeah, and she knows it too.'

'What was Paul O'Brien even doing at that party?' Caroline asks. 'He must have been at least ten years older than everyone else.'

'Olivia told me——'

'And how does Olivia know so much?' Caroline interrupts her.

'Her sister Mia was at the party,' the first girl says slowly. 'And I know you're on your period, but there's no need to get cranky with me.'

'Sorry,' Caroline says. 'I suppose . . .' She hesitates. 'Well, those photos are sort of weird, aren't they? Emma looked completely out of it. Was she asleep?'

'I don't know,' the second girl says.

'Yeah, neither do I. But Olivia said that Mia said that Emma was baloobas, that she had definitely taken something. She was dancing for ages, and her dress had fallen down and she was topless for, like, five minutes before Maggie Bennett noticed and pulled it back up again.' Something cracks inside me. Cutting everything up. 'And then she dragged Paul into Sean Casey's parents' room.'

'Ewww. His *parents'* bedroom? That is so gross.'

'I know.'

'Yeah.' Caroline still sounds unsure. 'But if she had passed out?'

'Car.' The first girl is losing patience. 'Come on. No one forced the drink down her throat, or made her take shit. And what guy was going to say no if it was handed to him on a plate?' She laughs. 'She was fucking asking for it.'

I place my lunch box on the floor and stand up, thumping the ground as hard as I can with my feet, slamming the toilet seat down and flushing the toilet. There's a hushed silence from the three girls, then whispered voices. Footsteps hurrying away, laughter once they're safely outside. Laughter follows me everywhere I go.

I am tired of it. I am so tired.

I am afraid to fall asleep. I am afraid of my dreams. Faces in the shadows, hands, so many hands. (You like that.) (Don't be such a pussy.) Those photos and those comments and more comments and more. (*Some people deserve to be pissed on.*)

I had told Mam this morning that I didn't want to go to school. I came down for breakfast in my pyjamas. Dad had left already. I felt as if I was trying to float away, float right out the top of my head and leave my body behind and I had to hold on to the back of her chair to anchor me down. *I'm sick*, I told her. *You do look sick*, Mam had said, her eyes worried as she brushed my hair away from my face, and I remembered when she would comb my hair as a child, running her fingers across my face, the joy in her voice when she told me how pretty I was. When was the last time she did that?

Please make this better for me, Mam, I wanted to say. *Please take this away.*

But her voice hardened as she said, *Well, it's self-inflicted, isn't it? Get dressed. You're going to school.*

And I knew that she couldn't help me.

I pack the lunch box back into my school bag, the uneaten goats cheese and rocket sandwich, the small bunch of grapes, the organic raspberry yogurt and spoon, all neatly packed in with a couple of paper napkins covering the top. (I'm not hungry.) I check my phone. Another dozen missed calls in the last half an hour, all from private numbers. I don't listen to the voicemails. There are so many new friend requests on Facebook and Twitter notifications, from accounts with no profile pictures and names like XYZ89u4.

Slut . . . Bitch . . . Skank . . . Whore . . .

We know what you are . . .

Slut . . . Bitch . . . Skank . . . Whore . . .

We know what you did.

A text message from Mam, asking if I still feel sick. None from Bryan. There's one from a number I don't have saved in my contact list, and I press delete without reading it.

The bell rings, the door to the toilets swings open and closed, open and closed, the sounds of a bulimic getting rid of her lunch in the cubicle next to me, toilets flushing, the taps turning on and off, one girl begs lip balm off another, panicked voices talking about a test in maths, *Oh my God, can I copy your answers? I didn't have time to study last night,* a half-finished assignment, complaints about what a bitch Ms Harrington is for giving her forty-five per cent in German, *my dad is going to kill me, especially after he paid for me to go to that German summer camp,* then silence. I walk out and stand in front of the sinks. The photos from the Easy Emma page sketch themselves on to the mirror, *pink flesh, legs, a collection of body parts (some people deserve to get pissed on)* and dance across the glass. I wash my hands, soaping and re-soaping my fingers, watching the red skin disappearing behind the suds, washing and washing and washing.

'How nice of you to join us,' Ms O'Regan says as I trudge into class, scanning the room for a spare seat. She's young and pretty, her blonde hair tied up in a neat ponytail. She waits for me to reply. 'Well. Don't just stand there.'

Rows of blank faces. Eyes staring at me like shiny coins, mouths sewn shut.

Did I enjoy this once, being the centre of attention?

'There's nowhere for me to sit, miss.'

She walks up and down the centre of the two rows of seats.

'You're right.' She looks confused. 'There does seem to be a seat missing.' She faces the class. 'Did one of you move a seat? There are always twenty-four seats in this classroom. Six rows, four seats a row.'

No one says anything. 'Come on, girls, you're all doing higher-level maths here. Six rows, four seats a row, twenty-four seats. I'm only counting twenty-three.' She's met with silence. '*Fine*. Emma, please go get another chair from the hall and come back here as quickly as you can. You've missed enough class time as it is.'

My hand is already on the handle when I see Ms McCarthy's face through the narrow glass pane cut into the side of the door.

'I'm sorry to interrupt your class, Ms O'Regan,' Ms McCarthy says when I let her in, 'but may Emma O'Donovan please be excused?'

No one goes *Oooooh* like they normally would.

Ms O'Regan nods, the two pretending as if they barely recognize each other, when we all know that they're housemates. Everyone knows that the two of them go with Miss Coughlan to the off-licence every Friday night and buy three bottles of white wine, a Pinot Grigio and two bottles of Sauvignon Blanc, that they go to Ahoy Matey's takeaway afterwards for two battered cods, two large portions of chips and mushy peas, but that Miss Coughlan doesn't get any because she does Weight Watchers with Sarah Swallows's mam and their weigh-in is on a Saturday morning. And Miss Coughlan needs to lose sixteen pounds by October because she's going to be bridesmaid at her sister's wedding and the dress that's been bought for her is Vera Wang but they got it on eBay and it was only available in a size twelve, and her sister's insisting that she lose weight to fit into it.

'Come on, Emma,' Ms McCarthy says, and I can see that all the other girls in the class are thinking the same as me. She's seen the photos (pink flesh) and the comments (*some people deserve to get pissed on*) and she's come to tell me that I'm expelled, that I'm a bad influence, that they can't have such a *Slut* . . . *Bitch* . . . *Skank* . . . *Whore* . . . in St Brigid's. You can almost feel the air in the room thicken, a noiseless buzz of energy starting to build up as I follow Ms McCarthy out of the room.

She turns left, walking down the five steps that lead out of this side of the school towards the gym, ducking into the religion room on the right. When I was in first year, there used to be a crucifix on the wall, and a font of holy water by the light switch, but that's all gone now. There's a circle of red chairs, a couple of limp beanbags, a narrow wooden bench running alongside the radiators below the three square windows. On the bench there's a collection of books on different religions from around the world and an ancient CD player with a stack of CDs, guided meditations and crap pan-pipe music to listen to when we're doing our relaxation exercises. The other three walls are covered in artwork, projects on racism and tolerance and compassion for all mankind, collages of pictures cut out of magazines, words written beside them in bubble letters.

'Take a seat,' Ms McCarthy says. Her dark curls are tied back with a pink barrette, matching her cheap pink blazer. She sits down, patting the chair next to her. She stares at me, her tinted contact lenses turning her eyes a strange milky blue. 'Do you feel comfortable?' she asks. 'Do you want something to drink? I can run up to the staffroom to get you a cup of tea if you'd like.' Her voice is quieter than normal, that sing-song Cork City accent somehow subdued.

'I'm fine.' I can feel my palms start to moisten. I wish she'd just hurry on and get this over with.

'Are you sure?' She rests her hand on my shoulder. 'Because if anything was wrong, you could tell me, you know. You can trust me.'

'I'm fine,' I say again, staring at a poster with photos of emaciated models, 'Dying to be Thin?' scrawled across it.

'Emma.' She clears her throat and says more firmly,

'Emma. I caught two third years looking at some inappropriate photos on Facebook.' The bones of my skeleton are shifting, moving in like a cage around my heart, squeezing all the air out of my lungs. 'Do you know what I'm talking about?'

All the walls are falling down. Falling apart.

(pink flesh) (legs pushed apart)

My body is not my own any more. They have stamped their names all over it.

Easy Emma.

'Yes.' The word feels like a slug on my tongue, fat and wet.

'Can you understand why I'm so concerned?'

I don't know why she doesn't just say it, that they're throwing me out, that I'll have to go to one of those grind schools up in the city to do my Leaving Cert, and that I probably won't be able to stay there either because there'll be someone who has a friend of a friend from Ballinatoom, and they'll send on a link to the page, *that page*, with all those photos and all those comments, more and more every second. It is a wildfire, out of control, and I am burning up in its path. *Don't read them, don't read them.* (Some people deserve to get pissed on.) In the new school there will be the same hush when I enter a room, the same rows of staring eyes, the same pockets of silence as I pass a table, the same explosion of laughter when I leave. The thought of it makes me want to lie down and fall asleep and never wake up again.

'Emma?'

'No one will talk to me.'

'No one will talk to you?'

'They won't let me sit with them at lunch, and no one wants to sit with me in class either. I had to eat my sandwich by myself in the toilets. And I can hear people whispering every time I pass, and I don't think I can cope with this, miss, I really don't.'

'OK.' She seems to be searching for the right words. 'Well. That must be hard for you. But is there anything *else* you would like to talk about?'

I pick at the perfectly ironed pleats of my skirt, trying not to cry.

'Back to the photos . . .' She wraps a ringlet of hair around her index finger, wincing as she struggles to let it loose again. 'I want you to know that you can talk to me. This is a safe space.' She waits for me to say something. I wish I knew what she wanted me to say.

'Am I going to get expelled?'

She leans forward until our faces are nearly touching. I can smell tuna off her breath. 'No. God, Emma, of course not. No.'

My legs begin to tremble, pent-up adrenalin flooding through my limbs.

'I checked your files. You're eighteen, right?'

It was my birthday two weeks ago. I had woken up to my parents sitting at the end of my bed, Dad telling me that I would always be his little girl no matter what age I was. Mam had made me blueberry pancakes, had let me eat them in bed without complaining that the crumbs would attract mice, telling me stories about the day I was born, about how happy she had been when the midwife had said I was a girl, because that had meant she had one of each, and that her family was perfect. She handed me a small box wrapped in silver paper. *Do you like it?* she asked me as I held Nana's gold locket in my hands. *I love it,* I told her, and for once I was telling the truth. For once I wasn't looking for the gift receipt while she moaned about how unappreciative I was. For once I felt like maybe she understood who I was. There was a pile of presents stacked at the bottom of my bed, a square box wrapped in pink-and-white pinstriped paper containing the Jeffrey Campbell shoes that I'd been begging for, an envelope with €20 phone credit in it from Bryan, a €500 Topshop voucher from my aunt Beth in London. Maggie and Ali had arrived to pick me up at seven that night. *Where's Jamie?* I asked. *Oh, she can't come,* Maggie had replied, *she has to work,* and I pretended to be disappointed. They had two helium balloons with the number eighteen on them and a huge hamper from Auntie Nellie's sweet shop. We got dressed up and went to Corleone's Italian for dinner, splitting two pizzas and sweet-talking the waiter into bringing us bottle after bottle of wine, using my 'Happy Eighteenth!' sash and crown as proof of our age. We abandoned Maggie's car in town, staggered up Main Street, but they wouldn't let us into Voodoo because I was the only one with ID, so we snuck around the back and scaled the eight-foot stone wall, landing into the smoking area with a clatter, our heels in our hands. Within minutes we were surrounded by boys, men really, all in their late twenties and early thirties. We let them take turns in trying on my plastic crown and the sash; made them buy us shots of tequila, and ignored the women they'd been chatting up before we arrived who were muttering under their breath that we 'should go back to the Attic Disco'. When I woke up the next morning, I was lying crossways on my pillows, my head squashed into my bedside locker. Maggie and Ali were sleeping top to toe on the bed. Mam was calling up from the kitchen to tell us that she had a fry on, but that she could make French toast or pancakes or frittatas if we'd prefer that. And I had felt happy.

'Yes,' I tell Ms McCarthy, 'I'm eighteen.'

She frowns. 'Well, legally then . . . I just, Emma – look, those photos really concerned me. Do you understand why I'm concerned?'

There's a long pause. I can hear the tick, tick, ticking of a clock and I look up above the collages on the wall to my left, above Ms McCarthy's head, until I find it. It's a flat white clock, the hands and numbers a stark black. I watch the second hand move around, and around, and around again.

'The reason why . . .' She clears her throat. 'The reason why I'm concerned is that in the photos you seemed to be –' she breaks off – 'unresponsive.'

I wipe my palms furtively on the sides of the chair.

'Do you remember what happened, Emma?'

I don't remember.

I don't remember.

I don't want to remember.

'I don't want to talk about it.'

'I respect that,' she says. 'But I have a duty of care to my students to make sure that they're safe.'

'It didn't happen in school, did it?'

'I can understand why you're upset.'

'Stop saying you understand, you understand, you understand. Is that what they tell you to say? Are you reading from some fucking manual?'

My hand jerks up to my mouth when I curse, as if I can just swallow it back down. 'I'm sorry,' I whisper. I wait for her to start yelling at me but she doesn't.

'Emma, do you think there could have been a possibility your drink was spiked?'

Yeah, spiked with more drink, I can hear Ali scoffing last year after a girl in our year claimed to have been roofied.

'No.'

'OK. I believe you, Emma, and I respect you. It's just that, in the photos, well, you look—'

Stop talking about those photos. (Legs spread apart.) (Pink flesh.)

'I was pretending.'

'Pretending?'

'Yeah.' I look over my shoulder at the door. 'I was pretending to be asleep. It was a joke.'

Neither of us says anything. I'm gripping on to the edges of my seat, my feet raised up on to my tippy-toes as if I'm waiting for the starting pistol to go off in a race. Please God, please just let the bell ring so I can go home to my bed, I'll give five euro to the missionaries' money box in Spar if you do. *Please, please, please.*

'OK, Emma. You can leave if you want.'

I'm at the door when I remember something.

'Miss?'

'Yes?' She turns around in her chair to look at me.

'Can we keep this between us?'

'That Facebook page is public,' she says. 'It's gone beyond that, I would think.'

But Mam and Dad don't know how to work Facebook, I think to myself, and I press her again. 'Yeah, but there's no need to tell anyone else, right?'

'Emma, I can't promise you that. You know that.'

I imagine Dad seeing the photos, his shock, then disgust. (He would look at me with disgust.) He would turn away from me. He would never be able to see me again without seeing those pictures. (Legs spread apart.) (Pink flesh.) He would never want to see me again.

I thought you were better than this, he would say. *I thought you knew the difference between right and wrong.*

'Please, miss.' I squat by her feet. 'What's the point in telling my parents?'

'I don't have a choice in the matter, I'm afraid, Emma. Once there's a suggestion of illegal misconduct, it's my duty to report it to the DLP.' I must look confused because she says, 'That's the Designated Liaison Person. In this case, Mr Griffin.'

Mr Griffin? She's going to tell Mr Griffin? She's going to show those photos to Mr Griffin?

'Please, miss. I'm begging you. I'll do anything, but

you can't tell Mr Griffin, or show him the photos.' I am going to get in so much trouble.

'I don't have a choice.' She repeats herself. 'He already knows. I believe he's been in contact with your parents. Emma, the guards will probably need to get involved.'

I forget my terror for a minute and almost start laughing. The fucking guards? Why would the guards care about some teenagers getting drunk and having sex?

'Come off it, miss.'

'I. Don't. Have. A. Choice.' She says each word slowly and clearly. 'Not when there's a possibility it could be rape.'

Rape.

It is like a whip cracking against my spine.

The word fills the room, until there's nothing left, and all I can breathe is that word (rape) and all I can hear is that word (rape) and all I can smell is that word (rape) and all I can taste is that word (rape).

'No.' I shake my head, trying to stop that word from echoing in my brain, over and over and over again, beating its drum inside me. 'What are you talking about?'

And I fall down. (The walls are falling down. Falling apart.)

'Are you all right? Do you need some air? Do you want

me to get you a glass of water?' She crouches down beside me, rubbing my back.

'You, you . . .' I lose my train of thought, all the images from the Easy Emma page crammed up inside my brain and my mouth and my chest and there is no room to breathe.

(Pink flesh.) (Legs spread apart.)

'You can't just *say* things like that. Have you said that to my parents?'

'Said what, Emma?'

I cannot repeat that word.

She sits back on her seat, drawing her knees into her chest, and she looks so young you could mistake her for a Leaving Cert student. 'I'm sorry,' she says. 'I really am. But I have to follow protocol. The DLP has to be notified, then he'll contact the HSE. And then, like I said, a report to the guards if the HSE think it's necessary.' She bites her lip. 'And Emma, I have to be honest with you here. I think it's likely that the guards are going to be involved.'

A low keening sound, one that I've never heard myself make before, is coming from the depths of my stomach. Ms McCarthy tells me to *breathe*, to *try and catch your breath*, but her face is dissolving before me. What are my parents going to say, and the guards, *the guards*, and what about Paul, are they going to contact him, he's going to think that I said he did *that*, and I didn't, I didn't, but he's not going to believe me, no one is going to believe me when I say this isn't my fault, that I never said that I was . . . *that word* . . . and my dad saying *I thought you were a good girl*, and I don't want this, and I hate Ms McCarthy, I hate her so much I want to ram her stupid hair barrette down her throat and shut her the fuck up, why did she have to see those photos, and why did I have to get so drunk, why didn't I go home with Jamie? I should have been a good friend and gone home with her (and when she tried to tell me about Dylan, and she used that word, or she implied it at least, and I told her not to say that, *when you say that word you can't take it back, J*, I told her, *you have to be careful*), what is Jamie going to say to me now?

'Come on, Emma.' Ms McCarthy raises her hand and then lowers it, taking exaggerated breaths as she does so. 'Come on now. Take deep breaths, that's a good girl, come on. Breathe in —' and she sucks her breath in — 'and breathe out.' And she lets it go again. 'Come on, you can do it. Come on now.'

She puts her arm around my waist and drags me back on to the chair. I flop over my knees, holding on to the backs of my ankles.

Last year they found a few pre-cancerous cells on my

mam's ovaries, and the doctors kept saying that it was lucky they found it early. They could just cut it out, a simple operation, no one need know anything about it, it would be easy. *That's the wonderful thing about catching it early*, Mam had told us over dinner, dolloping creamed spinach on to Dad's plate. *You'll know all about this, Dymphna.* I wanted to scream at her, to tell her to stop comparing her situation with Dymphna's, when she wouldn't even need to have chemo. (I imagined Mam dying, what I would wear to the funeral, the glamour the tragedy would give me. I thought about how much easier my life would be if it was just me and Dad and Bryan.) Dymphna and Conor were eating with us, Dymphna's bald head covered with a silk scarf, Conor sneaking concerned looks at me, and I didn't know how he could be worried about me when his mam was so much sicker. *The doctor says they can contain it, and get rid it before it spreads. Once it starts to spread into other organs, you're . . .* and Mam drew a line across her throat. That's what this feels like now, like a cancer is spreading, and I can't do anything to stop it. I don't have any control over it.

Ms McCarthy helps me to my feet, keeping her arm around my waist as we leave the religion room. I lean on her as we walk up the few steps, past the door to my maths class. I can see them through the glass panel, Josephine in the front row, her hand waving frantically in the air to answer a question, the others stifling yawns. Bored with it all, wishing the time would move faster, *wishing their lives away,* as Mam would say. And then they are gone, as Ms McCarthy guides me up the corridor towards the principal's office.

And I see them. My parents.

'They'll be expecting you at the station,' I hear Mr Griffin saying in his Midlands accent.

'And the boys involved?' Mam asks.

'Ah, here she is,' Mr Griffin says, his shovel-like hands twisting at his belly. I turn to Dad, wanting to apologize, or to reassure him, I don't know what. But he won't look at me. He just stands there, his shoulders hunched, staring at his feet.

'So, yeah . . . I hope we're cool, because I didn't have anything to do with this, obviously. Right. Well, call me back if you get a chance. OK. Bye.' I hang up. It's the fifth voice message I've left on Paul O'Brien's phone since I got home from school, pretty much identical to the messages I've left for Dylan and Fitzy and Sean. None of them answered the dozens of texts I sent, and I need to fix this, I need to fix this right now.

The principal's office, the huge window overlooking

the primary school and the sea beyond that. Mam and I sitting in the plastic chairs across the worn pinewood table from Mr Griffin, Dad standing behind us, drumming his fingers on the back of Mam's chair. *I don't understand*, Dad said. *I just don't understand this. Why can't they just delete the photos?* Mr Griffin sighed. *That's not really how it works, Mr O'Donovan.*

The Garda station. (Don't think about it. Don't think about it.) The silent car journey home after. I sat in the back, my fingers chubby and short in the window's reflection. The view is beautiful, but it feels wrong now, like *that word* has bled all over the glassy sea, shaping it blood red. My dad glancing at me in the rear-view mirror, looking back at the road whenever I caught him doing it. Mam's body was tense, crouched forward, her knuckles white as she held on to the edges of her knee-length beige skirt, random words and half-finished sentences coming out of her mouth. *I don't . . . non-consensual . . . good families . . . I didn't think Ethan was interested in girls in that way . . .* She said that at least five times, never using the word 'gay', although it's obvious that's what she's thinking. She often commented on how nicely he dressed, how well he spoke, asking me if he ever had a girlfriend, if he ever played sports, or if it was 'just the art' he liked. She kept muttering under her breath, twisting the fabric between her fingertips, until Dad turned up the radio to drown her out. We walked up our driveway in single file, Mam smiling at Dymphna O'Callaghan and telling her it was 'a shame the fine weather broke. Still, we can't complain, we were lucky to have it for as long as we did.' Dad opened the front door and went straight to his office. Shut the door. Mam went into the kitchen, closing the door behind her.

And I was left alone.

I hear a knock, then Mam's voice. 'You have a visitor.' I yank the door open. Maggie? Ali? Maybe even Sean Casey, come to tell me that this is all just a misunderstanding?

Oh.

'Hey.' Conor is still in his school uniform, the top three buttons of his white shirt undone, an angry rash on his neck. He always gets that when he's nervous, a dead giveaway when we told our parents that it wasn't us who cut the hair off his sister's Barbie, or ate the last of the brownies that my mam had made for the old people's home, or made prank phone calls to our neighbours.

I walk back to the bed, flinching when I see myself in the mirror. My hair is pulled up into a messy ponytail, my face still raw from crying and blistering sunburn, the baggy UL sweatshirt I stole from Bryan's room not exactly flattering.

'I'm a mess.'

He doesn't say anything, not like before this, when he would tell me I was beautiful. Boys are always telling me I'm beautiful, their eyes roaming around my body hungrily, as if looking for a place to plant a flag. When Conor said it he always looked me in the eye, as if he was saying an oath.

'I wanted to come yesterday,' he says. 'As soon as I saw the Facebook page I wanted to come, but I wasn't sure if you would want me to.'

'You saw the page?'

When we were little, Conor and I would take baths together, and I knew his childish naked body as well as my own. And then we became too big to do that, too grown-up.

(He has seen me naked.)

Neither of us says anything. We both know that everyone has seen that page. I think of all the people I know, and all the people in Ballinatoom, and all their friends on Facebook, and friends of friends of friends, looking at me (pink flesh) (legs spread) and reading all those comments, and calling me a *slut, bitch, whore.* I sit on the edge of the bed, tracing my finger over the pattern of the quilt. He sits next to me.

'Are you OK?'

'What do you think?' I try to sound calm but my voice quivers, yet another part of my body to betray me.

'I don't know what to say.'

'It's not that big of a deal.'

'Aren't the guards involved now?'

'How do you know that?' I can feel my breath becoming shallow. 'Who told you that?' He doesn't answer. 'Who told you that, Conor?'

'Fitzy rang me.' Conor tugs at his shirt collar to loosen it even further. 'Sergeant Sutton phoned him to say that he'd be called in for questioning in a couple of days.'

'I thought they weren't allowed to do that.'

'Well, you know. He's friends with Dr Fitzpatrick so . . .' He bites his lip. 'I hung up on him, Emmie. I told him that I didn't want to speak to him ever again, not after what he did to you—'

'Fitzy didn't do anything, not really. He was just there.'

'For fuck's sake, Emma, I saw the photos. I know what they did to you.'

And then I know that there is no way that I can stop all of this. I can't stop this now.

I bend over with the crippling pain of it, aware of nothing but the sobs hacking up through my chest and a blistering heat building behind my eyeballs, and I'm rocking back and forward. A bottomless grief. Black hole. Black space. Falling, falling, falling.

Slowly I come back into my body, into the room, and I can smell vanilla and coconut from my candles, and soap and apple shampoo (I don't use apple shampoo?) and then I remember that Conor is here with me, that he is still by my side, his hand rubbing my lower back, his head bent over mine, his lips against the back of my head, whispering *you're OK, you're OK, you're OK* into my hair.

'I'm sorry.' I sit up straight, turned away from him so that he won't see my ruined face. He keeps stroking the back of my hair, and I am four years old, and my daddy is holding me close, and telling me *I'm his little princess, I'm his little girl*, and that he'll love me forever.

'You're OK,' Conor says again, pulling me closer to him. 'I'm here. I'll take care of you.' I relax into him, burrowing my face in his chest, the worn wool of his school jumper against my skin. I listen to the beat of his heart, steady and slow, as he murmurs *shhh, shhh* against my head. He is so good to me. He has always been so good to me, and he never got anything from me in return. (*We thought we could trust you to be a good girl, Emma. We thought we had raised you better than this.*) I see my father's face and I am broken from the way he is looking at me, and I cannot think about it, I cannot bear to think about it. I wriggle my right hand behind Conor, nestling it in the small of his back, the other hand dropping to his knee, making small circles with my fingertips, working my way up to his inner thigh. His body stiffens, and he pulls away from me.

'What's wrong?'

'I'd better go,' he says, staring straight ahead.

I rest my head on his shoulder, swallowing a sob. 'Don't cry, Emmie,' he says, and he wraps his arm around me again. I can feel him relax into it, and I move so that my lips inch closer and closer to his neck. He gives an involuntary moan. I can do this. I know I can do this. I butterfly-kiss my way towards his mouth, ready to give him what he has been waiting for all these years. My fingers move higher on his thigh. He reaches down to grab my wrist, pushing me away, and stands up, turning away to adjust himself.

'Conor –' I reach out for him – 'there's no need to be nervous.' I undo the button of his school trousers. I know that if he's inside me, he can make me forget, he can make me clean. He's so good, he can make me better. He grabs both my hands to stop me.

'No need to be shy.' I tilt my head at his hard-on. 'It's

pretty obvious you want this too.' He blushes. 'What?' I say. 'Are you worried about someone walking in? I can lock the door.'

He crouches down to meet me at eye level. 'Emma. You don't have to do this.'

'I know,' I say. 'But I want to. Don't you want to be with me?'

Of course he wants to be with me. He *has* to.

He lays his hands on my shoulders, pushing me away from him gently.

'What the fuck is wrong with you?' I spit the words out.

'I just . . .' He looks at the ground before reluctantly making eye contact again. 'I don't want you to feel like you have to do this.'

'I don't feel like I "have" to do this, Conor. I want to do this. I thought this was what you wanted too.'

'I just want . . . I just want—'

'I just want, I just want,' I mock him, but he doesn't react.

'I just want to help you. I want to protect you, Emma.'

And he brushes a piece of my hair away from my face. I've never seen this look from him before. It's pity. He feels sorry for me. (I can't bear it.)

'Just go,' I say.

'Emma—'

'Just leave me alone for fuck's sake, will you?'

And he does.

And I watch him leave.

This year

Thursday

I am awake. And then I remember.

I am awake and I instantly wish that I was not.

(Life ruiner.)

(I have ruined their lives.)

Guilt paints itself on to my skin. I am tarred in it and feathered.

The morning is creeping under the curtains like it is hunting for me. Even the light seems different now. It is greyer, shaping itself into shadows that want to smother me.

I am thirsty. A chalky residue coats my tongue. I look around the room, at the mirror, and the desk, and the windows. I can see points and the hard edges, the bits I might cut myself open on.

There is an old-fashioned radio alarm clock on my

bedside locker, a cheap plastic square my mother bought to replace my iPhone. I'm not supposed to use my iPhone. I am not supposed to keep my laptop in my room any more either.

8.51 a.m.
I have slept for ten hours and fifty minutes.

That is a long time. (It was not long enough.)

I wrap the oversized dressing gown around myself. I sit on the desk chair, swivelling around once, twice, three times. I used to twirl my father's globe like this as a child, my eyes closed, putting my hand out to stop it. I insisted that wherever my finger landed told of my future husband, my future home, my future life. I was so sure then. I was sure it was that easy.

The chair comes to a standstill. I concentrate on the edges of the mirror first, at the tacky residue left behind from the torn-off Polaroids, postcards, tickets for gigs. I work my way slowly towards the centre until I see that girl. Her face is slightly rounder now, her eyes like pieces of broken blue glass glued on to a papier-mâché moon.

I pick up a hairbrush from the vanity table, my eyes watering as I try to wrench out some of the knots (*when was the last time you brushed your hair, Emma?*) and for a second I think I can see chunks of vomit in my hair, that

I'm covered in it, *so gross, like, Sean puked all over her, did you see that photo?*

I jerk forward, searching.

But there's nothing there.

8.57 a.m.

This is a normal time for breakfast.

I stand at the top of the stairs, looking down. If I fell . . . (Broken neck? Brain trauma?) People fall down the stairs all the time.

One. Two. Three.

I count each one until at last my feet touch the round mat at the bottom. It is new. I sit on the bottom step, curling my toes against the emerald-green fabric. My mother never did get the vomit stains out of the old one. This one is not as nice. It is cheaper, I think.

'Ah, here, it's as simple as this, Ned,' from the kitchen, I hear a man's voice saying in an inner-city Dublin growl. 'I'm not a judgemental man, I'm not. But if this girl was in bed with the lad anyway, what was she expecting?'

'I don't think she was expecting to get raped, Davey,' a nasal voice retorts. Posh. Dublin 4. 'Although yours does seem to be a popular opinion. You agree with him, do you, Eileen?'

'I do indeed,' an older woman says. She breaks into

a raspy smoker's cough before continuing. 'I see these girls walking around town here on a Saturday night, half naked, I tell you—'

'They are—' Davey chimes in, but she talks over him.

'Skirts up to their backsides, and tops cut down to their belly buttons, and they're all drinking too much and falling over in the streets, they're practically asking to be attacked, and then when it happens, they start bawling crying over it. As your other man said, what do they expect?'

'Hmm,' the presenter says. 'OK, it's time for the 9 a.m. news, but stay tuned to us here at Ireland FM because after the bulletin we're going to keep discussing the Ballinatoom Case.'

I get to my feet as the shrill jingle for *The Ned O'Dwyer Show* plays out. Ned O'Dwyer, self-proclaimed defender of the innocent. 'It's so important that we talk about this,' he tells his listeners. 'We need to have a national conversation about this.'

I wish another girl had been the one to start the national conversation.

I am a regular feature on *Ned O'Dwyer*. They cannot use my name so they call me the Ballinatoom Girl. They cannot use their names either, for legal reasons, but everyone knows who they are. Their lives are ruined because of this. I have ruined them.

The Ballinatoom Girl. Her story told and retold until it's not her story any more.

She alleges. She claims. She says.

I don't have anything to say, but they want to hear it anyway. Journalists from Jezebel, from xoJane, from the *Guardian*, from the *New York Times*. Everyone wants me to tell my story.

I don't have a story.

It's because of *The Ned O'Dwyer Show* that the 'Ballinatoom Case' became national news in the first place, then international, thousands of people tweeting about me. #IBelieveBallinatoomGirl

I am supposed to take comfort in that, I think.

A source 'close to the family' rang in to the show to tip the producers off. (Who? my father kept asking. Who is giving them all this information? And we close ranks. We talk less to the neighbours. We watch everyone for signs of betrayal.) The source asked to remain anonymous. 'It's a small town, everyone knows everyone,' they said. 'And no one wants to upset anyone else.'

People phone in to say that I deserved it. They say that I was asking for it.

At first I was hurt when I heard what they said about me. I cried a lot, in the beginning.

I probably shouldn't listen. But no one will tell me

anything. It feels like I am always trying to finish a jigsaw puzzle with a few pieces missing.

In the kitchen my mother is bent over on the counter, stretched out towards the old radio, fiddling with its busted antenna. A clipped female voice says, 'Good morning. Here are your news stories. One year on in the Ballinatoom Case, and it's . . .'

I cough and she slams her hand down on the radio to turn it off. She pretends she wasn't listening to it. I pretend I didn't hear.

'I didn't hear you come down.'

My mother's face is flushed, her eyes folding inside creases of puffy skin. She looks pale, faded, her features indistinct. Behind her I can see the calendar propped up against the cupboard, a picture of a French bulldog in a flowerpot. The anniversary is coming closer and closer. I want to mark it, put a big black X on the date. But I never know which day to choose. 'The alleged attack happened in the early hours of Sunday morning', the papers said, even though when I think about it, when I force myself to imagine what happened (what might have happened – I can't remember, I can't remember, I can't remember) I always think of it as Saturday night. When you can't remember something (and I can't remember, I have told them all so many times that I can't remember) it is as if it never happened at all.

But it did happen. I know that now.

'You're late for school.' My mother tightens her dressing gown around her, the white stripes yellowing, a splotchy tea stain on the lapel.

'I'm not going in.'

'But you promised me last night that you would go in today, Emma. Your exams are only a month away.'

'Maybe tomorrow.'

This is a game we play. I pretend that I might return to school. She pretends to believe me. We both pretend that I might sit the Leaving Cert in June. We're good at pretending now.

I take a seat at the dining table, willing my hand to stop shaking as I tip some Alpen into a bowl, pouring the milk in after. It folds out in thick lumps, plopping on to the cereal. I stare at it. I should get up. I should throw away the cereal. I should wash the bowl out. I go through all the actions in my head, watching my body move as if it's easy.

'The milk . . .' I break off, my voice drying up. I swallow some water. '. . . it's gone off.'

'Shit,' my mother says. She picks up the carton, sniffs it, pulls a face. 'Don't tell your father about this.' She throws the mess into the sink, opens the cupboards with a clatter, hands me a new bowl and a pot of natural yogurt.

'You'll have to make do with that until I get a chance to do a shop.'

I begin again. It is a process, and each step must be taken carefully. Alpen in bowl. Yogurt. Stir. I am focused on the present moment. Mindfulness, the therapist calls it.

If I do this right, if I get every part of this right, maybe today will be OK.

'Where's Dad?'

My mother turns away from me. She rinses out some dishes and puts them in the dishwasher.

'Where's Dad?' I repeat, forcing myself to take a spoonful of cereal. It tastes like glue and cardboard, but I swallow it. *Have to keep your energy up*, the doctor tells me. And starvation seems a long, slow route to death.

'He had to go to work early,' she says. She opens the cupboard door and stands on her tiptoes to reach the top shelf. 'Some problems at the office.'

'Oh.'

I stare out the patio door. Helen O'Shea is herding Ollie and Elliot into the car. They are both wearing raincoats over their school uniforms, jumping into puddles and screaming with laughter so loudly I can hear them through the glass.

I want to eat them. I want to make myself fat on their innocence.

It's not your fault, the therapist tells me, but she is wrong.

'Did Dad leave my phone for me?'

'I thought we discussed this.'

'I deleted my Snapchat. I changed my number.' My voice rises. 'What more do you want?'

I didn't want to change my number. I was afraid that one of the lads might change their mind, that they might want to apologize, that they would decide to plead guilty and then maybe I wouldn't have to go through with all of this, people would know I wasn't an attention-seeking whore, that this wasn't my fault.

(Kevin Brennan tweeted: *OK girls, just get drunk and slutty, and then shout rape the next day.* It had been favourited 136 times.)

'But it just upsets you, Emma, and—'

'I want my phone today.'

'Fine,' my mother says. 'I'll give it you after breakfast.' She fills another glass with tap water and brings it to the table, placing it in front of me. She holds her cupped palm out, a green-and-cream striped pill and a small round white one in it. They are like pearls in a seashell, tiny, precious. Valuable. I put them in my mouth, washing them down with the water.

'Still?' she asks as the glass almost falls out of my

191

trembling hand. 'Maybe we should go back to Jimmy and ask him to adjust the dosage.'

'Dr Manning.'

'What?'

'It's Dr Manning now. You said Jimmy.'

'Did I?'

She squeezes my right shoulder, a little too tight for comfort.

'Tongue?'

I stick out my tongue. I have to show her my intent to get better, my promise not to be foolish again.

'Good girl.'

The room is so silent, the noises from outside quietening when all the neighbours have gone to work and to school. Their lives continue as normal. Maybe I should tell her to turn the radio back on. We could sit here, listen to those strangers tell us where it is we went wrong.

— *She should have known better.*

— *She was asking for it.*

— *What was she expecting?*

— *Not to get . . .*

Not to get. Not to get *that word*.

I listen to the rhythms that make up the morning, the tiny slurp as my mother drinks her coffee, the ping of the spoon hitting the china bowl, the patter of rain against the glass pane.

'This weather,' my mother says, staring out the window. 'Goodness, do you remember . . . ?'

She stops herself. Do you remember this time last year? is what she was about to say.

This time last year, it was sunny. This time last year we were in the middle of a heatwave, waiting for it to break.

'What the . . . ?' She sniffs the air, her forehead creasing into a frown. She pushes her chair back and runs over to the oven, opening the door and waving at the black clouds of smoke that are wisping out of it.

'My muffins,' she wails as she rescues the tray, slamming it down on the hob.

I follow her into the kitchen area and we stand side by side, staring at the baking tray.

'They're not so bad,' I say. 'Just burned around the edges. It's nothing.'

And it doesn't matter anyway, I want to tell her.

'Are you still going to the farmer's market?' I say. 'Really?'

'Yes.'

'But—'

'Are you going to come with me?' she asks as she trims the blackened pieces off.

'No.'

The word comes automatically. *No. No. No.* It's all I say these days. It is as if I am making up for the time when I couldn't say it. When I wasn't given the chance to say it. *No.*

My mother faces me, her hands in fists at her hips. 'You haven't gone outside in two weeks, Emma.'

'I've gone to therapy.'

'But besides that.'

It's been a year, Emma. It's time to get over it, Emma. Don't you think it'd be best to just put it all behind you, Emma?

'It will do you good to get outside, pet.'

I left this house by myself seven weeks ago. My mother lent me her car, asked me to get some messages for her in town. There was an awkward exchange with the girl on the till in Londis, neither of us knowing how to act. I felt as if I was playing a part, like I should burst into tears at any moment, as if a smile or a laugh might be used against me. When the boys had first been brought in for questioning, I tweeted about watching reruns of SpongeBob with Bryan. *Wait*, Sarah Swallows had replied. *You say you were 'raped' and then you tweet happy shit? #IDontGetIt #DumbBitch.* (It was retweeted fourteen times. Paul O'Brien retweeted it. So did Dylan Walsh.)

I thanked her as she gave me my change. Then, as I was

leaving Londis, I saw Paul and two of his friends coming out of the bookies' office, shoving betting slips into their pockets. I went to dart back into the shop, but he saw me and he knew I had seen him. He nudged one of his friends, whose face darkened when he caught sight of me. I could read his lips mouthing a word. *Slut.*

There are certain words I can lip-read now. I know them so well.

Paul stayed where he was, calling out his food order as his friends crossed the road. He is supposed to stay away from me. *If any of them tries to harass you, intimidate you or assault you,* Sergeant Sutton told me in a bored tone, *contact the Garda station immediately.* A voice was screaming in my head to start walking, to get away from there as fast as I could, but I couldn't move. (My body doesn't belong to me any more.) 'Whoops,' one of his friends had said as he banged into me hard. My fingers released involuntarily and the plastic bag fell to the ground, a smash as a bottle hit the concrete. 'Careful, Timmy, she'll probably say you raped her too,' the other guy said, and I could feel my breath warp into a desperate wheezing.

You're not dying, the therapist told me, *or having a heart attack. They're just panic attacks. They're very common. You need to learn to manage them, to calm your breathing enough to withstand the attack.*

It feels as if I might die. (I wish, I wish, I wish.)

The two of them walked past me into the shop, ordering chicken-fillet rolls and spicy wedges, flirting with the girl on the till as they paid. Paul rested against the window of Molly's Bar, sucking on a cigarette, blowing smoke rings out of his mouth, his eyes never leaving me for a second. He had gained weight, but that was the only difference I could see. He stood and watched me, the girl who ruined his life, and he waited for his friends to come back. The three of them started walking up Main Street, and he turned around, walking backwards, and smiled at me. It was as if he had won already, and we both knew it.

'Where's the wine?' my mother had asked when I got home. 'I told you to get a bottle of that Shiraz that was on special offer.'

I wanted to tell her. But I couldn't. *What happened?* she would demand. *What did you say? I hope you didn't react, I hope you remained dignified, I hope you didn't show him you were upset. I hope you didn't give him the soot of it.* Then she would remember herself, what a mother was supposed to do, how the therapist had told her she needed to behave. She would wrap an arm around me, cover my head with soft, meaningless words that were supposed to comfort me, and I would want to ask her, *Do you believe I didn't want this, do you believe it wasn't my fault?* But I couldn't ask her that. I was afraid of what the answer might be. So I lied. 'I forgot,' I told her. 'I'm sorry. I just forgot the wine.'

'No,' I say again, more firmly. 'I'm not going out.'

My world has become smaller and smaller in the past year, shrinking to fit the parameters of this house.

My mother's mouth tightens. 'Well, it's either the market with me, or school. Which would you prefer?'

'Can't we get any closer than this?' I say as my mother indicates into the cathedral car park, waiting for an old lady in a tweed skirt to hobble past us on the zebra crossing.

'It's market day,' my mother replies. She reverses into a space and switches the ignition off. 'We won't get parking anywhere else. It's always chock-a-block in town.'

The journey had been quiet, my mother clearly not daring to turn on the radio. 'Allegedly . . . she claims . . . the Ballinatoom Girl has been making headlines all over the world . . . trending on Twitter . . .' *I don't understand why there's so much fuss about this particular case,* I overheard her saying to my father a few weeks ago, the hiss of the iron as it released steam. I muted the TV so I could eavesdrop. *People get . . . These things happen all the time.* My father didn't reply. I went upstairs, opened the diary that my therapist, a woman Hannah had recommended because she had *experience with this type of thing,* insisted I buy, and

I made a list.

Reasons why people are interested in the Ballinatoom Case:
1. Four boys, one girl.
2. The effect of social media on young people today.
3. When will young people learn the value of privacy?
4. Should the photos of the Ballinatoom Case be admitted as evidence?
5. The Americanization of Irish culture.
6. Does 'jock culture' support rape culture?
7. Does 'rape culture' even exist?
8. One in three reported rapes happens when the victim has been drinking.
9. We need to talk about consent.

These are just titles of editorials in newspapers. There have been so many. I have them bookmarked on my laptop so that I can find them easily whenever I want to read them again. My therapist thinks this is a bad idea.

'I want you to draw me a picture,' she said in our last session, the two of us holed up in a box-like room above a supermarket in Kilgavan, a town about fifteen miles from Ballinatoom. The walls are painted a cheerful yellow, two blue armchairs too close together, a box of tissues placed at the foot of my chair. There are framed posters on the wall, pictures of snow-capped mountains and horses galloping on beaches, inspirational quotes like 'Never give up!' and 'Don't let your wounds transform you into something you're not' typed in block letters across them. There are a couple of certificates as well, which my father had demanded to look at during our first, and only, family session. Once he had seen them he was satisfied. This woman was qualified. She would fix me. He could leave us to it. 'Draw me a picture of where you are in relation to your body,' she said, and she handed me a blank piece of paper and some crayons. 'Why do you have these anyway?' I asked her. 'For my younger clients.' She pushed her glasses up her nose. 'I have a degree in play therapy as well.' I wondered what these younger clients came there for. Were they being bullied? Had a parent died? Were they being sexually abused? Did they find the therapy useful? Did it cure any of them? The therapist pointed at the paper and cleared her throat so I began to draw. I drew the body that was to blame for all this. (I want to erase it. I want to make it disappear.) 'And where are you?' the therapist asked. 'Where are you, Emma?' I drew a tiny dot at the other end of the page, as far away as I could possibly make it, and the therapist shook her head. She spoke of the importance of getting back in touch with my body, of being present, of feeling connected. She recommended yoga and acupuncture and massage. I said I would think about it.

That was another lie. I tell her so many. (*This will only work if we're completely honest with one another, Emma.*)

I don't want to be 'in my body'. I am like a shadow, still attached to the thing that people called Emma, following it around wherever it wants to go, but I am lighter now without all the *stuff* that body had, the memories, the attention it attracted. I feel less substantial.

'Oh, Father Michael, how are you?' My mother uses her best phone voice as we take two large Tupperware containers full of cakes and scones and muffins and bread from the boot of the car. 'Miserable day, isn't it?'

The priest closes the side door into the vestry behind him. He's a small, neat man, three thin strands of oily hair combed over his bald head, flaking age spots on his cheeks and forehead. He looks at the sky. 'Only a bit of soft rain, Nora. Thank God.'

'Yes, that's true,' my mother agrees, resting the heavy Tupperware container back into the boot. 'Will you have a muffin? They're fresh out of the oven.'

'I won't, Nora.' He looks at me, and I know what he's thinking, he has seen the photos. Pink flesh. Legs spread apart. (I thought you were a good girl, Emma.)

I cannot remember, so those photos and those comments have become my memories.

The priest rests a hand on his concave stomach. 'Gluttony is a deadly sin, and all that. God bless now,' he says, walking away.

Father Michael used to say that my mother's baking was so good she should open up her own cafe, that she'd put the Cake Shack out of business in no time. We watch him scurry away, stopping to talk to an elderly couple by the cathedral gates.

'Come on,' my mother snaps. 'Will you hurry up for pity's sake? Why do you always have to be so bloody slow?' She pauses, takes a deep breath and tries again. 'Sorry, Emma. I didn't mean to snap, I . . .'

We carry the boxes through the small wrought-iron gate in the cathedral wall. My mother walks ahead of me by a few paces. I follow her up Main Street, tucking my head into my chin to shield my face.

There she is (whispers, an elbow to the ribs), *there's that girl who says she was . . . you know.*

I'll always be 'That Girl' now.

'Hey. Hey, you!'

A red Toyota, shiny with rain and newness, slows down beside me, a male voice calling out. I tense, my breath catching in my throat, and hurry to catch up to my mother.

'You. The girl in the navy sweater. Hello? Can you hear me?'

It's going to be a group of boys leering at me. They will be holding their fingers up in a V around their lips and sticking their tongue out, asking how much I charge, telling me that they'd heard I was good for it, that I liked it rough, that I liked it hard. They will be laughing at me. But it's not, it's only a young couple, one of them holding a map out. I forget myself for a minute and smile. Who uses maps any more?

'Hello, we are looking for the Sheep's Head,' the man says, his girlfriend or wife bringing the car to a standstill. They sound German, fair and tanned in matching navy anoraks.

'I don't know.' My voice is barely a whisper, and the man frowns at me and asks me to speak up, but I can't. I leave them there, calling after me.

'What was that about?' my mother asks when I catch up to her.

'Just a German couple looking for directions to the Sheep's Head.'

'Well, I hope you helped them. It's very important to be friendly to the foreigners. We don't want them going home to their countries and saying that the Irish weren't nice to them. We could do with all the tourism we can get.'

Ballinatoom used to be popular with tourists. Before this, it was known for its friendly locals, the folk club, the beautiful beach. Tourism is how towns like ours survive.

Business has been down, they say. No one wants to spend their holiday somewhere like this now. Less money around the place. (My fault.)

We walk into Camden Lane, where the farmer's market is held. My mother calls out thanks to the apple seller for setting up a table for her under the roof of the alleyway, shielding us from the rain. She arranges a selection of her baking on to mismatched floral plates, cutting off chunks of cake for free samples, placing them on a large white plate in the middle. The other vendors are setting up too, the man selling veggie burritos firing up his grill, the fishmonger in his white apron and green wellies piling mounds of ice on top of the salmon and cod and mussels to keep them fresh, writing the specials on his blackboard with a piece of broken chalk, a moustached man with a jaunty scarf around his neck picking out folk tunes on his guitar. Then the customers begin to arrive. The older women in biscuit-coloured clothing, clear plastic headscarves tied around their heads to protect their freshly set hair from the rain, complaining about the bruising on the apples. Small children running around in neon-coloured rain boots, jumping into puddles, ignoring their harried mothers pushing babies in prams, telling them to be careful. Hipster couples who had moved down from the city for a better quality of life, always with their reusable bags in hand, the fathers proudly toting their babies in cotton slings around their chests. They joke and smile, nodding as the organic pig farmer shows them some pork chops, pointing out the fat marbling and giving them a 'special price'. I picture them at home, making kale chips for their children, delighted with themselves for integrating fully into small-town life, oblivious to the fact that they were still, and always would be, blow-ins. There were other strangers too, Polish accents asking the price of a jar of local honey, women with intricately braided hair haggling with the butcher for weird cuts of meat that no one else would want anyway. No one ever seemed to know where the refugees actually came from, their black skin marking them both as different but as one, an indistinguishable mass.

Not Eli, though. He was one of us.

I shake my head. I don't want to think about Eli.

My mother and I stand by our table, watching the people mill around the market. Some pause when they see me. They stop at our stand to buy an apple tart, place a hand on my arm. They look hurt when I flinch. Others talk to my mother in hushed tones, asking about the court case, the chances of prosecution, *sure you can see them walking around town, not a care in the world, it's a disgrace is what it is, an absolute disgrace,* eyes wide with the drama of it all. They want to hear that I had taken enough drugs to fell a small animal, they want to hear that I was assaulted by the entire football team, that I got pregnant with triplets and had to go to England for an abortion, they want to hear that I try to kill myself every day, twice on a Sunday for good luck.

I catch a young couple looking in my direction, their cheeks burning when they realize I've spotted them. They approach our stand, he with his bushy brown beard, she in printed harem trousers. 'Do you use agave in your baking?' she asks. 'Or maple syrup?'

'It would have to be top-grade maple syrup though, one hundred per cent,' the husband interrupts.

They grimace when my mother tells them she doesn't, that she's a plain, traditional baker, but do they want to try a sample anyway? They back away as if she has offered them rat poison, but it's clear they're disappointed, as if they wanted to show me their support in some small way.

I wake in the middle of the night. I remember. I am pink flesh. I am splayed legs. All the photos and photos and photos. I open my laptop. I read the articles on Jezebel and xoJane and the Journal and the *Guardian* and the *New Statesman*. And then I scroll down to the comments.

  — *She went into that room.*

  — *She drank too much.*

  — *She took drugs.*

  — *No one else knows what happened except the people who were in that room.*

  — *She told the guards she was only pretending to be asleep.*

  — *She went to another house party in Dylan Walsh's house a month after it happened. Would she have done that if she was really raped?*

  — *I know for a fact that she texted Ethan Fitzgerald the next morning. You wouldn't do that if what she said happened really did happen.*

  — *She changed her story.*

  — *Boys will be boys will be boys.*

Some of those commenting claimed to be from Ballinatoom, to know me, to know my family, that they'd always thought I was a little slut who was just asking for trouble, that I had been easy with my favours and had regretted it in the morning and decided to yell rape, and that I was ruining those boys' futures, that I was an attention seeker, that I was embarrassing the town, that I deserved it, that they hoped I got AIDS and died, that I was a dirty slut.

I look around at the people walking around the market, buying groceries, throwing a euro coin into the open guitar case, the busker smiling his thanks. Did any of these people write those comments? Did all of them?

'Hello, Karen,' my mother says as Karen Hennessy tries to pass our stall without stopping, her eyes focused firmly on a point in the distance. She hesitates just for a second, then spins on her heel.

'Nora! Emma!' she says, pushing her sunglasses up into her hair, tied in a bouncy ponytail. She's make-up free, her clear skin taut, her forehead slightly waxy. 'Excuse the state of me,' she gestures at her lean body in the lululemon yoga pants that she buys in bulk every time she goes to London. 'I've just had Yogalates.' She shifts her wicker basket full of vegetables from one arm to the other.

'Emma,' my mother admonishes me, 'say hello to Karen.'

'Hi, Karen.'

'Hi, Emma.' She smiles at me. 'How are you, sweetheart? You look exhausted.'

(*You look stunning*, she said. We are in Mannequin. I am standing in front of the mirror in a dress that I will never be able to afford. *You could be a model*.)

The memories flutter in my brain like moths.

You could be a model. You could be a model. You could be a model.

I make my mind go blank. I am not that girl any more. I am an It. I am a collection of doll parts, of pink flesh, of legs spread open for all to see.

'You poor thing. I hope you're taking care of yourself.' She turns to my mother. 'Why isn't she at school? God, all I hear from Ali these days is the Leaving this and the Leaving that.'

'Oh,' my mother says, 'Emma wasn't feeling very well today, and it's just, well, things . . .'

'Yes,' Karen says when my mother trails off, 'I understand. It's awful really. Mind yourself, Emma, and you too, Nora. I can't even imagine how stressful all of this must be for you.'

She starts to walk away. 'Wait,' my mother calls out. 'Do you want to buy anything?'

Karen looks at the stand. 'Oh, I can't, Nora, I'm on a cleanse at the moment. Maybe next week?'

An hour passes, then another, and the other vendors start packing up their stands. 'How did you get on today, Mrs O'Donovan?' the apple man asks when he comes over to dismantle our stall.

'A little quieter than usual, Pat. You know how it goes,' she says. She looks old all of a sudden, and so thin. 'Do you want to take some home for Cathy and the girls?'

'Was it quieter today?' I ask my mother once we're back in the car.

'Ah, it'll pick up again next week, I'm sure of it.'

'Do you think it's—'

My mother sighs. 'Emma, don't worry, OK? Some days are better than others; that's just the way it goes.'

Maybe my mother's baking isn't that great after all.

Maybe it has nothing to do with me.

My mother stops the car outside Spar, and then Centra, and then SuperValu, dumping a little bit of the leftovers into the steel bins located outside each shop, two loaves of bread here, a few muffins there.

I stare at her.

'Don't.' She tightens her grip on the steering wheel. 'I can't dump it all in one bin,' she says. 'People notice that. They'll talk.'

'Emma. Time for dinner.'

I am lying on the sofa. The curtains are closed. It is dark. I like it better that way. The dark is softer. I tap my foot against the armrest, beating out a tune for my mind to dance to so I don't have to think.

'Emma.' The door to the TV room opens, a shaft of

light from the hall carving a square panel on the floor. My mother switches on a lamp. I blink.

'What are you doing in here by yourself in the dark? Dinner is ready.'

She leaves. The light is still on. I look at all the furniture. That is a sofa. That is a seat. That is a lamp. I say the words over and over again until they no longer have any meaning. I need to sit up. I need to get off this sofa. I need to turn the light off as I leave, shut the door behind me. I need to walk into the kitchen for dinner. I need to act normal.

I am tired just thinking about it.

Precious has shit at the foot of the coffee table. Small hard pellets. I can smell it.

'Emma, I'm not calling you again.' My mother's voice floats in from the kitchen.

I pull the rug over and cover the mess with it.

The room is cold. My mother is sitting at the dining table, a plate of steaming hot food and a glass of wine in front of her.

'What is this?'

'Chicken stir-fry. They make it ready-made for you in the butcher's. It's in a sweet-and-sour sauce.'

'What's there for me?'

'I put one of those vegetarian meals in the microwave.'

My mother takes a sip of her wine. 'I don't know what Paul was doing getting together with that Heather one. It was obvious he'd never got over Linda, don't you agree? At least the new wife is a little more age appropriate.' She gestures with her fork, bits of chicken falling on to the table but she doesn't seem to notice. I take the ready-meal out of the microwave, peeling off the plastic covering, and sit next to her. I eat it straight out of the container. I want my mother to notice and to demand that I *at least put it on a plate.*

But she doesn't say anything. She walks into the kitchen area, takes the wine bottle from the door of the fridge and drains what's left of it into her glass.

'Where's Dad?'

'He's working late.'

She spears a piece of chicken with her fork, cutting it up into smaller bits, then moving it from one side of the plate to the other. I shovel the food into me as fast as I can. It turns to ash in my mouth.

'Oh.' My father stands in the doorway, his leather briefcase still in his hands. 'I thought you would be finished by now.'

'Why are you apologizing?' my mother asks him. 'I think it's fairly normal for a man to eat dinner with his family. Don't you *want* to eat dinner with us?'

The room goes very still.

'Of course I want to eat dinner with you,' he says. There's a bang as his briefcase hits the ground. He hasn't looked at me yet. 'You know I do.'

She softens and kisses him on the cheek. He instinctively goes to wipe away the lipstick stain, but there is none there.

'How was work anyway?' my mother asks as she goes into the kitchen to prepare his dinner.

'It was . . .' he lets out a sigh, his body sagging with the weight of it, 'stressful.'

'Oh dear,' she says. 'Why so?' He doesn't reply. 'And I can't believe you went to the office in that suit, it's as wrinkled. What were you thinking, Denis? What will people be saying?'

'But you . . . Don't you remember . . . ?' He picks up his knife, and frowns. He breathes on to it, wiping it clean with his napkin. My mother said the same thing about his suit last night and she had promised to steam it for him before work this morning.

'Remember what?' my mother asks as she dishes out some stir-fry on to a plate for him.

'Never mind.'

I push my seat back from the table, dumping the food container in the bin. As I open the door to the hall I can hear him ask, 'And how did you get on in the market today, Nora?'

'Oh, brilliantly,' she says. 'Sold out completely.'

Upstairs, I draw my curtains closed and lie on my stomach on the bed. I put my hands over the back of my head, pushing my face into the pillow, but I can't do it. I come up, gasping for air.

My phone vibrates against my bedside locker. My mother forgot to take it back off me. My phone use is supposed to be strictly monitored these days. *It's to protect you*, my father told me, *We just want to protect you*.

It is not now that I need to be protected.

I unlock my phone, waiting.

Subject: Your side of the story

Subject: We Believe You

Subject: It happened to me too

Subject: Liar

Subject: Dirty Whore

Subject: Fucking Slut

Subject: Kill Yourself.

It goes on and on. I delete them. I see Conor's name in my inbox. He emails me every day, talking about the pre-exams, or the open day at Trinity he had gone to, how impressed he had been with the School of Medicine there, what his sister Gemma had said about his new haircut (and I had wondered what it looked like, and I had wanted to see it), about how some kid in school had gotten into trouble for calling Mr Canniffe a 'dick' for saying that the likelihood of a man developing superpowers after being bitten by a radioactive spider was zero. He told me how Eli was still miserable after the break-up with Maggie. I knew all about that already, of course. Maggie had come to see me straight after it had happened, her eyes swollen and bloodshot, crying and saying, 'I had to do it. He refused to go and speak to the guards and tell them what happened that night at the party, he kept saying he didn't know, he wasn't in the room with you, so how did he know what happened?'

Eli had been in the room, someone said afterwards. He had come in to take the keys off Fitzy to make sure that he didn't drive. Drink-driving is bad, we had always been told. Drink-driving is dangerous. Drink-driving kills people, it ruins lives.

There are other ways to ruin lives. We were never warned about those. (*Are you sure that the Boahen boy didn't have anything to do with it?* my father had wanted to know in the beginning. It would have been easier for him to understand if it had been Eli.)

'I had to break up with him.' Maggie was sobbing now. 'You're my best friend.' She stared at me, as if she was waiting for me to say something. Did she want me to congratulate her? To say thank you? To tell her not to be silly and to get back with Eli?

I stood there in silence, staring out the window. *This view is amazing*, people used to say when they came to my house. *You can see the entire bay. You are so lucky.*

People used to say I was lucky.

Conor just tells me funny stories and silly jokes, and he keeps sending the emails, despite the fact that I have never answered. He never mentions Sean or Fitzy. He never said that Dylan has dropped out of school and had to get a job in a local garage. *Your father refuses to go there now,* my mother told me, *he goes all the way to Kilgavan to get his petrol.* It was as if she was trying to prove my father's love for me when really it is just one more reason for him to resent me.

I wonder if Conor knows how grateful I am for these emails. I wonder if he knows that they're the best part of my day.

Hi Emmie, the email message starts, and I can't believe I ever found that nickname annoying –

I was looking through old photos on my laptop the other day and I found some of you and me. I'm pretty sure that they were taken after my eleventh birthday party. Do

215

you remember? Mom took us to the cinema to see the first Iron Man movie and you threw such a tantrum Mom said her eardrums were still ringing when we got home. After Caoimhe had driven all the other lads home, you and I watched Home and Away and ate leftover birthday cake, and you said that you were glad it was just us again.

I had wanted to see some other movie, the name of which I can't even recall now. *Iron Man* is for boys, I pouted, and Conor had said that he didn't mind, we could go to whatever I wanted. That didn't last long, Fitzy and Eli kicking up such a fuss that Dymphna had to split us up, making Conor's oldest sister, Caoimhe, take me while Dymphna brought Eli and Fitzy to see *Iron Man*. Conor had come with Caoimhe and me. He said his birthday wouldn't be the same without me there.

I'm looking at one photo of us, side by side on that crappy old couch we used to have, you know the one, with cream and pink and yellow swirls that you said looked like melted Neapolitan ice cream, and I've got chocolate stains all over my mouth and I look like such a baby sitting next to you. Even then, Emmie, you were so beautiful. It's easier to say that to you by email, when I don't have to look at you. But you are, you know. You're still the most beautiful girl I've ever known. And I miss you.

I delete the email and place the iPhone carefully on my locker. I don't like these types of emails as much as the other ones he sends. When he tells me I'm beautiful, it feels as if he's saying that this was all my fault, that if I didn't look the way I did then this wouldn't have happened to me.

I turn the light off. I used to have glow-in-the-dark stars stuck to my ceiling. My father spent hours painstakingly arranging them in the exact shape of my favourite constellations. *Anything for my little princess,* he had said.

I scraped them off a few months ago. I wanted everything to be clean. I like it better when my room is pitch black, when the dark is so thick it swallows me up and I feel as if I could drown in it.

It's too early to ask my mother for my sleeping tablet. I will the clock to move faster, for it to be 10 p.m. That is the time that my mother has deemed suitable for bed. Normal.

I live for bedtime. Some days it is all I can think about. That blissful moment when the sleeping tablets start to kick in, when I can feel my mind going loose, when there are no edges to hurt myself on and I can fall into my dreams. For that moment I can pretend that I'm dying, that I'm letting go of all this, slipping into the next world, whatever that might be.

That's what I want to believe death will be like. I want to believe it will be as simple as falling asleep.

Friday

'And what time do you call this?' my mother demands as I sit down. The dining table wobbles. My father keeps saying he'll take a look at it. He says he'll do a lot of things. I shake some Alpen into a bowl.

'Where's the milk?' I ask her.

'I forgot to get any,' she says. I sigh and she bristles. 'That's neither here nor there. You're an hour late for school.'

'I'm not going.' I walk into the kitchen and rummage through the bread bin. I find the heel end of the sliced pan, and put it in the toaster, filling up a pint glass with water and gulping it down.

'Emma, you're going to have to start going in. You're in sixth year, remember?'

Exams. Points. Books. Studying. I remember when it all seemed to matter.

'Why didn't you wake me then?'

'I . . . I, well, I . . .' She's flustered. '. . . well, that's not really the issue, is it? Ms McCarthy rang again this morning, wanting to know where you were.'

Ms McCarthy came to the house a lot at the start. The doorbell would ring, and the three of us would tense. There had been problems. Phone calls. Anonymous letters. A bag of dog shit left on the front porch. *Harmless pranks*, the guards said. *Keep track of it. Contact us again if it escalates.* We were nervous. We stared at one another, wondering who would crack first. My father would push himself out of his chair as I rushed upstairs, hissing at my mother to *tell whoever it is that I'm not in.* I always kept my bedroom door open so I could listen though, the low murmur of voices from downstairs as my mother made tea, offering biscuits and cake. Afterwards, there were study notes left behind and brochures from UCC and UL, shiny kids with American-style white teeth on the cover, clasping books to their chests.

'What did you tell her?' I say.

'I told her you were getting through the curriculum at home.'

I nod. That was the right thing to say.

'You missed a call from Beth as well.'

'Did I?'

My aunt phones every week, giving me pep talks on how I *need to create public sympathy* and how *this is all about how other people perceive you, you have to spin it the right way.* She keeps promising to visit, because she wants to give *my poor goddaughter a big hug,* but there never seems to be a good time, what with work, and her friends, and her agreeing to participate in the London Marathon and her need to train properly for that because she's running for *the Cork Rape Crisis Centre, darling, I want you to know that. I'm doing this for you.*

My mother sighs as she hands me the two pills.

The toaster pops and I start.

'It's just the toaster, Emma,' she says. 'Deep breaths, OK?'

I take the slice of toast, grab the marmalade from the fridge and sit back at the table. She follows me. 'Wait. Show me, Emma.'

I ignore her, opening the jar.

'Emma. Show me, I said.'

I stick out my tongue. 'See? Gone.'

'Good girl.' She sits beside me, still grasping a mug in her hands. Her bob is frizzing, sprinkled with coarse white hairs around the hairline. *Oh, I don't see the point in getting my hair done every week any more,* she told me a few months ago. *It just seems like a waste of money when I can do it myself.* She slurps her tea, loudly, and I cannot cope with how disgusting she is, *disgusting*, and I want to knock the cup out of her hands.

(You're so like your mother, aren't you?)

(Oh, you're the image of your mother!)

'And remember,' she says, 'your therapist session is at five.'

'I'm not going.'

'Yes, you are.' There's a shadow of something in her eyes, a glimmer of panic forming. 'Your appointment is at five. And you will be there, Emma.'

My parents are insistent I go to the therapist every week. They seem to think that it keeps the problem contained in some way, that it stops it from touching them, their lives. *What is 'it'?* the therapist asks me. *Use your words.* It is nothingness. It is a desire to sleep forever. My parents are afraid that if I stop taking the tablets, if I stop going to see the therapist, I might start talking instead. I might start to remember.

They need not worry.

I don't remember. I don't remember. I don't remember.

'And we have a meeting with the solicitor at two.'

'What's the point? He can't take my case anyway.'

'I know, Emma, but Aidan said he'd meet us anyway. Just to discuss the news from the guards.'

What is there to discuss? I am a life ruiner.

'It's important to get an expert opinion,' she says. 'So remember – two o'clock.'

'Why did you schedule an appointment in the middle of the day if I'm supposed to be at school?' I ask. She stares out the window. She doesn't like it when I ask questions like that, when I go off script. My mother gives out to me for not going to school, and I pretend that I'll go next week, and my mother mentions a tutor, and I nod, and my mother gives me the new batch of college brochures that Ms McCarthy has sent, and I take them to my room, promising to look at them, and I throw them in the bin, and the next morning the bin has been emptied, but my mother never mentions the discarded brochures, and on and on and on it goes, and my world gets smaller, wrapping itself around me.

'Two o'clock,' she says. 'Be ready.'

'Nora. And Emma. Come in, come in.' Aidan Heffernan waves us into his office, winking at the middle-aged secretary sitting at the desk outside his door. My father had been determined to hire Aidan Heffernan. 'He's the best solicitor in Ballinatoom,' he kept saying. 'We need to get him before the O'Briens do.' Not that it had mattered. 'I can't take her case, I'm sorry to say,' Aidan told us the first time we came, me, my mother and my father sitting in his office. He didn't look very sorry, probably afraid that the golfing trips to the K Club with Ciarán O'Brien would disappear into thin air. 'Under Irish law, Emma doesn't have the right to separate legal representation. The DPP –' he broke off – 'I'm sorry, the Director of Public Prosecutions – will bring the accused to court and prosecute on behalf of the state. Not on Emma's behalf per se. The only time you'll be entitled to a solicitor is if an application is made to bring up Emma's sexual history.'

'They won't do that though, will they?' I said, and my father had looked sick. My mother began to babble: 'We don't need to worry about that, Emmie is a good girl, we raised her to know better than that.' I tried to look like a good girl while I counted my sins.

(How many boys?)

(What were you wearing?)

(How much did you have to drink?)

My father spoke again, ignoring the secretary's offer of Scottish shortbread. 'And what about those boys?'

'They'll get to choose their own solicitor,' Mr Heffernan said. 'The accused's right to legal representation is safeguarded under the Irish Constitution.' We left soon after. The bill for a consultation had arrived the very next day, my father wincing as he opened the envelope. It must cost a lot to keep a man in fancy biscuits.

'Thank you for seeing us,' my mother tells Aidan as he sits down in his burgundy leather chair, gesturing at us to sit in the two chairs opposite the oak desk, which is covered in mounds of files and paper and a PC. There are framed certificates on the bottle-green walls, and one large window that runs from ceiling to floor, a beige sash blind covering it.

'You've a fabulous colour,' she says, and he waves a hand at her in denial. 'Did you have a nice time?'

'Three weeks of sunshine and Margaux, how bad.' He fiddles with the cufflinks on his crisp white shirt. 'Have you any holidays planned this year yourselves?'

My mother simpers at this, as if we're planning an all-inclusive trip to the Maldives for the whole family.

'Did . . .' she hesitates, 'Sheila enjoy the holiday too?'

'Oh, she did,' Aidan says. 'She was well in need of a break. Did she not phone you?' My mother shakes her head. 'Oh. I know she meant to. It must have slipped her mind.' There's an awkward pause. 'Anyway.' He opens a cream-coloured file on his desk and looks through some pieces of paper. 'I see we've had some news while I was away. The DPP has decided to prosecute.'

'Yes, the guards contacted us last week,' my mother says.

'You must be thrilled.'

This case will be on their permanent record forever. Fitzy won't get into his course at that place in Rhode Island, *and what did he do?* they say. *He didn't take part, not really.* I can't remember. Their lives will be ruined. (I am ruining their lives.)

'Oh, we are. We're delighted,' my mother says. 'Although to be perfectly honest, I don't understand why it has taken them this long.'

'Nora, I know it seems that way, but a year isn't that long I assure you. Not in a case this complicated. And of course, there was some difficulty in getting all the evidence together.'

The guards had asked anyone who was at the party to come forward and to give their statement. No one did. The guards asked anyone who had photos saved to their phones or computers to email them to the station. I don't think anyone did that either, except for my brother, who had had the foresight to save them all to a flash drive. *Lucky*, the guards said. *Very lucky that he did that.* Lucky. Does Bryan think of those photos when he looks at me now? Does he see pink flesh, splayed legs? Have I ruined his life as well?

'It could take another two years for this to come to trial, you know. That wouldn't be unusual,' Aidan says, and my mother blanches. 'It's just a shame that Emma was over eighteen at the time or they could have prosecuted them for possession and distribution of paedophilic images. So much easier to prove than the issue of consent.' (Yet another thing that I've done wrong.) He shakes his head while he speed-reads through the file. He drops the file on his desk. 'But still. It's good that the DPP has decided to prosecute. They don't do that very often, you know. Rate of conviction is terrible low in this country.'

What's the point then?

'Yes,' he laughs, and I realize that I've spoken out loud. 'I guess you could say that.' My mother's lip starts to quiver and he says quickly, 'But this is great news. Great news altogether. The Book of Evidence must be very strong.'

'What's the Book of Evidence again?' my mother asks him. I could have told her. The lady in the Rape Crisis Centre explained it all to me when I finally went there. *It's not your fault*, she kept telling me. My mother picked me up after the appointment, but she didn't ask me how it went, or what they were like, or if I was feeling OK, or if I thought it had helped me. She didn't say anything at all.

'It's the evidence compiled by the Gardai,' Aidan

explains to her. 'It's the charges made against the accused, a list of witnesses, statements, any physical evidence that is going to be introduced at the trial, that sort of thing. There would normally be forensics, of course, but since Emma refused to go for tests in the Sexual Assault Treatment Unit . . .'

That was in the very beginning when I didn't want to be in a waiting room with other girls who had been . . . *that word*. I kept saying that I had been pretending to be asleep in the photos, that it had all been a joke. I still thought it might go away then.

'Well, we've plenty of other physical evidence.' My mother sniffs. 'All those photos.' Those photos are all I see. They are my thoughts and my daydreams. They are my nightmares and my memories. 'Surely it'll be an open-and-shut case once the judge sees those,' she says.

'Well,' Aidan says, 'we don't know if they'll be admitted.'

'What?' My mother's head snaps up. 'What are you talking about?'

Aidan spreads his fingers out and presses them into the dark wood. 'This is all unprecedented, Nora. It's a whole new world, all these camera phones and Facebook pages and whatnot. I have no idea whether the judge will allow it.'

'Can't you check? Can't you check this book thing and see if the photos are in it?'

'I'm sorry, Nora.' He shrugs. 'Only the prosecuting solicitor, the accused and their representation will be allowed to see it.'

'What? But if it's all about Emma—'

'I'm sorry.' Aidan cuts her off. 'That's just the way it is.'

I can't be told too much, the woman at the Rape Crisis Centre explained. *We can't talk about what evidence you will give in court,* she said. *Otherwise, they could claim I coached you about what to say.* But I can't help but try and imagine what the court case will be like. Will it be like what they show on *Law and Order: SVU*? Will I have to swear on a Bible, stand in front of Paul and Sean and Fitzy and Dylan and their families, all of them staring at me, hating me, whispering under their breath, *slut, liar, skank, bitch, whore*?

'You had how many drinks?' their barrister would ask, the jury gasping when I told them. (Would there be a jury?)

'There were reports you took MDMA, a Class A illegal substance,' he would say (surely it would be a he, no woman would be so cruel, right?). 'What do you say to this? You claim that Mr O'Brien gave it to you? Mr O'Brien – an upstanding citizen and exceptional athlete,

who was on track to play football for Cork senior team –
you're trying to tell us that he gave you Class A drugs?
Have you ever taken drugs before? Remember you're
under oath.' (That's what they always said on TV: *Remember
you're under oath*.) 'We have statements from your friends
that swear that they saw you taking illicit substances on
numerous occasions before then. And you admit that you
had sex with Mr O'Brien voluntarily? You admit that? And
why did you change your story? In your initial statement
to the Gardai, you said that you were pretending to be
asleep, is that correct? I have that statement here. In it
you say that those boys were your friends, that they would
never have done that, that this was all a huge mistake.
Why did you change your statement? You were afraid, you
say? You were embarrassed? Is that why you changed your
statement to say that you had, in fact, been raped? Were
you embarrassed by what you had done? Were you ashamed
of yourself once the pictures began to circulate? You seem
confused to me. You say you can't remember. Well, I put
it to you that it was consensual, that you gave consent, but
you can't remember now. Does that seem fair?'

I imagine myself standing in front of a courtroom of
people, saying *I don't remember* to every question. Members
of the press would be allowed to be present, the lady at the
Rape Crisis Centre told me, and witnesses, but she would

be there with me for support, she wouldn't leave my side for a second. It would be hard, she admitted, and her face was grave. I would have to be brave.

And it could take another two years for the case to come to trial. I would wake every morning for the next two years, looking at my parents, worry lines scored into their faces. I have ruined their lives as well.

I grasp the armrests of the chair, feeling as if I might vomit Scottish shortbread and tea all over Aidan Heffernan's plush carpet.

'How was it?'

My mother had been parked outside the supermarket in Kilgavan, reading one of those magazines full of baking tips and knitting patterns, waiting for me to finish my therapy session. She had a takeaway cup of coffee in one hand, and a packet of pink wafer biscuits open on her lap, crumbs all over her skirt.

Terrible, I want to say. Pointless.

It wasn't your fault, the therapist keeps telling me. *You were the victim of a crime, it wasn't your fault.*

Doesn't she read the papers, listen to *The Ned O'Dwyer Show*? Doesn't she realize what Emma O'Donovan was wearing (I hear she was wearing a skirt so short that you could see her knickers . . . Wait, I heard she wasn't even wearing any underwear . . .), that she drank too much (I heard that she had a bottle of vodka before she left her house . . . No, I heard that she had twenty tequila shots and then went on to the vodka . . .), that she had taken drugs (coke . . . pills? . . . No, I heard it was heroin, but she only smoked it . . .), that she was so fucking stupid? Too stupid to live really.

And now Emma O'Donovan wants to ruin their lives.

There was silence as I read one of the affirmations on the wall. *Life isn't about waiting for the storm to pass, it's about learning to dance in the rain.* I tried to give the therapist what she wants. 'You're right,' I lied. 'You're right. It wasn't my fault.'

'I hope it's working,' my mother brushes the crumbs off her skirt, 'with what we're paying her.' She places a hand on mine. 'Not that we mind about the money, Emma. All we want is for you to feel better.'

All they want is for me to have been a good girl that night. All they want is for me to have been different.

'It was grand,' I say and she looks relieved, as if she's marking it off on her mental to-do list. #3 – Prevent Emma from having a complete nervous breakdown.

I stare out the window as we drive home, following the meandering river that flows between the two towns, people out jogging, a dilapidated petrol station, the soggy edges of the fields. What would happen if I pulled up the handbrake? (Car flipping over. And over. Necks snapped.) Or if I grabbed the steering wheel and forced us into the way of that truck? (Crushed. Unidentifiable. Mangled.)

It would all be over. We probably wouldn't even know what was happening.

After the second time I tried, people around town said that I didn't really mean to do it, that I was looking for attention. I don't think that was the reason. I think I just wanted some silence. But I don't know.

I got an anonymous text message (how did they get my new number?) while I was in the hospital: *Try harder next time.*

'Damn it, anyway,' my mother says when she sees Bryan's red Golf in the driveway. 'I wanted to be here to welcome him home.'

She slams the car door behind her, not noticing that the end of her thin floral scarf has gotten caught. She hurries up the driveway, holding her leather handbag over her head, almost tripping over Precious on the porch.

I need to open the car door. I need to walk into the house. I need to meet my brother and ask him how his week was. I need to look normal. As I wait for this body to cooperate I watch the drops of rain dribbling down the car window. It looks like it's crying.

The door to the O'Callaghans' house opens. It's Conor, staring up at the sky, grimacing at the rain as he pulls the hood of his jacket up. I try and sink down in my seat but he's seen me, a hand held up in hello. I look through my satchel for my iPod and stick the earbuds in, pretending that I'm listening to music as I get out of the car and that I can't hear him calling my name, *Emmie, Emmie?* as I open up the Ballinatoom GAA umbrella to hide from him, moving my satchel strap from one shoulder to the other, ignoring Precious's miaows for attention, repeating *left leg, right leg, left leg, right leg* in my head, until I can shut the front door behind me. I lean against it, shaking.

'Hey, Emmie,' Bryan says as I walk into the kitchen. 'How are you?'

He's sitting on a stool at the island. At his feet he's thrown his navy Adidas gym bag and a black plastic bag with a tear down the side, bed-sheets and socks seeping out. He looks thinner, bluish smudges under his eyes. He needs a haircut. He gets up to hug me, his arms wrap around me tightly, and I can't breathe. I want to tell him to stop touching me, but it's Bryan, it's only Bryan. He lets go, as if he can sense my discomfort.

'How *are* you?' he asks again.

'I'm fine.'

'Did you go to school this week?'

'Your scarf got caught in the car door,' I tell my mother. She is pulling packets of pasta and a jar of white sauce out of the cupboards, apologizing to Bryan for not having time to make her own today.

'What was that?' my mother asks me, raising her voice to be heard over the whirr of the extractor fan. She heats some oil in a frying pan on the hob and throws in a couple of salmon fillets. The smell is strong. Nauseating.

(*Bet it smelled fishy!!!!!!!!* one of the comments on Facebook said. *I am an It. I am an It. I am an It.* Seventy-six people liked the comment. I made my mother go out the next day and buy vaginal cleanser in the chemist. I used it again and again and again. I wanted to be clean. I wanted to smell of nothing.)

'Your scarf,' I say, 'it got caught in the door on your way in.'

'Did you bring it with you?'

'No.'

'What is wrong with you? That was *expensive*, Emma. Your brother gave it to me for my birthday. For God's . . .' Bryan frowns at her, and she tries again. 'OK. Can you go out and get it for me, please?'

'No.'

'Why not?'

I don't want to explain to her about Conor.

'What am I supposed to eat for dinner?' I say instead. 'Is that all you're making?'

'There's a vegetarian ready-meal in the freezer,' she says, her eyes flicking to Bryan, but he doesn't comment, too busy texting.

'Any plans for the weekend?' she asks him as she gets two wine glasses from the dishwasher.

'No.'

'Are you not meeting up with the lads?' She opens the fridge door and takes out a bottle of white wine, pouring herself a large glass.

'None for me, Mam.' Bryan looks up from his phone just as she's about to pour wine into the second glass. 'Thanks.'

She doesn't offer any to me. I am not allowed to drink any more.

'Oh, come on, Bryan.' My mother waves the bottle at him. 'It's your favourite, a lovely Pinot Grigio – that wine critic in the *Sunday Times* recommended it. Just one little glass. It'll relax you after the long drive.'

'My favourite?' he says. 'I don't even like wine.'

'A beer? I have Heineken.'

'No, honestly, I'm grand, Mam.'

'What about a Coors? Or a Budweiser?'

'No,' Bryan says firmly. 'I'm grand, I said.'

A key scraping in the front door, my father muttering under his breath *that blasted cat*, wiping his shoes on the mat. 'Bryan?' he calls out. My mother puts the wine bottle back in the fridge, hiding her glass behind the kettle. She picks up the wooden spoon and stirs the jar of white sauce into the pasta.

'In here, Dad.'

My father shakes the wet out of his hair, walking from the door to where we are sitting in three strides. He stands between Bryan and me, his back to me, one hand on Bryan's shoulder, asking him question after question, *how's college, have you thought about getting back on the football team, how did that exam go, how are the lads in the house, do you have enough money, I see you brought your washing home, good lad, your mother will take care of that for you.*

'Come on, son.' He walks away, gesturing at Bryan to follow him. 'The match is about to start.'

'That's a wonderful idea,' my mother says. 'I love it when my boys spend some quality time together.'

Bryan doesn't get up. 'What about Emma?'

My father's face pinches at my name, then he smooths it away so quickly I wonder if I've only imagined it. 'What about Emma?' His words are careful, exact.

'You haven't said a word to her since you arrived

home. Aren't you going to ask how her day went?' Bryan looks at me. 'You didn't go to school, did you?'

'She had to meet her therapist today,' my mother says, ignoring my father's tight expression at the word *therapist*.

'But surely she should be going to school?' Bryan persists. 'It's her Leaving Cert in a month. Is she sitting her exams? Or is she going to take a year out and sit them next year?'

'Bryan, we talked about this last weekend.'

'Yeah, Dad, we did, and we talked about it the weekend before that, and the weekend before that too, and I still haven't heard a proper answer.'

'Well, she couldn't go to school today; she had to go visit the solicitor,' my mother pipes up. 'Much good that it did us, when he can't tell us anything anyway.'

'I still can't believe she's not allowed her own solicitor.' My father shakes his head.

Not unless they make an application to bring up my sexual history, I think, and they will. Of course they will.

How many people have you had sex with?

What counts as sex? Full penetration? Oral?

(Remember you're under oath.)

Mam's face, Dad's face, Bryan.

(Remember you're under oath.)

'Did he say anything about their performance in the

District Court?' Bryan asks. 'I can't believe those fuckers are saying they're not guilty.'

'Language, please.'

'Sorry, Mam, but as if anyone is going to look at those photos and not convict them.'

'Hmmm,' my mother says. 'Well, Aidan Heffernan isn't sure if the photos will be admitted as evidence.'

'*What?*'

'Please don't shout at me, Bryan. I'm only repeating what the man said.'

'Why not?'

'I don't know.' She looks at me for support. 'They might be allowed, he's just not sure. They probably will be. I'm sure they will be.'

Bryan's teeth are gritted. 'After all that . . .' *Hassle*, he wants to say. *Trouble. Effort.* He has seen all the photos. He has seen my legs splayed, pink flesh. (I bet it smells fishy.) He has seen me as a *slut, whore, bitch.*

'I've started seeing a therapist too, this woman at UL,' Bryan told us last month over dinner. My father pushed his chair back from the table and left the room without saying a word. I am infecting them all with my sadness. I am ruining their lives too.

'I'll phone Aidan tomorrow,' my father says. 'He'll tell me.'

'He can't.'

'Nora, I've been friends with Aidan Heffernan since national school.' My father's chest is puffed out. 'He'll tell me.'

'He can't, Denis. He doesn't get to see this Book of Evidence thing either. It's only the other side will get to see that.'

'The other side? You mean Paul O'Brien and those scumbags will get to see this before Emma?' Bryan asks, and my mother nods. He looks sick. 'We've got to do *something*; we can't just sit around and watch Emma fall apart while—'

'She's not falling apart,' my mother says sharply.

I am not falling apart. I am being ripped at the seams, my insides torn out until I am hollow.

'That's none of your concern, Bryan,' my father says.

'Well, Dad, since I'm the only one who is prepared to face up to the reality around here, then I think it is my concern. It's my *sister* we're talking about.'

I wish Bryan would leave it alone. It's because of him all of this is happening anyway. He was the one who persuaded me that I needed to press charges, that I needed to change my statement to say that I couldn't remember what had happened that night. And if I couldn't remember, how could I have given consent? And I did what he said. I thought it would be better for him to think of me as the victim (helpless, blameless, stupid) rather than a dirty slut (*slut, liar, skank, bitch, whore*) like everyone else.

And it spiralled out of control.

'Hi, I'm a producer from *The Ned O'Dwyer Show* – we'd love to have you on with us?'

'I'm with xoJane – we want you to write a piece for us. It will give you a chance to share your side of the story. I've attached some articles that we've run previously, girls with similar stories to yours.'

(I read the articles. I want to find stories that are worse. I need to know that there are girls who have been through worse. Did they survive?)

'I work for Jezebel. We want to support you. You are not alone in this, Emma.'

I feel as if I am alone.

'And I just think it would be nice to know that there's some sort of plan for her future,' Bryan says, 'and not just everyone sticking their head in the sand and pretending like—'

'Bryan –' my father's voice is firm – 'just quit while you're ahead. Your mother and I will deal with this. And that's that. Now, are we going to go watch the match?' He stops in the hall doorway, looking back over his shoulder at me. 'Sure, Emma doesn't want to watch soccer, do you, love?' he asks me out of the side of his mouth, his gaze hovering at a point an inch above my head. 'It's not really her thing.'

My mother waits until they've left before rescuing her glass of wine. 'Why don't you go upstairs?' she says. 'No point in you waiting here. Go on now, out of my sight.'

I'm lying on my bed looking at Facebook when I hear my mother call us for dinner. Sean has commented on Ali's wall about the poetry question for English Paper Two, Ali replying that she's betting on Heaney to come up. Jamie commented underneath that she's prepared an answer on John Donne too, just in case. Sean liked Jamie's comment.

'Should you have your laptop in your room?' It's Bryan, standing in the open doorway. I shut the computer.

'You again?' I joke weakly.

He has come into my room every fifteen minutes for the last hour, asking if I had seen his old Ballinatoom jersey, or if he could borrow my phone charger, or wondering if I had heard about this new comedian and wanting to show me a clip on YouTube. 'Aren't you missing the match?' I asked him, and he shrugged it off. He's always like this when he comes home, following me around, keeping an eye on me. He is the only one who looks at me any more and he looks too closely. I am afraid of what he must see.

'Just wanted to check that you heard Mam calling us for dinner,' he replies, walking before me down the stairs.

I don't want to be caught, I want to tell him. Let me fall.

My parents have already started eating when Bryan and I sit at the table, the sounds of biting and chewing and slurping unbearably loud. I cut the tofu-burger up into little pieces, placing each one in my mouth gingerly and making myself chew it and swallow, washing it down with the rest of my juice.

'No good?' Bryan asks.

'Food tastes a bit grey these days.'

My parents stiffen. *Medication = depression = things we do not talk about in this family.* That's why I go to the therapist.

'Well, it's tofu, what can you expect?' Bryan says, and my father guffaws, as if it's the funniest thing he's ever heard. I go to the fridge to refill my juice. There is a different bottle of wine in the fridge door now. I check the label. It's a white wine from Chile, a quarter of it gone already. I sit back at the table and I say nothing.

'Now tell me this, and tell me no more,' my mother says to Bryan, 'have you been on any dates recently?'

'No one goes on dates, Mam.'

'Well, any romance? A gorgeous-looking boy like

you – they must be queuing up.' She sucks her lower lip. 'Unless you're not ready. Are you still upset about Jennifer?'

'I don't want to talk about that.'

'You poor thing, it's only natural—'

'The boy said he didn't want to talk about it, Nora.' My father drops his cutlery on his plate with a clatter.

Bryan looks sad. That's my fault too.

'Oh, don't worry. You're my beautiful boy. You'll find someone yet.' She reaches across the table to take hold of his hand, knocking over my juice as she does so. I try and catch the glass, scrambling to my feet to grab a dishcloth.

'Have you been drinking?'

'I had one glass, Denis. Surely I'm allowed to have *one* glass of wine?'

I wrap my legs around the feet of the chair to stop myself from running out to the utility room and getting rid of the recycling bin, all the empty bottles, *clink clink clink*, before my father can see it. What if he decides that my mother has a drinking problem and that she needs to be sent to a clinic somewhere to get sober? Will she have to go up to St John of God's like Jamie's uncle Billy had to do a few years ago, everyone in town joking that the publicans would be put out of business if he went on the dry. I could already hear them gossiping, saying *like mother, like daughter, sure everyone knows that girl was demented with the drink when this 'attack' happened, and I mean, who poured the drink down her throat? No one forced her to drink that much.* I imagine my mother at an AA meeting, sitting around in a circle talking about her feelings, and maybe she would want to start talking to me too, talking about things I don't want to remember. (I can't remember, I told you.) The therapist tells me that I need to *stop engaging in Catastrophe Thinking*, that I should *visualize a large Stop sign whenever your thoughts start to spin in this way*, but I can't, no one will tell me anything, no one will tell me what's *really* going on, so of course I have to imagine it for myself. What if my father doesn't want to have a lush, a *stupid, ugly, fucking lush*, as a wife any more? (Why can't she be strong? Why can't she pretend like the rest of us?) What if he decides that he wants someone who has her make-up on in the mornings, and who cooks dinners from scratch for her family, not just for show at the farmer's market? (*We can't let them think they've got the better of us, Emma.*) What if he meets someone else, and doesn't want to have anything more to do with this family, with his stupid, drunken wife and his stupid, damaged daughter? And my mother would blame me. She would wish that I had never been born. She would hate me for breaking up her perfect family. After all those years of wishing my mother was different, that she would just leave me alone, it's strange how panicked I feel at the thought of her giving up on me.

And it would be all my fault.

'So, Em, are you heading out this weekend?' Bryan changes the subject.

I pretend to give this some consideration. 'No, I don't think so. Not this weekend.'

'I met Maggie at Centra earlier, and she said she and Jamie are going to hang out at Ali's later, watch a movie. Nothing too hectic, she said, because of –' he hesitates – 'the, eh, Leaving being so close now, you know. Anyway, she said that she'd tried to text you to ask if you wanted to come, and she phoned too but she couldn't get on to you.'

'Oh, wait.' My mother slams her hand down on the table. The knife jumps off her plate and hits the floor with a clatter. I jerk back in fright. 'She rang the house phone earlier looking for you.'

'And why didn't you tell Emma?' my father asks. 'Why didn't you pass on the message?'

'I forgot. I'm sorry.'

'You're forgetting a lot of things these days,' my father mutters.

'And what's that supposed to mean?'

He doesn't answer.

'I'll ring her later,' I say. The girls had come to visit at the beginning, filing into my room like mourners at a wake. I could tell a small part of them loved this, the drama of it all. 'Yes, she's my best friend,' they could say. 'Yes, I was there that night.' 'Yes, I know what's happened. Emma talks to me. She trusts me.'

Maggie had been distraught, her eyes welling up, constantly reaching out to hug me. (I didn't want to be touched.) I was stiff, my arms stuck to my sides. She broke away, embarrassed, apologizing over and over again for leaving the party without me, for not insisting that I go home with them, for being mean to me in school.

'But I didn't know, Em,' she had said. 'I didn't know about all of this. I thought you had fucked Ali over, and with the whole Eli thing . . .' I stared at her and she flushed. 'Well, you *did* kiss him, Emma. Not that it matters now, obviously, but can you understand why I was cross with you? Even a little bit?'

I turned to watch Ali tracing her fingers over the Polaroids I had glued to my vanity mirror, and I knew she was counting to see how many she was in.

'Ali,' Maggie had hissed at her. She joined us on the bed, sitting with her legs curled up underneath her, telling me she forgave me for sleeping with Sean. She was restless, uncomfortable. She wanted things to go back to normal.

So did I.

'Wait, are those my sunglasses?' she said, picking up the Warby Parkers. I remember taking those. I remember thinking she could afford a new pair, I remember feeling it wasn't fair, why weren't my parents rich too? I remember caring about stuff like that.

'Yes,' I said. I didn't even feel embarrassed.

'Ali, for fuck's sake.' Maggie's face was turning red. 'Will you just cop on?'

'It doesn't matter,' I said. And it didn't. None of it mattered.

We were silent for a few moments. Silence follows me everywhere these days.

'But are you sure, Em?' Ali blurted out. 'You were pretty wasted.'

'Ali.'

'What? Mags, I have to ask. Sean is a good guy, I just want Emma to be, like, totally sure.' She wrapped her arm around my shoulder. (I didn't want to be touched.) 'You know I'm on your side, right? I was just asking if it was, like, *rape* rape.' (I don't want to hear *that word*.)

'Do you want to go out?' I said. 'I heard Dylan's throwing a party in his place.'

'What? Why would you want to go—'

'Or we can just go out,' I said. 'Do you want to go out for a few drinks?'

'Eh, sure,' Maggie said, looking at Ali in confusion. 'If that's what you want.'

I wanted things to go back to normal.

Ringing the doorbell of Dylan's house. Walking into the kitchen to put our beer in the fridge. Silence. We go into the living room. One person leaves. Another. And another. It is only Maggie, Ali and me left. Sarah Swallows saying, 'I think you had better leave. Dylan doesn't want *her* here.' We go to Reilly's. I drink and I drink and I drink. I try to forget my shame. (I can't remember.)

Maggie and Ali came to the house again the next day, wanting to 'discuss last night'. *We couldn't find you, someone said you went down that alleyway, who was that guy, Emma?*

The next time they came to visit, I refused to see them. And the next time, and the next. They had too many questions, and I didn't have any answers.

I never heard from Jamie. Maggie told me that she was *just so busy, I know she wants to see you but things are crazy for her at home, and she's still working, and she's studying her ass off because she's been offered a scholarship dependent on her results.*

I wish I could tell Jamie that I did her a favour. I wish I could explain to her that she is the lucky one. If I could go back, pretend like nothing had happened, I would.

'You should go meet them,' my mother says to me, walking into the kitchen and opening the fridge door. 'When was the last time you saw the girls?'

'I think it's nearly time for *The Late Late*,' I say, and she checks her watch, gasping when she sees the time, shooing all of us out, leaving the table laden down with dirty dishes.

In the TV room, the four of us stand, unsure of which seats to take, which combinations to follow. Bryan sits down first, on the sofa, pulling me down beside him. I can smell his aftershave, and nausea shudders through me. I shift away. My mother sits on the edge of the sofa, on Bryan's side.

'This is nice, isn't it? It's nice for all four of us to be at home together,' she says as my father folds himself into the recliner chair. He puts the leg-rests up, gesturing impatiently at her.

'Yes, Denis?'

'Remote.'

'Pardon?'

'Can. You. Give. Me. The. Remote. Control.'

Bryan digs it out from under his seat and leans forward

to pass it to my father. 'Didn't you hear what I said, Denis?' my mother says again.

'Well, good evening and welcome to *The Late Late Show*!' the presenter says, smiling into the camera. 'Coming up on the programme, we have rising star Sasha Peters here to sing a song from her debut album, described by *Hot Press* as the "best Irish record of the last three years"; best-selling author Roisin Flewett will talk about her newest release, *Did You Ever Really Love Me?*; we're going to meet the man who's swapping horses for tractors; and we'll be talking to one of the greatest rugby legends this country has ever produced.' A photo of Padraig Brady flashes on the screen. 'We'll also be discussing the Ballinatoom Case. One year on, what happens next? We have legal expert Sean O'Reilly here, as well as child psychologist Suzanne Meade, and Lorna Sisk from the Rape Crisis Centre in Dublin to debate whether—'

My father pushes himself out of the recliner and leaves the room. My mother slams her glass on the coffee table, jabbing at the buttons of the remote until the screen cuts out. I close my eyes, something heavy coursing through my veins, grating against my bones.

I need something sharp to cut it out with.

'It's disgraceful,' Bryan says, his fists clenching. 'Fucking *disgraceful*. I'm going to make a complaint, I'm

251

going to write an email to RTÉ tomorrow and tell them that they can't just do that, it's traumatizing for people, there have to be trigger warnings. Right, Emma? Shouldn't they have put a trigger warning before it?'

When did we all become fluent in this language that none of us wanted to learn?

'It's not cool, they can't just do that, what about other victims of rape, what do they think?'

Was there always this much of (*don't say the word, don't say that word ever again*) before, on TV and on the radio, and in songs and in movies and in the papers and I just never noticed?

'Well,' my mother says, 'I'm not in the form for *The Late Late* anyway.' She picks up a copy of the *RTÉ Guide* from the coffee table and leafs through it. 'Look, there's a film on Channel 4, some romantic comedy. That'll do, won't it?'

Neither Bryan nor I says anything.

'You OK?' he asks me, but I can't look at him. (He has seen the photos. He has seen me, pink flesh, *slut, whore, bitch.*)

My mother turns the TV back on. 'I hate the term chick-lit, I find it pejorative,' the red-headed author is saying while the presenter nods. My mother switches channel.

'Here we are,' she says. 'This is better now, isn't it?'

It's about fifteen minutes into the film, but it's easy enough to catch up. It's about a girl, petite and pretty, whose younger sister is getting married before her, and everyone acts like this is a terrible tragedy. At the hen party the women, all emaciated with sleek hair, start talking about their 'numbers'.

'What's your number?' a bitchy girl asks the main character, the other girls at the hen party giggling in anticipation.

What's your number? What's your number, Emma?

(Remember you're under oath.)

Does it count if you can't remember? Does it count if you didn't want it to happen in the first place?

Saturday

I can hear my parents arguing as I come downstairs for breakfast. I tiptoe nearer to the door, pressing my ear against it. It's the only way I can find out what's happening these days.

'It's just not good enough, Denis. Beth says that—'

'Jesus Christ, will you stop talking about Beth? Beth this, Beth that. Where the fuck *is* Beth?' My breath shortens. My father never swears. 'Have we seen her since all of this happened? No. All we get are phone calls giving us bloody PR advice.'

'You can't blame Beth for this, Denis. It's not like she's the one leaking Garda information. "A source in the local Garda station says that the alleged victim was well known locally for her promiscuous behaviour." Why are they bringing it up anyway? Didn't Aidan Heffernan say that they'd have to make a special application to bring up any of that sort of thing?'

'I'd say it's fairly likely they're going to apply for that, isn't it? Have you *seen* what the papers are saying about her? How did you not know what she was up to, Nora? You're her mother for God's sake. Christ, I feel as if we never knew her at all. I'm just glad my parents aren't still alive to see all this. The shame would have killed them.'

I hear a low sob, and then my father saying, 'Please, Nora. Please. Don't cry. I can't . . .'

When I first changed my mind and decided I had been *that word*, Joe Quirke had come to the house. He was wearing plain clothes, driving the 'undercover' cop car whose licence plate every kid in Ballinatoom had memorized by the time we were fourteen. A big man with thinning grey hair, he always seemed to have a sheen of sweat on his brow. He wanted to talk to Nora and Denis, he said, he would bring the ban-garda the next time to speak with me in private. It wasn't usual, he said, to do this in people's homes, and he would have to do it again in a more formal setting, but his sister Bernie had asked him to help out so he was prepared to bend the rules a little. Just for us. I was told to leave, to go upstairs, and I did, making a big show of banging my bedroom door so they would hear it downstairs. Then I had crept back down, wincing as the wooden boards of the stairs creaked, and listened in to the conversation. My father's answers had been monosyllabic, 'Yes. No. Yes. No. I don't know. Are we done here, Joe?'

(I started to log in to my father's email account, scan through his text messages when he wasn't looking. I needed to see what he was saying about me, what he was thinking. If he thought this was my fault. I check them again and again, each time bracing myself for the worst. But my name is never mentioned. It as if I have been erased.)

Then my mother began.

Please give me your name for the tape recorder: Nora O'Donovan.

Where were you the night of the alleged attack? We, sorry, that is Denis and I—

Who is Denis? Joe, you know who Denis is, for God's sake—

Please, tell me who Denis is, for the tape recorder. Oh, right. Sorry, Joe. Denis is my husband. Emmie's father. Denis and I had gone to Killarney for the night. Bryan, sorry, Emmie's brother Bryan, had given us a voucher for a deal for a hotel down there. For our anniversary.

Continue. Well, we'd had a lovely night, but Denis was anxious to get home. He had a few meetings on the

Monday that he wanted to look over his notes for, and you know what he's like. And it was such a gorgeous day. I mean, who'd want to be in a car on a day like that is beyond me—

Can we please stick to the relevant information. Sorry, Joe. So we arrived home, and I saw something on the porch, but you know, my eyesight isn't the best, so I asked Denis. I said, 'Denis, what *is* that on the porch, it looks like a black plastic bag or something,' and he stopped the car, well, stalled really, and I went flying forward and I was giving out to him, I was saying, 'Denis – for God's sake, Denis – are you trying to give me whiplash?' and he said, 'Shut up, Nora.' And then he said, 'That's Emmie.'

Just lying on the porch? I'm surprised none of the neighbours found her before that. Well, they couldn't have. There's no way they would have just left her there. We look out for each other on the estate.

OK. What happened next? For a moment, all I could think of was that she was dead, that she must be dead, sure why else would she have been collapsed on the porch like that . . .

Take your time. Do you want a glass of water? No, Joe. Thank you. I'm fine. So I ran out of the car, I can't remember the last time I ran that fast, until I got to her, and she was so sunburnt there were blisters forming around her hairline, and her dress was on back to front, I remember that distinctly because I kept thinking, did she go out with her dress like that, and she, and she . . .

Yes? You're OK, Nora. This is all confidential? You won't tell Bernadette?

Of course. It's just that, Emma wasn't, she wasn't wearing any . . . *underwear.* And I pulled the dress down as quickly as I could before Denis could see it, and her skin was so hot, she was burning up. And she wasn't making any sense, she was talking gibberish, and she was like jelly, she kept falling over, and her knees and hands were bleeding, gushing blood, it was like something out of a horror film.

What did you do then? Denis said that we'd better bring her to SouthDoc, that she must have sunstroke. It was just a coincidence that Jimmy was on duty. And sure, we've known Jimmy for years, he went to school with Denis, he was Denis's best man, you know that. He's like family. He said Emma had sunstroke all right, and that she wasn't the first he'd seen that weekend, that so many people lost the run of themselves with this heat. And I tried to tell him that Emmie wasn't like that, that Emmie was obsessed with taking care of her skin, that she wore factor fifty on Christmas Day.

Did you tell Dr Fitzpatrick about your concerns? Did you ask him to run any other tests? No. No. I didn't even think, how would I have thought that . . . I don't know. But with his son being implicated . . . Not that he would have known that at the time. Not that we—

And what about Emma? What about Emma?

Did she say anything at this time that might be of relevance to the case? No. We kept asking her . . . We kept asking her questions but . . . she just kept saying she felt sick, that she couldn't remember what had happened, how she got home, that she didn't know why she was lying on the porch. But—

But what? Joe, you should have seen her there, on that porch. Just lying there. It was as if she was a bag of rubbish, ready to be thrown away.

I was crammed full of rubbish, of shit, of the stuff that was no use any more, that no one wanted, or could ever want again. I was dirty. (I should be thrown away.) And as I listened it was as if I could feel myself crack into two, me and her, and now it was she who was Emma, Emma O'Donovan. I was the Ballinatoom Girl.

The female guard had arrived two days afterwards, wearing jeans and a white shirt. As soon as she came in the door of the TV room I recognized her – she was one of Susan Twomey's best friends. (Elaine? Tracey? Jess?) She had been with her after that match, had snickered when Susan had pulled at my top and told me to cover myself up. She was polite, refusing my mother's offer of tea and biscuits, waiting until my mother said, *OK, I'll let you alone so. I'll just be in the kitchen if you need anything.* She had been businesslike, talking me through the questions briskly.

'It's all a misunderstanding,' I told her again and again. 'It was all a joke. I was pretending to be asleep.'

Afterwards, once more refusing my mother's baking, she asked if I had taken the morning-after pill, if I had gotten tested for any sexually transmitted infections. 'Sure, why would she need to do that?' my mother had interjected. 'They were all good local boys, from good families.' The guard raised an eyebrow.

Then the blistering began. I didn't want to do it, but I had to so I grabbed a hand mirror, holding it up so I could see myself (pink flesh) (splayed legs) and (the photos, the photos, Bryan saw those photos, Conor saw those photos, my father saw those photos) I could see open sores, oozing. I dropped the hand mirror. I should take a pair of scissors and cut it off, and get them to sew it back up. What would it matter? It didn't belong to me any more anyway.

I had to go to a doctor in Kilgavan. I couldn't go to Dr Fitzpatrick, for obvious reasons, and I couldn't face anyone else in town with something this embarrassing, someone that I would see in the supermarket afterwards or at Mass. They would know that I was tainted, riddled, dirty, dirty, *slut, liar, skank, bitch, whore.* I sat by myself in the sterile waiting room, staring at a black-and-white poster on the wall, a photo of a girl lying on the ground, her make-up smeared over her face. One in three reported rapes happens when the victim is drinking, it said. It was her own fault. (My fault. My fault.)

'Morning.'

My parents are sitting at the table, glaring at each other, but as soon as I walk in they stop. My father crumples up the newspaper he was reading and walks out into the utility room, throwing it into the recycling bin.

'Morning, Emma,' my mother replies. 'Did you sleep well?'

I grunt in response. My father leans over to kiss my mother on the cheek, asking her to hand him his briefcase. He pauses, as if he's about to kiss me too.

'Bye then,' he says. 'I'll see you this evening.'

(I am six years old. I have woken early because it is my birthday, and I want to see what presents I got, and I want to have pancakes for breakfast, and I want to be spoiled rotten. Everyone at school will want to sit next to me at lunch today. They all want to be my best friend. They are coming to my birthday party, even though I won't have a magician and a bouncy castle and a chocolate fountain like Ali did at hers. *Why can't I have a chocolate fountain too?* I ask my parents, as my mother ties my hair up with a pink ribbon. My daddy gives me a big hug. *You are the prettiest girl in Ballinatoom. You don't need a chocolate fountain.* I looked at myself in my mirror. *You'll always be Daddy's little girl, do you know that?* he told me. *You'll always be my princess.*)

'But why were you there?' he kept asking me in the first few weeks after it happened. 'Why did you drink so much, Emmie? Why were you in that bed in the first place, Emmie? I thought you knew better. I thought we had reared you better than that. Why, Emmie?' he kept asking, and asking, and asking, only stopping when I started to cry. 'Crocodile tears,' he snapped. 'Oh, just get out of my sight. I can't stand to look at you.'

The first time I tried I was in my bedroom. I lock the door behind me. I take a towel, and I place it underneath me. I don't want to make a mess.

I am going to make it end.

When I woke up in the hospital, Bryan was there. He had left Limerick as soon as he heard, he told me.

He held my hand, bandages covering the new tattoos on my wrists, my parents behind him. 'Emmie, please, I'm begging you . . .' Bryan said, dashing away tears with the back of his hand. My father had told him, 'That's enough of that now, lad.' We went home, and we didn't talk about it again. (Until the next time.)

My mother waits until we hear the front door close behind my father.

'Your tablets.' She doles them out on to my palm. The dark shadows and crow's feet around her eyes seem to be more pronounced every time I look at her. I remember watching her when I was a child as she patted and stroked her face, applying layers of creams and gels. *You have to take care of yourself*, she would tell me. *I can't expect your father to stay interested in me if I just let myself go.*

'Tongue?' She nods afterwards. 'Good girl. So, what's the plan for today?'

What does she want me to say? That I'm going to meet the girls for lunch, maybe go to Style Magpie to pick out an outfit especially for tonight? Something revealing, that shows off my body; the perfect outfit that will attract the attention of a boy I have my eye on? *Slut, liar, skank, bitch, whore.* Does she want me to grumble about homework, to beg her for fifty euro for my vodka fund?

'No plans,' I say. She gets up and walks into the

kitchen area, takes a dishcloth from the sink and makes small circles on the counter for a few seconds. 'Where's your brother?'

'Still in bed, I think,' I say, looking at the box of cereal on the table. I run through the routine carefully in my head. Take box, pour in bowl, milk on top. Take spoon and eat it, the nothing taste of cardboard flakes in my dry mouth. If someone stops eating completely, they would only survive for thirty days. Wikipedia says that death by dehydration is quicker, but more painful. During terminal dehydration, the usual <u>symptoms of dehydration</u>, such as <u>headache</u> and <u>leg cramps</u>, can occur. Dehydration can be hard to bear, and requires patience and determination, since it takes from several days to a few weeks. Those who die by terminal dehydration typically lapse into unconsciousness before death, and may also experience <u>delirium</u> and altered <u>serum sodium</u>.

You would tell me if you still had suicide ideation, wouldn't you, Emma? the therapist asks me after each session. I smile and tell her I would. I am lying. I would never tell her. She might try and stop me.

'Emma? Emma, are you listening to me?' I look up to find my mother staring at me.

'Sorry. What did you say?'

'I was just saying that I'm going to meet Sheila for elevenses. Will you be OK by yourself?'

'I thought she was supposed to come here?'

'Yes, well.' Her smile doesn't reach her eyes. 'She said she feels like the Cake Shack today.'

'Fine.'

I wait until I hear her footsteps on the stairs before I tiptoe into the utility room. I crouch down on my haunches, rummaging through the recycling bin to find what my father has hidden in there, wiping fingers sticky with dribbling honey and tomato sauce off the ends of my dressing gown, *And I've told you time and time again, Nora, please wash out the containers properly before you put them in the recycling. Jesus, is it so hard to remember? Is it, Nora? Do I have to do everything myself around here now?* Sitting back on my heels, I quickly scan through the *Ballinatoom News*. There's a piece in the sports section about the team's chances of winning the county this year. Sean and Paul had kept playing for the seniors last year. Paul had started a few of the championship matches on Ciarán O'Brien's insistence, some of the crowd cheering when he was brought on, according to a caller on *The Ned O'Dwyer Show*. But when the case started to blow up, and the national newspapers got hold of it, Ali's father had threatened to withdraw sponsorship from Hennessy's Pharmacies if they weren't benched for the rest of the season. They lost to Kilgavan in the quarter finals, the earliest they had ever gone out. That night, our house phone rang. The caller hung up when we answered. It rang again. They hung up. I stood barefoot on the landing at 1 a.m., watching from the top of the stairs as my mother answered the phone yet again. 'Who is it?' Her voice was wavering, and even from that distance I could hear the jeers and screams at the other end. We went back to bed. And the phone rang again. Then the doorbell began to ring, a long shrill note as someone held it down, screams of laughter when they ran away before my father could catch them. 'Ring the garda station.' My mother was getting hysterical. My father told her to calm down, that he couldn't ring the guards over some stupid kids acting the maggot. The phone rang and rang. At 3 a.m. my father took it off the hook. And we pretended to go to sleep.

My father was exhausted the next day at work. He made stupid mistakes, he said.

(My fault.)

I thumb through the paper (a photo of Bernadette and Sheila at a charity event – where was Mam?), a drizzle of olive oil turning the paper transparent in the middle of the page, stopping when I find what I'm looking for. 'As many of my loyal readers will know,' Veronica Horan writes, 'I have been writing about the degradation of Ireland's ethical value system for some time now. Spoiled by indulgent parenting during the Celtic Tiger years, the youth of today show no sense of community spirit or civic duty. Nowhere is this more clear than in our young women. You can see them on a Saturday night, falling over in their high-heeled shoes, skirts worn so short that you can see their knickers. That is if they deign to wear underwear. You can spout all the nonsense you like about equal rights, but the truth is – women have to take responsibility for themselves and their own safety. If they are going to insist on wearing such revealing clothes, if they are going to insist on getting so drunk that they can barely stand, then they must be prepared to bear the consequences. The so-called "Ballinatoom Girl" should ask a few questions of herself. Did anyone force her to drink so much? Did anyone force her to take illegal drugs, as it has been alleged she did? No. And yet she is asking us to place the blame upon four young men. These youngsters have continued to protest their innocence And I believe them. I've never experienced anything like it before. I have watched as their lives have fallen apart, I have watched the effect this heinous accusation has had on their families. The mother of one of the men, vulnerable after the death of a son many years ago, is reported to be suffering from a nervous breakdown. Has the Ballinatoom Girl given any thought to this poor woman and her emotional well-being? I think not. I doubt that she cares that as a result of her actions our community is being torn apart at its very foundations.'

'What's that?'

'Jesus.' I gasp in fright as Bryan creeps up on me, a cereal bowl in his hands. He's wearing a grey wife-beater and old football shorts, shovelling cornflakes into his mouth. 'You scared me.'

'Sorry.' He puts the bowl down on top of the washing machine and leans over to grab the newspaper off me. 'Why are you reading that out here?' He scans through the article, his lips almost disappearing as he reads the last lines. My mother walks back into the kitchen, in a neat blouse and trousers, her bob held back with a black hairband. She rifles through drawers and under stacks of old magazines and unopened letters until she finds her car keys.

'OK, kids, I'm off—'

'Have you read this?' Bryan confronts her, holding up the greasy, stained paper. My knee joints crack as I stand up and follow him, leaning against the door frame between the utility room and the kitchen area.

'Yes,' my mother admits.

'And you weren't going to tell me?'

'Tell you what?'

Bryan stares at her.

'What was I supposed to say?' she says. 'I'm surprised you hadn't heard from one of your friends anyway.' She snatches the paper from him. 'A nervous breakdown. Oh, wouldn't I have loved the luxury of a nervous breakdown. And using the memory of poor John Junior for sympathy, as if that could excuse things, as if that . . .'

Everyone knew that Deirdre Casey had never recovered after John Junior died. Their house was always cold, silent. Jennifer spent most of her time with us. 'It's nice to be around a *real* family,' she would say.

'John Senior has to cook all his own meals,' Sheila Heffernan had tutted to my mother a few years ago, 'and he coming in from a hard day's work on the farm.'

'Ah, Sheila,' my mother had replied. 'She lost a child. There's no greater loss than that.'

I wonder if she still feels like that. Maybe she wishes that I had died too. Would that have been an easier grief than this, looking at me every day and knowing that this was only a shell, that Emmie, the real Emmie, was never coming back and that there was a new Emma that she had to learn to love all over again?

Maybe they would all rather I was dead.

Maybe they wish that Bryan hadn't found me in time.

Maybe they're hoping that it'll be third time lucky.

'I can't believe you didn't tell me.' Bryan shoves past her and storms upstairs.

'What good would it do? Jennifer isn't talking to you, is she? She doesn't want to have anything to do with this family, and we don't want to have anything to do with hers, so just *grow up*, Bryan.' My mother follows him out into the hall, standing at the bottom of the stairs and yelling up at him, 'Where are your loyalties? This is your *sister* we're talking about here –' as Bryan slams his bedroom door.

She shuffles back into the kitchen, her skin flushed. 'Oh, don't *you* look at me like that, for God's sake. I was defending *you*, wasn't I? None of this would even . . .' and she stops herself just in time.

None of this would even be happening if it wasn't for you.

I feel like I did when I was a very small child and I lost sight of my mother in a crowded shopping centre. I looked up at the lady next to me, putting my hand between her knees, but then I saw it wasn't Mam, and panic began to pool in my throat. The seconds slowed down, everyone walking past me as if they were wading through water, and I believed, at that moment, that I would never find my mother, that I would never see her ever again.

*

'Emma. *Emma.* Wake up.'

Someone's hand is on my shoulder, shaking me out of my nothingness dream. I open one eye to see Bryan and I blink, that grey in-between sleep and waking space sharpening into shapes, colours, memories that I don't want to look at. I turn away from him.

I wish I was dead. I hug the thought to myself.

'Why are you asleep? It's only three o'clock in the afternoon.'

'I was tired,' I say. My mother had gone to meet Sheila without putting the padlock back on the medicine cabinet. I had taken one of my sleeping tablets, counting out the rest. Twenty-six little white pills. It must have been a new bottle.

One, two, three, four, five, six, seven, eight, nine, ten, eleven, twelve, thirteen, fourteen, fifteen, sixteen, seventeen, eighteen, nineteen, twenty, twenty-one, twenty-two, twenty-three, twenty-four, twenty-five, twenty-six. I look at them all in the palm of my hand.

(I am dead.

There is a funeral.

People come. They cry.

Would they be sorry?

Would my sins be forgiven?)

But I couldn't do it to Bryan again. He had been the

one, my mother told me afterwards, who found me when I tried the second time. He screamed. He phoned the ambulance. He put his fingers down my throat to try and make me get sick. He thought I was dead. And he had been the one by my side, once again, when I woke up. *Please, Emmie*, he said. *Please, stop doing this. Promise me.*

I had promised. (But I didn't want to stop.) (I don't want to stop trying.)

(I want all this to end. I want all this to be over.)

'Fine,' he says now, and I hear the sound of my desk chair being rolled across the floor, feel his knees nudging against my back as he sits beside my bed. 'So, any plans for the day?'

I see the photos etched through the thin veil of my eyelids. (Bryan has seen those photos.) Pink flesh. Splayed legs. Slut, bitch, whore.

'Or tonight?' he continues. 'I wouldn't mind going to the cinema. Do you want to come?'

'No,' I say. 'I'm not in the mood.'

'Well, what about heading to the arts centre?' he says, even though he hates the theatre. 'The Players are doing *Mole*. You'd like that, wouldn't you?' He pauses, checking his phone again. 'Mole? Molly?'

'It's pronounced Moll.'

'Will we go? You enjoyed that other play, didn't you?'

We had gone to see the Toom Players' production of *Juno and the Paycock* last year. We arrived at the arts centre ten minutes before the show was about to start, Bryan's face turning pale when he realized the playwright's name was Sean O'Casey, taking a sneaky look at me to see if I had noticed. I still thought then that it might all die down.

'Shit,' Bryan had said when his phone rang, a photo of Jen coming up on the screen. 'I have to take this.'

He stepped away. A surge of people pushed from behind.

'Sorry,' I said to the person I bumped into, before realizing that it was Danny the Taxi, one arm wrapped proprietarily around a girl who had fake tan staining her elbows. He didn't turn around, too busy arguing with the ticket seller, huffing in disgust when he was told that it was all sold out.

'I have two spare tickets,' I told them.

Mam and Dad were supposed to come too, but they had decided against it at the last minute. Bryan and I had left without them, neither of us mentioning Mam's red-rimmed eyes and Dad's stony face. Danny the Taxi turned, physically recoiling when he saw me.

He went back to the girl at the ticket office. 'Are you sure there are none left? Any at all?'

273

She looked from him to me, and then back at him. 'Did you not hear that girl behind you? She has two spare tickets.'

'Yeah, well,' he said. 'I'm not that desperate.'

Bryan came back.

'Bryan, my man,' Danny punched him lightly on the shoulder. 'What's this about spare tickets?'

Bryan gave them to him, refusing to allow Danny to pay for them. 'Nah, sure they're paid for by the parents, don't sweat it.' Danny promised him a free spin home after his next night out. We went into the dark theatre, and no one turned to look at me, most of the audience were Mam and Dad's age and probably hadn't even seen the Easy Emma page. (They haven't seen it, Emma. They haven't seen it, that man isn't looking at you, he isn't, he isn't, he isn't. He hasn't seen your tits and thought they were too small. Pink flesh and splayed legs. He didn't comment that at least your ass was amazing. Stop it, stop it, stop it, stop it.)

'You all right, Emmie?' Bryan had asked me as we took our seats. 'I'm fine,' I replied automatically. Danny and his date sat in the seats directly in front of us, where my parents should have been, and he leaned over to whisper something in her ear. She stiffened, slowly turning her head to look at me. (I had thought he was my friend.)

274

Slut, liar, skank, bitch, whore. The lights went down and we stood for the national anthem. *Slut, liar, skank, bitch, whore.* The curtains drew back and the actors appeared on stage. *Slut, liar, skank, bitch, whore.* At the interval we had tea in the club bar, we bought tickets for the raffle. It was for a good cause, they said. *Slut, liar, skank, bitch, whore.* In the car on the way home, Bryan asked me what I thought of the play, had I enjoyed it, wasn't I glad that I had come out after all? And I realized he hadn't even noticed.

'I'm not really in the form for the theatre tonight,' I tell him now, still curled on my side facing the wall. He reaches out to touch my shoulder, and I can feel my breath clotting again, getting shorter and tighter. It's only Bryan, I tell myself, but I can't, *I can't*, and I have to shrug him off me.

'Everyone is always looking at me,' I whisper, the words breaking from my throat.

'People have always looked at you. Remember when we were kids? Mam couldn't take us to the park to feed the ducks without twenty different people stopping her to tell her you should be a child model.'

I had liked it before. I had encouraged them.

(Maybe I had been asking for it.)

'I'm not going, Bryan. Just leave it.' I close my eyes

again and start counting silently. I only reach five when I hear my bedroom door close quietly behind him.

'Where's Dad?' Bryan asks my mother when we're having dinner. 'Shouldn't he be home at this stage?'

'He's gone to the pub for a few drinks.'

With who? I want to ask her. Who does he have to drink with any more, since Ciarán O'Brien declared war against him? (My fault.)

'Maybe you could go meet him for one,' she says. 'I'm sure he'd like that.'

'No, I'm grand,' Bryan says. He smiles at me. It's a collection of teeth, *all the better to eat you with, my dear,* and I have to remember to breathe. Bryan is safe. Bryan is good. Bryan would never hurt me.

'You sure?' she asks, and Bryan nods. Does he want to go out for a drink?

I count the things he could do if it wasn't for me.

1. Hang out with Jen.

2. Remember what a genuine smile feels like.

3. Have a good time.

4. Be normal.

He could be happy. They could all be happy.

'OK, then. The two of you go on into the TV room, and I'll just clear up here,' my mother says, reaching for her glass. Bryan raises an eyebrow but I shake my head. It is funny how quickly we have become accustomed to this new life, and this new mother.

'What do you want to watch?' Bryan throws himself on the sofa, opening up the Doritos he took from the cupboard. He holds the bag out to me as I sit next to him, curling my feet underneath me. I shake my head.

He changes channel again and again. Mam and Dad finally gave in and got a satellite dish after years of saying it would only be *a distraction, and it's unhealthy for growing teenagers. You should be outside with your friends, getting fresh air.*

'What do you want to watch?'

I don't reply, and the silence expands, yawning like a chasm between us.

'Emma,' he says again. 'Emmie. I'm trying, OK? Can't you just try too?'

But I don't want him to try. I don't want him to have to *try* all the time.

He reaches over to take my hand. The sound of our breathing filling the room. His breath, then mine, his breath, then mine, just a beat out of sync.

'Emma?' He needs me to say that I'm OK. He needs to know that I won't do anything stupid.

'I'm going to bed.'

'But you slept for most of the day . . .' he protests as I walk out of the room.

My mother closes the fridge as I come into the kitchen. 'Oh, it's only you.' She puts her hand over her heart and reopens the fridge door, draining the last of the wine bottle into her glass.

'I want to take my sleeping tablet.'

She nods at me. She doesn't say, *But it's so early*, or *Why do you want to go to sleep already?* or *Is there anything that you want to talk about, Emma?* She takes the small key off the necklace around her neck, standing on tippy toes to reach the cupboard that used to contain homeopathic remedies and plasters and vitamins and out-of-date cough syrup and now looks like a mini-chemist, countless clear bottles with 'Hennessy's Pharmacy' emblazoned across them.

'What the . . . ?' she says, when she finds the cupboard open. She gives me a sideways look to check if I've noticed and I pretend to be innocent. She takes down the small yellow bottle, and I can feel myself relax just at the sight of it. She counts them.

'I thought there were twenty-six?'

'I don't know,' I say as I grab the tablet off her.

'Tongue?'

I show her my empty mouth gladly.

Sunday

'Morning.' Bryan takes an exaggerated look at his phone when I walk into the dining area. 'Or should I say, good afternoon?'

I make myself smile at him. It seems to mean so much to him now, that he can make me smile.

I wonder if he knows I'm pretending. I wonder if he prefers it that way.

'It's a nice morning,' he says. The rain has stopped and the entire room is bathed in sunshine, but it's too bright. The sun shows up all of our messiness, the streaky smears on the window panes, the sprinkling of dust like ashes over the counter, the small piles of crumbs gathering in the grooves between the floor tiles. Precious is licking at the ground. When was the last time she was fed?

My brother is sitting at the dining table in the same

outfit he was wearing yesterday, tracksuit pants and an old Ballinatoom jersey, flicking his unruly curls out of his face while he eats a breakfast roll, the Sunday papers spread across the table. He should shave.

'Yuck.' He fishes out a tiny piece of tinfoil that he accidentally chewed and removes the rest of the packaging from the roll before taking another bite. 'I got you one too,' he says after he swallows. 'It's on the counter. It's vegetarian, just eggs and mushrooms in a wholegrain roll.'

I remember when I used to worry about being healthy.

'I got them to put Ballymaloe Relish in it instead of ketchup. You like that, don't you? It's better for you than ketchup. Right, Emmie?'

Stop calling me Emmie, I want to say. I am the Ballinatoom Girl now. I am That Girl.

'Thanks.' I pick up the silver-wrapped roll and brandish it at him like a baton. He pushes his chair back and walks into the kitchen area, takes a key from his pocket and unlocks the medicine cupboard.

'There you go.' He gives me the tablets, picking up a glass from the draining board and filling it with water. He watches as I swallow.

'Show me?' His face relaxes when I stick my tongue out at him. He believes that each tablet I take will cut away at the fog that is obscuring me from him. He wants Emmie. He wants his real sister back, not this imposter.

'Hey, did you see this?' He picks up a magazine section of one of the papers. 'Karen Hennessy is covering *Sunday Life* magazine.'

'She always does this time of year,' I say. Karen is wearing the bottom half of a gold lamé bikini, a waist-length wig covering her naked breasts as she sits on top of a huge horse. 'The new Lady Godiva', they're calling her. Ali will be embarrassed. 'Oh, thank God you're here,' Karen had said last year when she opened the door to see me, Jamie and Maggie on the front porch. 'She's in a terrible state. I don't know what to do with her.' Ali had texted that morning, begging us to come rescue her as quickly as possible when the photos of her mother styled as a topless Marie Antoinette started to flood her Instagram feed. The other two girls went ahead of me, but Karen put her hand on my shoulder, holding me back. 'What did you think of the photos?' she asked me. She pulled out her iPhone, scanning through the camera roll. Her body was perfect. I wouldn't be so afraid of getting older if I thought I would look like that. 'They're unreal,' I told her. We looked at one another. Did she feel the same way I did? Did she think that Ali was a changeling, that it was really *me* who should have been her daughter? It should have been me living here with her, sharing clothes and make-up, and never having to hear, *It's too expensive*, and, *Do you know how much that costs?*

That was the last weekend before everything changed.

I read a little of today's interview. They asked her about the Ballinatoom Case. *It's heartbreaking*, Karen said. *My daughter is very close to the girl involved so I can't say too much. I've tried to give her and her poor family space. I don't want to be in her face, you know?*

I push the magazine away.

'Do you not want your breakfast roll?'

'I'm not hungry.'

He sits next to me. Clots of black pudding and tomato ketchup are oozing on to the plate, and something turns in my stomach, like a live thing. Before I would have wailed about the smell of pigs' blood – *You're, like, so disgusting, Bryan* – but I don't have the energy.

'Where are they?'

'Mass.' He takes a gulp of his milk, turning the page of the paper. 'Should be home soon.'

They never ask me to go to Mass any more.

'What time are you leaving for Limerick?'

Soon, I hope. At least my parents just leave me alone now, the silence pouring around us like water, covering our mouths and our ears, muffling the noise outside.

'I think I might stay around for a bit.'

I want to tell him to go back to Limerick, to escape from here and never return. There is no need for him to drown in the silence too.

The front door is thrown open with a clatter, and I jump, my heart starting to race.

'Jesus Christ, Nora,' my father says once the door is slammed closed again. 'Would you just calm down?'

'Don't you dare tell me to calm down, Denis. Don't you *dare*.'

'Well, what am I supposed to do about it? No, go right ahead and tell me exactly what you think I should do about this?'

'She's *your* daughter and I'd like you to be a fucking man and—'

'Hey!' Bryan calls out to them. 'Emma and I are in here, you know.'

Your daughter. No, *your* daughter. *Your daughter.* No one wants to claim me. I understand. I wouldn't claim me either. I would give myself away to the first person who wanted me. (No one would want me now.)

There's a sudden hush in the hall, as if they had forgotten that Bryan and I might be in the house.

'We'll be in in a minute, dear,' my mother calls out. 'We're just chatting about something.'

They continue their argument in heated whispers. Then we hear the front door open, a hoarse, 'No, Denis, come back, I didn't mean it, I'm—' and a loud slam. The rev of the car engine outside, tyres screeching as it backs down the drive. Something soft hitting the carpet in the hall, so quietly you could almost ignore it. (Easier to ignore it.) Moments pass. Then slow, soft footsteps on the stairs. Isn't it funny how you can tell your family members apart just by the sound of their footsteps on the stairs? Bryan's are usually sluggish in the morning, bounding later in the day, two steps at a time. My father's are more deliberate, taking his time with each step. My mother's always used to be quick and light. Cheerful, I guess. They used to sound cheerful.

One hour later. Two hours. Five hours. And my father still hasn't come home.

I am hiding in my room, waiting until it is time to take my sleeping tablet. I watch movies on Netflix, darker and darker fare, a fist to the face, a knife to the throat, blood and blood and blood. But it's not enough. I start looking at porn. I go for new channels these days. I watch videos filed under *Reluctance* and *Non-consent*. (They don't use that word either.) I watch for clues. Is that what happened to me? Is that what I looked like? (Pink flesh.) (Splayed legs.)

I want to see these girls cry too.

I can do this for hours and hours. The videos are something to hold on to, something to ground me, to make sure I don't float away. (I wish I would float away. I wish I could cut myself up into so many pieces that there would be nothing left of me.)

I promised Bryan I would try. (I don't want to try.)

I read the magazines Beth sent over in her latest care package, *Grazia* and *Vogue* and *Elle*, accompanied by Lush bath bombs wrapped in floral printed paper from Liberty, six bags of Percy Pigs and salted caramels from Marks & Spencer, a tin of Darjeeling first-flush tea from Fortnum & Mason, two BADgal eyeliners from Benefit and a tube of Elizabeth Arden Eight Hour Cream. *For my darling goddaughter!* she wrote on one of those Papyrus greeting cards she buys when she's on a business trip in the US. *Hopefully this will cheer you up! Much love, Beth xxxxxx.* It doesn't look like her handwriting. She probably gave her personal assistant a credit card and told her to go buy stuff that a 'normal nineteen-year-old' would like.

I try to remember what normal felt like.

I turn each page with care. I want to sear these new images into my mind to replace those photos and those comments but . . .

I am pink flesh.

I am splayed legs.

I am a thing to be used.

I pad downstairs as softly as I can. I don't want to attract any attention. They will want to talk to me, and there are no words any more, there is only one word, *that word*, and I cannot say it out loud. I fill up a glass of water to soothe my mouth. I pull at the handle of the medicine cupboard, but it's locked. I curl my hands into fists and practise my deep breathing like the therapist showed me, but something is throbbing in me. It is a yawning mouth in my belly, sharp teeth, and it needs, and it needs and it needs. I have to make it stop.

Breathe in. *One. Two. Three.* Breathe out.

In the silence I can hear the faint echo of music seeping out underneath the door to the TV room. I strain to listen.

You fill up my senses . . .

My mother's tuneless voice croaks along to that old song she and my father love so much. They used to laugh every time it came on the radio, and they would dance in the kitchen, while Bryan and I groaned with embarrassment. 'No one waltzes any more,' I would say. 'You are so lame.'

'Just you wait,' my mother told me. 'Some day you'll have a special song with your own husband and your children will say it's "lame" too.'

I had believed her.

I will never have children now. I would not allow them to grow inside me, where I could infect them. I would not allow them to grow up in a world where bad things could happen to them, such very bad things, and I wouldn't be able to protect them.

My father used to grab my hands and pull me to my feet and twirl me around, telling me that 'Annie's Song' was the song they played at their wedding. 'Your mother was the most beautiful girl in Ballinatoom.' He would blow a kiss at her.

'It was the best day of my life,' he would always say.

I look out the window, but only my mother's car is in the drive.

I walk into the hall. My mother's voice is thick, choked. She stops singing every so often to hiccup.

'. . . *Let me die in your arms . . .*'

Her head spins when I push the door open, the hope in her eyes dying when she sees it is me. She is curled up on the sofa, the coffee table pulled over near her, a glass of wine placed precariously near the edge. No coaster.

'Emma!' I remember her saying when I put a glass of her home-made lemonade down on the wooden table. 'A coaster, please. That table was expensive and I don't want any watermarks on it.' Ali and Maggie had looked at the ground, but I could see Jamie smirking. 'Cool, will do, Mam,' I said, grabbing a coaster, pretending that I didn't care.

She has an old biscuit tin full of photos on the seat next to her, most of them the yellow-tinged prints of the seventies and eighties, and their wedding album is open on her lap. I used to love looking at it before. The thick wooden sleeves, a love-heart cut into the front of it, the date of their wedding swirled underneath. I would turn each page, laughing at the mullets and drop waists and padded shoulders. They all looked so young, standing outside the cathedral, waving at the photographer.

I should ask my mother why she's crying but I don't want to know. I am afraid. (I am always afraid now.)

The song comes to an end, pauses for a second and then starts again. *You fill up my senses . . .*

'Look at this one,' my mother says to me, but I don't move closer. I don't want to be near her. She holds up the album, pushing back a thin layer of tissue paper, and points at a photo caught in the thick cream board. 'Look at that. D'you see that? Do you?' She doesn't wait for my response, just drops the album back on to her lap, knocking the glass over, wine slopping on to the pages. She wipes at it with the edge of her dressing gown, hissing *shit* under her breath. 'Old Jimmy Fitzpatrick, how are you, boy?'

she asks the photo album. She looks back at me. 'He was our best man, do you know that? Do you, Emma?'

Of course I knew that.

'Some best man,' she snorts, and turns the page. 'Oh, and there *you* are.' She raises a glass in mock salute at the photo. 'My dear, darling Father Michael. Man of God. Man of the cloth. The fucking prick.'

'Calm down.' I don't know what else to say.

'Calm down? Calm down! Don't you tell me to *calm down*.'

'I'm sorry,' I say. And I am.

'You're sorry,' she says in a sing-song voice. 'Little Emma is sorry. Poor little Emma.'

I want to leave. What is she going to say? More words that can never be unsaid, more images that will never leave me.

'Where do you think you're going?' she says when my fingers are on the door handle.

'I just . . . I just came downstairs for my tablet. The cupboard was locked.'

'Oh yes. Your tablets. Have to keep them under lock and key, don't we? Can't trust you not to do anything stupid. Again.'

She doesn't mean this, I tell myself. She doesn't mean any of this.

'Maybe I'm sick of having to keep my medicine cupboard locked, did you ever think of that? Maybe I would like to be able to relax in my own fucking house without worrying about what you're up to in your bedroom. Whether I'm going to go upstairs and find you lying in a pool of your own blood. The *mess* of it.'

'Please.'

'Selfish, that's what you are. Don't care about upsetting your brother, or your father, or me and—'

'Please, Mam, don't—'

'Please don't what? What, Emma?' She laughs. Why is she laughing at me?

I don't know what to say.

'Do you know what happened today at Mass? I'm surprised you didn't see something on Facebook.'

I haven't been online today. Sundays are the hardest, when photos from the night before are uploaded, the girls glittering like prizes to be won, short skirts and high heels and I feel so very afraid for them (don't they know what could happen? Don't they know that they need to be careful?) and I feel so jealous of them. (Why me? Why did it have to happen to me?) And Sean and Paul and Fitzy are always there and they are always smiling, laughing. (I have ruined their lives.) Smiling and laughing and smiling and laughing. (I have ruined their lives.)

'So you don't know what I'm talking about?' She shakes her head. 'Of course you don't. We have to protect little Emma. We have to make sure little Emma is OK, don't we? But what about *me*? What about me, Emma? Who is making sure that *I'm* OK?'

I don't know what to say. Tell me my lines, please.

'He shook their hands,' she says. 'He actually went up to them and shook their hands. Some days I really wish . . .'

'What are you talking about?' I ask her.

'And after all the times we've had him to the house,' she continues, as if I hadn't spoken. 'He baptized you. He gave you your first Holy Communion. I arrange the flowers for the cathedral. And he went and shook their hands.'

'Whose hands, Mam?'

She looks up at me. 'Are you sure you want to know?'

I don't know what I want.

'Because I can tell you if you really want to know,' she says. 'Well? Do you? Do you want to know what happened today?'

I don't know what I want any more.

'But I'm not supposed to tell you. Don't want to upset Emma, do we?' There's a pause, both of us staring at each other, and her eyes narrow. 'Well, I think you should know.' She grabs the page of the album, as thick as a board, and starts to tear at it.

'Don't!' I cry out, but she ignores me, pulling the page from the old wooden book-frame, the spine of the album tearing, letting the other pages fall loose too. She throws the offending page at me, and the sharp corner of it hits me square in the forehead.

'Take a good look at it,' she says. 'That man, that man gave a speech at our wedding talking about love and gentleness and kindness—'

'Please—'

'And then today, do you know what he did? Do you?'

'Please stop—'

'His sermon was about not judging others, and how important it is to assume that everyone is innocent until proven guilty. He didn't use any names – oh, he couldn't do that, could he? – but everyone knew who he was talking about, and your father and I like idiots in the top pew, after giving fifty euro to the collection plate.'

They are all innocent until proven guilty. But not me. I am a liar until I am proven honest.

'As if we can afford fifty euro at the moment, when we don't even know if your father is going to get fired—'

'What?' My throat closes up and I can't get enough air in. My father is going to lose his job? (My fault.)

'And everyone staring at us, and muttering under their breath—'

'Please, Mam—'

'And I passed Ciarán O'Brien on my way to take Holy Communion, and he winked at me, he actually winked—'

'I don't want to—'

'And then, oh, I'm keeping the best till last, young lady. Just wait until you hear this. Then Father Michael waited at the church door until Sean Casey and Paul O'Brien . . .'

(What was Paul O'Brien doing at Mass?)

'. . . came out, and he shook their hands, and offered his condolences.'

Father Michael has been the Monsignor in Ballinatoom for twenty years. He christened me, he heard my first confession as I listed off the fights I'd had with Bryan and the time I had found a five-euro note stuck down the back of the couch in the TV room and didn't tell my parents. He was there for my first Holy Communion and Confirmation. He would come to our house for dinner and he would tell me how pretty I looked. When he gave me his plate after he had finished eating, he would smile and tell me that I'd make some lucky man a fine wife someday.

He doesn't believe me. None of them believe me.

'It's pretty obvious he's chosen sides,' my mother says. 'And it isn't yours.'

Yours. Not ours.

I try to think about what the therapist told me. You're not going to die, Emma, it's just a panic attack. Breathe in love, *slut, liar*, breathe out fear, *skank*, breathe in love, *bitch*, breathe out fear. *Whore.*

I try and remember but my brain is crammed up with that word and those photos and those comments (her tits are tiny, aren't they?) and I don't have any room for anything else.

Slut, liar, skank, bitch, whore.

I turn my back to her. I need to walk away. I need to go upstairs and pull the duvet over my head, diving into the darkness as if I was diving into water.

But I can't. I am full of this shame, and it is weighing me down, holding my feet in shackles. I can see Father Michael shaking their hands, and I do not know if I can survive this. I just want it to stop. I just want it all to stop. I want the opinion pieces in the newspapers to stop, and I want the phone calls at 3 a.m. to stop, and I want #IBelieveBallinatoomGirl to stop trending on Twitter.

All of those strangers who believe that I am a victim, that I am innocent. (And they are the only ones.)

I stare at my wrists. (I want them to bleed.) I imagine my life oozing away from me, my body weakening, until this could be over.

My mother is gasping, *sorry, sorry, sorry*, begging me to talk to her.

'Please don't tell your father, please, Emma, I didn't mean to tell you, I swear.'

But she did mean to tell me. She wants me to hurt as much as she does.

'Please, Emma? Promise me. He'll kill me, he'll, well, I don't know what he'll do.'

He'll divorce you, I think. He'll pack his bags, and leave this house, without a backward glance. He would be happy to have an excuse to escape. He will leave you alone with me.

'I can't take it any more,' she says, 'I just can't take it any more, I can't, Emma, I can't take this any more, I just can't, I can't take it any more . . .'

She babbles while I stare at a photo on the wall. It is the four of us, taken before Bryan's grads ball in sixth year. We look happy.

I want to rip it from the wall and smash it.

She whimpers, then starts to cry again, but it's softer now, a low gurgling in the back of her throat. I stay still. I hear shuffling, the thud of something heavy hitting the ground, and then my mother's breathing eases from tightly wound gasps into longer, slower sighs. I wait until I hear the chafing sound of snores before I turn to look at her. She's stretched out on the sofa, her mouth slack, a little pocket of fat gathered at her jawline. Her glass has tipped over on to her chest, the liquid seeping into her dressing gown. I bend down and collect all the sheets of photos, hiding the wine glass behind the sofa so my father won't see it when he comes in. I take a photo out of the old biscuit tin. My father with a pint of Murphy's in one hand, a cast on the other from a broken bone during a GAA match. My mother in a shapeless dress, a long pearl necklace around her neck, holding her glass of orange cordial out to the camera. They look so young.

I take the patchwork quilt from the back of the sofa and shake it out, tucking it around my mother's body and up as far as her chin, and she curls into it like a child. I make myself walk away from her.

'What are you doing?' I say on the landing. Bryan is closing the door of my room, a laptop stuffed under his armpit. 'What were you doing in my room?'

'Nothing.'

'You're not supposed to go in there if I'm not there,' I say. 'I'm entitled to some privacy.' Even if the lock has gone from my door, removed after the last time . . . after the last time. 'Is that mine?' I ask him, pointing at the laptop.

'Sorry.' His jaw is moving back and forward as if he's grinding his teeth. 'I had to . . .' He breaks off. 'Well, I had to, and you weren't there.'

'Is that mine?' I repeat myself.

'Yes,' he squeaks, and he coughs to clear his throat. 'And, eh, I was wondering if I could borrow your laptop?'

I need it. I need it to block out the argument with Mam and all the other images and those photos and the comments, and *no, no, no*. I need it.

'Well,' I try to be calm but I can feel the panic climbing up my throat, 'I can't sleep and I was thinking of watching—'

'No,' he yells, and I back away from him. 'You're not even supposed to have it anyway, are you?'

'What's *wrong* with you?'

'I just need to borrow your laptop.'

'But you have your own laptop.'

'Yeah, I know. But, it's, eh, it's, eh . . .'

'It's what?'

'Broken. It's broken.' He swallows hard. 'And I need to do research for a project.'

'A project?'

'Yeah.'

'What type of project?'

'What do you mean, what type of project?'

'Well, what's it about? What subject is it for? Are you working in a group or are—'

'It's just a project, OK?' he snaps. 'Just a project for college. End of.'

'OK.' I don't like it when Bryan gets angry with me. 'Just take it. You can sign in as a guest. I'm not giving you my password.'

Closing my bedroom door behind me, I go to the vanity table and fumble around in the top drawer. There's a pile of diaries there, cheap hardback copybooks that my mother buys for me. The therapist says that I should try and use the journals as a way of processing this experience. As a way of remembering. They all want me to remember. (I don't want to remember.)

The phone is hidden beneath the diaries. My mother forgot to take it from me, again. I sit on the ground with my back pressed against the door in case Bryan decides he needs to come back in.

I have thirty new emails, and as I scroll through them (m248sh@hotmail.com, thisbetheverse@gmail.com, youareaslutandeveryonehatesyou@gmail.com) I only recognize two names – so I delete the rest. (How did they find my new address?) One is from Conor,

Emmie,

I was thinking about you today. I saw you getting out of your car on Friday evening. I wasn't going to say anything . . . I don't know why I am saying anything. It was nice to see your face. I miss you. x

I read the email three times before making myself delete it. The other email is from Maggie.

Hey hunnie,

Listen, I just wanted to tell you to ignore all that crap on Facebook, people are so pathetic. It's this stupid town, they have nothing else to do with their time, you know? Please phone me. I really want to see you and make sure you're doing OK. I need to talk to you about something too.

Love you. xxx

I shut down my email, and I click into the Facebook app. There are about one hundred new private messages, but I don't look at them. I know what darkness they will hold. *Kill yourself. Run away. Leave here forever. Everybody hates you. Slut, liar, skank, bitch, whore.* I promised my parents that I would shut down all my accounts, but I can't. I would be erased. It would be as if I never existed. (Isn't that what I want?) I'm tagged in ten new photos.

I am afraid every time I open my computer or look at my phone.

I know I shouldn't look. Of course I shouldn't look. I am afraid of looking but I am afraid not to look too. (I am afraid all the time.)

In each of the photos there are girls, loads of them, each picture with a different group, all of them wearing plain white T-shirts. I know most of them. There's Sarah Swallows and Julie Clancy, surrounded by six or seven other girls from my year. In another there's Susan Twomey, and a few of her friends, and I can barely make out the rest, my eyes blurring. Scrawled on the T-shirts in black marker are the words #TeamPaul, #TeamDylan and #TeamSean, one or two have #TeamFitzy, but not as many. I look at the comments underneath.

Slut, liar, skank, bitch, whore. Slut, liar, skank, bitch, whore. Slut, liar, skank, bitch, whore. Slut, liar, skank, bitch, whore.

Over and over and over.

She was asking for it.

What did she expect?

I see legs splayed. I see pink flesh, delicate. Bruised. Ripped apart.

Any #TeamEmma T-shirts? someone had written, and Julie Clancy replied, *Bitch, please.*

I blink, and I can see Jen Casey, her face paler than I

remember, fingers pointing at the #TeamSean across her chest.

'I wish you would get together with Sean,' Jennifer said to me. It must have been two years ago. She and I were watching TV, waiting for Bryan to come home after football training. Her mother had come off her meds without telling anyone again. She began showing up at school in her pyjamas, she started bulk-buying tinned tomatoes until their garden shed was full of hundreds of cans. She had gone back to hospital for a 'rest', and Mam insisted that Jen come and have dinner with us as often as she wanted. 'I would, you know I would, Jen,' I told her. 'But Ali really likes him, and I wouldn't do that to a friend.' The truth was, I would do that to a friend, and I *had* done that to a friend. But not for someone like Sean, someone whom no one else wanted.

If this was a movie I would start crying now. Wouldn't that be the normal reaction?

My eyes are dry. They are burned out.

(I wish I could cry.)

All I have now is a feeling of falling, like you do in a dream, where you are falling and falling and falling into a pit of nothingness, and you keep waiting to wake up before you hit the bottom, before your brain splats all over the concrete floor of your nightmare. But I don't wake up. I'm falling, falling forever, always waiting for the ground to meet me.

Monday

My dreams are heavy, bloated things. My crusted eyelids peel apart as I wake, my mind a-shimmer with the haze of disintegrating images. It's always the same these days, the world turning sideways, oily black ink spilling down the walls and flooding the square box that I'm trapped in, pooling around my ankles, then my knees, then my chest, until it's over my head and I can't breathe.

There you are. There's a good girl. You like that, don't you? Don't you?

'Emma? Are you awake?' It's my mother, the door opening just a crack, a strip of light opening into the room. I remember what happened last night. I remember her face and her words. And remembering feels like gathering pieces of broken glass in my hands.

I wonder if she can smell it, if the darkness has its own

particular scent, or if my room smells the way it always did in the morning, of stale breath, vanilla candles and traces of perfume. People always asked me what perfume I used. I would refuse to tell them. I wanted to be unique, to stand out. I wanted to be different.

Now all I want is to fade away.

I slow my breathing down, making my inhale catch in a whistle at the back of my throat. Does she know I'm pretending to be asleep? Is she pretending to believe me? Is it easier that way? The door closes with a gentle click behind her. I curl up underneath the duvet, holding my knees into my chest, rubbing my belly. The therapist says it's important to *process the memories, it's important to feel your feelings, Emma*, but if I don't even know what I actually remember, what are real memories, what are *mine*, and what's been implanted inside there by the Easy Emma page, and Ms McCarthy, and the guards, and Bryan, and Ali and Maggie, and my parents, and the newspapers, and the outraged callers to *The Ned O'Dwyer Show*. What if I *am* just making it all up, like Paul claims? Veronica Horan wrote about the increase in false accusations, how women were claiming that they had repressed memories of sexual abuse, when in fact it was all in their imagination. Fathers thrown in jail. Mothers devastated. More lives ruined.

'The intransigence of memory', that article had been called. I read it ten times.

I think of my mother last night, her voice with that edge in it, somewhere between a sob and a scream. I think of how she looked at me. I know that this memory is real, this one is mine, and it feels like desperation standing before me, whittled skinny and hungry for me.

What will the trial be like? The book they gave me at the Rape Crisis Centre said it could be a 'traumatic experience for the victim'. What does that even mean? My therapist uses the word 'trauma' to explain away everything that is happening to me.

I can't eat. *That's because of the trauma.*

I can't sleep. *That's because of the trauma.*

I can't breathe. *That's because of the trauma.*

What sorts of questions will they ask in court?

How much did you drink that night? Did you take drugs? Witnesses say they saw you leading Paul O'Brien into the bedroom, do you admit that? Do you admit that you consented to have sex with him? How many other people have you had sex with? Would you say that you're promiscuous?

I imagine my parents, my father looking at me with those new eyes of his, faded, listless. I want to climb up his body like I did as a child, feel his arms around me as he carries me. I want to hear him call me his princess, just once more. When was the last time he said it to me? Another thing I can't remember.

I'll have to go to Dublin. 'Rape (don't say *that word*, don't use *that word* about me) and aggravated sexual assault are tried in the Central Criminal Court,' Aidan Heffernan told me. 'The court case could last up to two weeks at least,' he said. But they do not know how long it will take this time, with all 'the photos, and the media attention, and the complex nature of the case'. 'There is no precedent,' the reporter will say on TV, small boys in tracksuits jumping up and down in the background, making grotesque faces and waving at their mams watching.

I have to stand up and be counted.

I have to set a good example. I have to be brave for other victims.

#IBelieveBallinatoomGirl

I don't want to be their champion. I don't want to be brave. I don't want to be a hero.

I'll have to dress respectably, make sure I look like a good girl. *You're not wearing that, are you, Emma?* I wonder if the barrister that the State provides will bring up that I tried to swallow death or the time I scored lines into my wrists. Will that count in my favour? (The pain pulsing in me, begging to be let out, needing something sharp to help it escape. The dribble of blood. Then gushing, faster and faster.) Or will they say it was a sign of a guilty conscience? Guilt over ruining lives. What will my friends have said in their witness statements? She was drunk, she was high, she was asking for it, she wanted it, she wanted it. And I did want it, didn't I? I took Paul into that room, I knew what I was doing.

Didn't I?

And you phoned the accused on the following Monday, did you not? You left voice messages, friendly voice messages. Why would you have done that if they had, as you claim, raped you?

I see myself standing in a witness box, and it's the exact same one as on *Law and Order: SVU*, my lips mouthing words, but I'm not making any sound.

And you went to see a doctor the day after, a Dr Fitzpatrick, the father of one of the boys you accuse. Why would you have gone to him, if his son had been involved, as you claim, in a brutal gang rape?

Fitzy didn't do anything. But he saw. He watched.

He has seen my splayed legs showing pink flesh.

(So has everyone else. *Everyone*.)

And after the alleged rape took place I see you sat your summer exams and your grades were excellent. Nothing below seventy-five per cent, and all higher-level subjects. If you had just endured something as traumatic as you claim, surely you wouldn't be able to concentrate on your studies?

School corridors, people parting like the Red Sea, shoulders banging into mine and then the whispers, whispers, whispers, *slut, liar, skank, bitch, whore.* Screenshots of those photos printed out and stuffed into my locker. Ali, Maggie and Jamie not talking to me, it was early days then, the guards hadn't approached them for their witness statements yet, they didn't know what I was claiming, what I was *alleging.* They didn't know about *that word* yet so I was still just a disloyal slut. Lunch eaten in a toilet cubicle, forcing it down my throat. New graffiti on the wall. (About me. It's always about me.)

And your social life continued unabated, wouldn't you say? You met friends for drinks, you went to nightclubs. We have statements from a number of different men saying that you slept with them after the alleged 'rape'. You even went to a party in Dylan Walsh's home, one of the men that you accuse of assaulting you. Does that sound like the behaviour of someone who was violated in the most horrific way?

Dizziness, my knees sliding on the damp floor of the club toilets, falling in a slump over the cistern, a fist banging on the door, someone saying, 'Hurry up, for fuck's sake. Who's in there? Would you hurry up?' The silence when I open the door and they see it's me. My smeared face in the bathroom's mirrors. Cold air outside, a wind cutting through me, arms linked with some faceless man, ignoring my phone ringing and ringing and ringing in my bag, because they were my friends again, they knew what had happened (that word) so there were awkward hugs, and good-listener faces, and *you can talk to me, I'm here for you, I'm here for you.* The beeps of texts. *Where are you Emma, where are you?* On my knees again, the concrete cold and hard. I try to reclaim that night. I try to make new memories to replace the ones that were stolen from me. I try to make it my choice, my decision.

It could be another two years before it comes to trial. Two years. 730 days. Will every one of them be the same? Bitter-tasting dreams, like I'm sucking on lemons. The crushing disappointment when I awake and find myself still alive, my heart still beating, my lungs still gasping in air. 730 breakfasts where my father has rushed out the door before I can wake up so he doesn't have to look at me, 730 days with microwaved Linda McCartney meals for dinner, watching my father stare suspiciously at the food on the table, biting his lip so he won't ask my mother what the hell this is supposed to be. 730 days of him looking out the window at the ruined vegetable garden, choked with weeds, then glancing at me, so quick you'd almost miss it. But I always catch him (because I hope that he'll look at me and it'll be the way it was before, *you're my princess*) and I always see it. His eyes, rat-black when he looks at me now, gleam for a second, full of *your fault, why were you there? what were you wearing? they say you slept around, did you? did you did you?* And I know that I'm not his princess any more and I never will be again.

In two years I'll be twenty-one. I thought I would be at college then. I saw myself in winter, wrapped in matching hats and scarves, my nose and cheeks tinged with red, clutching a takeaway Starbucks as I made my way to a lecture. I thought I'd walk across campus in short skirts and bare legs in the summer, pretending that I don't notice the men staring at me. I would go to parties with glow sticks and beer kegs and cute boys. I would be living in some awful, damp house, six of us probably, three guys and three girls, and we'd all hook up with each other. One couple would start dating and the rest of us would mock them, but we would secretly think it was cute and hope that they would get married so we could attend their wedding and talk about our 'wild college years', like Karen Hennessy and her friends did. In years to come we would laugh about how we couldn't keep that house clean, but that we didn't care because we drank vodka for breakfast and watched *Home and Away* before our afternoon naps, then starting all over again, another party to go to, another nightclub to check out, new boys to meet. I would come home at the weekends to get my mother to wash my clothes, and to see Ali and Jamie and Maggie, and I would talk about my new friends so they would know that I was popular, that I was making a success of college, that I didn't need Ballinatoom or anyone in it.

I never thought that this would be my life, the small, small world of this house, and my parents and Bryan taking care of me, wrapping me up in their words and kind gestures, tying me down to this life, *this existence*. There is no escape.

I can't take it any more, my mother had said last night. *I just can't take it any more*.

I don't think I can take it any more either.

'You look wrecked,' Bryan says to me at dinner.

'Do I?'

'Yeah, your eyes are really red. You all right?'

My mother and I briefly make eye contact, and I can read her mind, *Please, Emma, please don't say anything*, as she passes me the mushy peas.

'I don't know,' I say, spooning a portion of the peas next to the burnt chickpea-and-spinach sausages. 'I guess I didn't sleep very well.'

A key in the front door. A high-pitched miaow from Precious. A door slamming.

'You're late,' Bryan says, glancing at his phone to

check the time as my father drops his briefcase at the door. Everything about him seems to droop, from his limp hair to his moustache; even his clothes are too big for his frame. He's lost weight. He sinks into his chair and Bryan turns to our mother.

'Mam?'

'Yes?' Her eyes drift out to the garden and she frowns. She gets to her feet and Bryan half smiles, but she only closes the curtains.

'It's too bright outside.' She takes another sip of wine as she sits back down. 'The glare was hurting my eyes.'

Bryan walks into the kitchen area, neither he nor our father saying anything when he returns with a plate of shepherd's pie. The scrape of a knife on my father's plate, shallow breathing and waving a hand in front of his face when he realizes how hot the food is, gulping down water to cool his mouth. We eat in silence. I wonder if it will always be like this. Will it just be me, my mother and my father, eating our dinner every night at the same time, shepherd's pie on a Monday, bacon and cabbage on a Tuesday, lasagne on a Wednesday, stir-fry on a Thursday, salmon-and-broccoli bake on a Friday, quiche and salads from the Organic Kitchen Project on a Saturday, a roast dinner on a Sunday, whatever vegetarian dish my mother has bought me for that night twirling around in the microwave until I hear it ping? Bryan would come home every weekend for a while, pulling me on to the sofa on a Friday night to watch *The Late Late Show* or a movie with him, asking how my week went, did I have any plans for Saturday, had I given any more thought to my Leaving Cert, or college, or an evening class, or an online course, or some other idea he would come up with to try and force me to leave the house and be normal. But he would start to dread it. He would start to hate opening the door into this house full of ghosts. There would be one weekend missed, then another. He would start to come home once a month, then for birthdays and bank holidays, then maybe just for Christmas and Easter. He would move away, to Canada or Australia or Japan, somewhere far enough that he wouldn't feel guilty about not visiting more often. There would be emails, promises to Skype, packages arriving in the post full of expensive, useless items that he 'saw and thought of you'. Then he would meet someone, someone who laughed a lot, and her family would be close, loving. They would welcome him as if he was one of their own. He would bring her home to meet us and her eyes would be wary, and she would speak to me in gentle, low tones. They would have children, and they would visit less often. *Children are so sensitive to energy*, they would tell each other. *We don't want them to absorb the negativity in That House.* And he would tell himself not to blame me (my fault). He would tell himself not to wish that he had a different sister (one who wasn't a *slut, bitch, whore*). More emails. More phone calls. More Christmases spent with her family, while my parents and I ate Brussels sprouts and stuffing in front of the television, numbing ourselves on carbohydrates and reruns of classic movies. I would look at my mother and my father, and marvel at how old they had become, how they had turned 65, 70, 75, 80, 85, 90, and I hadn't even noticed. And then I would realize that I was old too, my bones starting to creak as my skin sagged around them. I would lie awake in the same single bed that I had slept in since I was a child, staring at the blank ceiling, wondering where the stars had gone.

My father clears his throat. 'I have some news.'

My head snaps up. News. *Two years, it might take. Two years.* But maybe they heard something, maybe Fitzy decided to change his plea to guilty and they just rang Dad instead of me. Maybe it's all over.

'News?'

'Yes.' He fidgets with the edge of the tablecloth. 'Nora, this tablecloth is filthy.'

'Really?' We all look at the grubby linen tablecloth. (*Be careful!* she used to shout at us before. *That was expensive.*) 'That's odd. I washed it yesterday.'

'Are you sure?' my father persists.

'I said I did, didn't I? I don't know why you feel the need to question every little thing I say and do.'

'Nora, I just asked a question. Look at—'

'You have news?' I interrupt them. (Maybe it's all over.) 'What is it?' (Maybe things will go back to normal.)

My father frowns (maybe I can forget all of this ever happened) as if trying to remember what he had been talking about. 'Ah,' he says. 'Yes. Well, the area manager came in to the branch today.'

Disappointment is a spear through my chest, puncturing my lungs. I can feel them shrivelling inside me. *Stupid, stupid, stupid.* Of course it's not over.

'And, well, we had to discuss the recent spate of transfers from the bank.'

'That's not your fault.' My mother's voice is fierce. I wonder if she is going to turn around and say, *It's Emma's fault.* She grips the stem of her wine glass. 'The fees of current accounts are so high now, loads of people are switching to Ulster Bank or to one of those other banks. They were discussing it on *The Ned O'Dwyer Show* the other day and I'm sure I read an article about it in the *Examiner* as well. That's hardly your fault, Denis, is it?'

He looks as if it's taking all of his energy to keep his

body upright. (I used to think you were like an oak tree. I used to think you were tall and good and strong, and that you could never be broken.) 'Well,' he says, 'they've made their decision.'

'What decision?' Bryan asks.

'They're transferring me to another bank, in the city.' He tries to smile at us. 'The assistant manager of the Douglas branch is retiring, and it's so busy there that they want someone with experience to take over.'

'*Assistant* manager?' Bryan says.

'Well, it's a much bigger branch than Ballinatoom.' My father shrugs. 'It's fine.' He turns to my mother, puts his hand over hers and squeezes. 'It's a good thing, Nora. Sure, what difference does it make? Work is work, wherever I do it, right?'

My father has worked in the Ballinatoom branch for nearly forty years. He started there when he left school, working his way up from a teller, to assistant manager, and then manager. He used to joke about how the bank was his mistress, and my mother would roll her eyes, but I'd hear her on the phone to Sheila Heffernan saying, 'Oh, Denis works so hard – that place would fall apart without him.' Apparently it was my father who insisted that they start using computers in the banks before anyone else in town, it was my father who persuaded head office to give him the money for a complete refurbishment a few years ago, it was my father who made sure the flower boxes were done beautifully every summer, who organized special treats for the staff Christmas party to show his appreciation for their loyalty. When people asked him what he did for a living, he would answer, *I'm a bank manager,* and it was as if he was saying, *I'm a professional footballer with Man. United,* or, *I'm the President of the United States.*

'So that's that,' he says. We start eating again. I look at them, and I see how tired they are.

I have done this. I have done this to us all. I am ruining their lives.

And, I can see the boys' defence lawyer saying (would they share one? No, surely Ciarán O'Brien could afford a better solicitor for Paul than Dylan Walsh could get?) *You changed your statement, didn't you, Emma? You admitted that you were lying in your first statement. How are we supposed to trust the word of a girl who has admitted to being a liar? The men that stand accused have never lied. They have given honest accounts of their actions. Their character witnesses have spoken, they have told the court about what upstanding members of the community these boys are, how dependable they are, what respectable families they come from. And you want to ruin their lives, ruin their futures.*

They couldn't say that. Could they?

Liar, liar, pants on fire. Emma O'Donovan is a liar.

She was asking for it.

'Wait,' I say, and my family look at me.

The men have said that you agreed, that you consented. They say that it was your idea. They say that you wanted it.

But I can't remember. How can they prove I gave consent?

How can I prove I didn't?

Did you know the rate of conviction for rape is only one per cent in this country?

What's the point then?

'What's the point of what?' my mother asks. I didn't realize I had spoken aloud again. Is this going to become more common? Will Bryan's future children be afraid of me, whinge at the thought of coming to visit Ballinatoom. *She's weird*, they would say. *She talks to herself. She smells.*

I do smell. When was the last time I took a shower? I don't like getting undressed or seeing my body in the mirror. It is not my body any more. (Her tits are tiny, aren't they? Yeah, but her ass is great.)

'Emma?' My mother is getting impatient. 'Do you have something you want to say?

Father Michael has stood as character witness for Paul O'Brien today. Would a man of the cloth do that if he had any doubts about the veracity of Mr O'Brien's statement? Father Michael christened you, did he not? He was a regular visitor to your house, a good friend of your parents'. Would you say that he had reasonable opportunity to get to know you, appraise your true character?

I am Eve. I am the snake in the garden of Eden. I am temptation.

Would you say you were promiscuous? Would you say that you slept around? Would you say you are a slut and a whore?

Mother Mary, blessed virgin. O Mary, conceived without sin.

They can't say that, can they? Can they? They said at the Rape Crisis Centre that the case wouldn't be open to the general public. But would people come anyway? Would a crowd wait outside the court, baying for my blood?

'Emma?' Bryan looks worried. I am a constant source of worry to him now. I will make him old before his time. I will make him broken too. 'Are you OK?'

I didn't want to ruin anyone's life. Fitzy was going to art college, and Paul was going to be on the Cork senior football team, and I shouldn't have made a fuss, and everything would have gone back to normal, and everyone would have forgotten about me and about all this. I wouldn't be That Girl.

I can't take it any more. I need it to stop.

'I just wanted to tell you that I have news as well.' My

voice goes up at the end of the sentence like I'm asking a question. And maybe I am asking a question, maybe I'm asking them if this is what they want from me, if this will make it all better. 'I've made a decision.' I take a deep breath, getting the words out in a rush. 'I've decided to withdraw my complaint.'

I stand up, scrape the leftovers into the bin and rinse the plate clean before putting it in the dishwasher. Turn around, I tell myself. Turn around and face them.

Tick, tick, tick, tick. The kitchen clock moves on, counting the seconds for us. And still no one says anything. The air feels dead, like it's made of weeds.

'Did you hear me?' I say. 'I'm going to withdraw my complaint.'

'We heard,' my mother says, her voice so very careful. 'What's prompted this decision?'

'Oh,' I say, and I sound like I mean it, 'you know what the statistics are like for conviction. I just don't see the point of putting myself through all that when I'm never going to win anyway.'

I hesitate, waiting, *waiting* for my mother or my father to rush in and tell me not to be silly, that of course I'll win, that I have to win because I'm innocent in this, because I am the victim, because this wasn't my fault. But no one speaks.

319

I watch the clock, the second hand going around once, twice, three times, four times.

'I don't know, Emma,' my father says finally. I force myself to turn around to look at him. He's almost glistening with hope. I haven't seen hope in this house in a long time. 'This is something that you'll need to think about very seriously.'

'I am serious,' I say. *Please tell me not to, Daddy. Please tell me I should go ahead with this, please, please, please.* 'I just want to get on with my life.'

'It might . . .' My mother is speaking so quietly I have to lean over the counter to hear her properly. 'Well.' She rubs her hand across her forehead wearily, pressing her fingertips into her eye sockets. 'It might be . . . easier, I guess.' She starts at the word *easier*, as if shocked it came from her mouth. *Easy Emma. She was always easy, easy, easy.* 'Better. I mean, it might be better. For you, Emma, I mean. It might be better for you. If that's what you want, of course.'

She is hopeful too.

Will this make it better? Will this make everything go back to the way it was before?

My parents start to eat again, my father's jaw clicking as he chews, she takes a sip of water, a dab of her mouth. I sit down again.

'Wait, so this is it?'

The three of us jump when Bryan speaks, startled by the roughness of his voice. 'Is this fucking *it*?'

'Language, Bryan,' my mother hisses.

My father throws his napkin over his plate. 'Have you anything valid you would like to add to this conversation, Bryan? Or are you just going to use profanities?'

My brother shakes his head, his cheeks filling with blood. 'After all this, you're just going to give up?'

After the meeting in Mr Griffin's office, we had gone to the station. They were waiting for us. The guard had said I should get a forensic examination. 'It'll be routine,' he told me. 'They'll just get head and pubic-hair samples, check under your nails, and take some swabs. That'll be oral, vaginal, and, eh, anal.' At the word anal my mother had left the room. I told the guard that I didn't need to go to the sexual-assault treatment unit, because there was no sexual assault. I had been pretending to be asleep in those photos. I told them it was all a joke and I wanted this to go away.

They took down those words to use against me.

Bryan arrived home the next day. I could hear him and my mother having a low muttered conversation, his voice getting louder. He came into the TV room to see me, muting the television and taking my hands in his.

'Why didn't you tell me?' he asked. 'I've been so awful to you, calling you . . .' He coughed to hide a hint of a sob. 'I thought this was your fault,' he said. It *was* my fault, but I couldn't bear for Bryan to think that.

'I thought you wanted it,' he said. And maybe that was true as well. (Maybe I had been asking for it.) But he looked at me, and he looked heartbroken. And he wasn't angry any more. He didn't look like he hated me. I needed that. I needed Bryan to love me. I needed someone to take care of me. So I agreed with him. I said it was not my fault.

I said it was *that word*.

I said it was rape.

'She's not giving up, Bryan,' my mother says. 'She's—'

'Even if you do decide you want to withdraw your complaint, what's to say the DPP won't prosecute anyway? They're doing it on behalf of the state, right?'

I turn to my father in panic. 'They won't make me testify, will they? They can't make me if I don't want to.'

'I wouldn't think so.' He puts his hand on mine. 'But I'll give Aidan Heffernan a ring later and ask what he thinks.'

'Well,' Bryan says, 'they might still be able to use your statement. And the photos . . .' He trails off, looking sick at the thought of the photos, at the comments under-neath.

(She's deader than a doorknob. She's deader than Oscar Pistorius's girlfriend.)

(Fuck, Emma O'Donovan's tits are tiny though. I thought they'd be way better than that.)

(Her ass looks good though ☺ ☺)

All I am is a thing.

All I am is a collection of doll parts to be filled in and plugged up and passed on.

After one photo, twenty different boys gave my body marks out of ten. Twenty boys that had been in my kindergarten class, that had come to my birthday parties. Twenty boys I had thought were my friends.

(Serves that bitch right. She friend-zoned me in third year.)

I looked at the marks to see what they really thought of me. And I wished I was dead.

'We don't even know if they would admit those photos in court; I told you that already,' my mother says. 'There's no precedent and—'

'Well, maybe we should make a precedent,' Bryan spits. 'What if this happens to someone else?'

I am supposed to set an example. I am supposed to tell my story to the feminist blogs, to feel encouraged by the support on Twitter from people that I have never met, who wouldn't even be able to point out Ireland on a map, let alone Ballinatoom.

I would like it if this happened to someone else. I would like it if someone else was ruined too. I wouldn't be alone.

'I'm sure it won't,' my mother says. 'They're good boys really. This all just got out of hand.'

And I look at her, and I look again, and she doesn't even realize what she has said. I need to get up. I need to leave this table. I need to find something sharp to play with.

'*What the fuck* did you just say?' Bryan screams at her, and she stutters, 'I didn't mean it that way,' and she turns to me. 'Oh, Emma, I didn't mean it that way – you know I didn't.'

'Please lower your voice, Bryan, and treat your mother with some respect,' my father says. 'This is *our* house, and I'll not have you speaking to us like this.'

'OK, forgetting the disgusting piece of *shit* she just came out with, that the animals who fucking gang-raped my sister' (that word) 'and posted photos on Facebook for the whole world to laugh at' (I knew they were all laughing at me), 'tell me this – what about Emma? What's going to happen to her now?'

'What do you mean?' My father's shoulders tense up around his ears.

'She's not getting better. When was the last time that she went to school? When—'

'She's being home-schooled,' my mother interrupts, and Bryan laughs, a harsh, guttural sound that scrapes against his teeth.

'Oh really? So she's going to be sitting her Leaving, is she? And where's she going to do that? Is she going to do it in St Brigid's? Has she got her exam number? How did her pre-exams go? Has she filled out her CAO form? What college is she hoping to go to? What course is she thinking of doing? Where's she going to live? Come on, Mam, the queen of home-schooling, you should be able to tell me all this, shouldn't you?'

'I, I . . .' Her eyes are watery. 'Well, I—'

'You don't know. You don't know because you've given up on her, haven't you?'

I wait for my mother to deny it. I wait for her to tell him not to be stupid. I wait for her to tell him, *Of course I haven't given up on Emma, I love her, we want to take care of her.*

I wait and I wait. I will wait forever.

'And when was the last time she went outside?' Bryan says. 'When it first happened, at least she still went to school, she met up with her friends, she had a fucking life—'

'The therapist says that's normal.'

My mother didn't think it was 'normal' at the time. She thought if I was telling the truth, I should have been up in my room, taking endless showers and scouring myself with a Brillo Pad. 'Apparently lots of people who claim to be raped can be strangely calm at the beginning,' she says.

Claim.

'But she's in therapy still?' Bryan continues, as if I wasn't in the room at all. 'Shouldn't that be making a difference by this stage? What does the therapist have to say about all of this?'

'Well, Emma has only just said it to us, Bryan, so how do I know what the therapist would think? I'm not a mind-reader, you know and—'

'They can't get away with this, with what they've done. How can you even be thinking about letting Emma—'

'Enough.' My father bangs his fist on the dining-room table with such force that my mother's wine glass falls to the floor, smashing into splinters. 'Enough, Bryan,' he says, almost pleadingly. 'You have to respect Emma's decision.'

'But—'

'I said, you have to respect Emma's decision.' My

father looks at me, straight in the eye, for the first time in months. 'Is this what you want?'

I can feel the word in my mouth. It feels as if it's drawing blood from my tongue. It feels as if this word is a sacrifice.

He and my mother look at me, *say yes, say yes, say yes*, and I can almost taste their fear that I might change my mind.

'Yes,' I say. 'Yes. This is what I want.'

Tuesday

'Emmie.' A hand gently brushes my hair away from my face. 'Emmie, wake up, sweetheart.'

I blink the sleep out of my eyes, and it's my mother, holding out a floral china cup and saucer. 'Here you go,' she says. Her voice sounds far away. 'I thought you might like a cup of tea.'

I sit up, my back against the headboard, and take it from her.

'How are you feeling today?'

I feel heavy. My limbs are aching, like I have the flu.

'Drink your tea,' she says, 'and then come downstairs to have breakfast with Daddy and me.'

'He's still here?'

'Yes.'

My fingers grip around the teacup. 'I'm not very hungry.'

'Well, Emma, it's the most important—'

'. . . meal of the day,' we say in unison.

'Exactly.' She bends over to give me a kiss. I close my eyes as she does so, inhaling a clean soapy smell. She must have showered already.

I keep my eyes closed as she walks away.

'Emmie?'

I open one eye to look at her, standing in the doorway. 'Yes?'

'You look really . . .' She hesitates, just for a second. 'You look really beautiful this morning.'

I bang the cup down on my bedside locker.

'Has someone been putting pressure on you to change your mind?' Joe Quirke asked last night when I rang him to tell him I'd decided to withdraw my complaint, brushing aside my apologies for ringing him so late. 'No,' I told him. 'I just don't want this to go ahead.' 'Well, Emma, it might be too late for that,' he said. 'The DPP might still want to prosecute.' 'But they can't make me testify, can they?' I said. 'I don't know,' he admitted. 'They can't *force* me to do something I don't want to do,' I said. (Not this time. Not now.) Bryan stormed upstairs then, yelling, 'I refuse to participate in this fucking charade.' Neither of my parents said anything, or went after him. They had stayed right by my side for the whole conversation.

'Emma?' Joe said after a long pause. 'Are you still there? Are you sure this is what you want?' I pressed the pencil into the paper so hard the lead broke off. 'Yes,' I said, 'I'm sure.' And my father reached out then, and he touched my shoulder. I closed my eyes, feeling dizzy.

My father is sitting at the dining table. There's a plate of scones in front of him, a carton of orange juice, and a big teapot covered in a striped tea cosy next to them.

'Take a seat,' my mother says to me. She pours me a glass of juice, handing me my tablets. I roll them between my fingers.

'Denis?'

'Yes?'

My mother jerks her head at me. 'Aren't you going to say good morning to Emma?'

He clears his throat. 'Morning.' He reaches out and takes another scone, spooning out a large dollop of strawberry jam on top of it. 'Have a scone. Your mother made them fresh this morning.'

'For us?'

'To celebrate,' my mother says, and he frowns at her.

'It's too early to celebrate, Nora. We still have to wait to hear back from the DPP.' I concentrate on my breathing. In. *One. Two. Three.* Out. *One. Two. Three.*

'But you're doing the right thing, you know that,

don't you?' my father says. 'We're proud of you, Emma.' He holds out the plate of scones to me and I take one.

I wait until he turns away before I swallow my tablet. 'Where's Bryan?'

My mother fumbles with the cap of the orange juice and it falls to the floor. She crawls under the table to retrieve it, letting out a small cry when she hits her head as she goes to stand up.

'He's gone back to Limerick,' my father answers when she's sitting upright again. 'We're paying good money for him to go to college and he already missed enough lectures yesterday. It's time for him to grow up.' He pushes his chair back, takes his suit jacket from the back and puts it on. 'Thanks for that, Nora. They were delicious.' He leans over to kiss her on the cheek. And as he leaves he grazes his hand against my neck, so lightly I could have imagined it.

'What do you think of them?' my mother asks me.

'What?'

'The scones. What do you think? I went back to an old Darina recipe.' She leans back in her chair, reaching a hand behind her and grabbing a few of her old cookbooks from the island counter. 'Speaking of which,' she says, thumbing through the well-worn pages covered in sugar granules and flour, and stained with egg yolk, 'I found this stuck behind the cover.' She hands me an envelope. 'It's addressed to you.'

She looks down at the envelope and back at me, nodding her head as if to give me permission to open it. She looks happy. That is what I wanted.

'I think I'm going to go upstairs,' I say.

'But you haven't finished your—'

'I'm not hungry.'

The smile on her face fades away. (I am glad.)

You were supposed to protect me, I want to say to her. You were supposed to be on my side.

I want them both to acknowledge what I've done. I want them to tell me that I did the right thing, to tell me that they're grateful, and that they'll spend the rest of their lives making it up to me. Do you believe me? (Believe what? I can't remember.) Did you ever believe that this wasn't my fault?

I don't ask them that. I will never ask.

Bryan has left my laptop on my chair, the lead wrapped around it to keep it shut. I place it on the vanity table, and sit down, turning the grubby envelope over in my hands, recognizing my own handwriting on the front beneath a dusting of flour. There's a warning on the back in capital letters – DO NOT OPEN UNTIL 30TH BIRTHDAY –

but I ignore it and slide my finger underneath the flap to open it, wincing as I give myself a paper cut. It's an A4 page, folded in on itself about twenty times. I smooth it out, trying to iron away the creases, and as soon as I see it, I remember what it is.

'It will be a time capsule of sorts,' Ms McCarthy had told us as she wrote 'Where Do I See Myself at Thirty?' on the whiteboard. 'I did it when I was in Transition Year myself, and I can't wait to open my letter when I turn thirty.' She added hastily that it wasn't for years yet, and I saw Jamie elbow Ali, making a face at Ms McCarthy's constant need to remind us of how 'young' she is, *It's not that long since I was sitting in your seats, you know.* Ali's shoulders started to shake. 'What's so funny?' Ms McCarthy demanded, as J let out a guffaw of laughter, Ali breaking next, then Maggie and me, infecting one another with our giddiness. 'Nothing,' we spluttered, in gasping breaths, 'Sorry, miss, sorry,' another round of giggles tearing through my chest as she rolled her eyes to heaven and told us to cop ourselves on. We had finally calmed down when Jamie started again, a laugh scraping through her nose in a snort, which made Ali laugh out loud, and I had to bend over to pretend I was getting something out of my bag to hide my face. After a few minutes I sat up straight, turning away from the other girls and stared out the window to control myself before she could send us to Mr Griffin's office. 'Where do you see yourself at thirty?' Ms McCarthy asked again, and as the sound of pens scratching against paper filled the room, I just knew that it couldn't get any better than this.

I look at the letter. The words are smudged, the ink running in parts. *Married to a multi-millionaire, two kids — a boy called Harry and a girl called Hazel, a nanny to take care of them, a personal chef, a mansion, a cleaner every day*, and then down at the very end I've scrawled, as an afterthought. *And I intend to be really happy.*

My fingers spasm, as if they're too weak to hold the page any longer, and it drifts to the floor. I stare at it. It's just words. Just words on a page.

I unwind the lead from around my laptop and open it, logging on to Facebook. I scroll down, photos of suntanned legs against a bone-white beach, Ladurée macarons, half-eaten pizza from Domino's, status updates with multiple emojis and exclamation marks, everyone smiling, smiling, smiling. Everyone is so happy.

I intend to be really happy.

Sarah Swallows has uploaded seventy photos into a new album called 'Graduation Ceremony'. I click through them, at the girls in their uniforms, hugging teachers, teary-eyed, one of Mr Griffin giving a speech in the hall. (I should be there.) Another photo, of Sarah with her jumper off, her shirt covered in scrawled signatures of every girl in our year (except for mine), then one of Sarah and Julie in Reilly's pub, bleary-looking, thick black eyeliner smudged around their eyes. Now they're back at Dylan Walsh's *epic party, woohooo*, and there's another photo of all of them, Sean and Eli and Maggie and Ali and Jamie and Jack and three or four other lads, holding plastic shot glasses up in salute at the camera. Maggie and Eli are holding hands. They must be back together.

(I wish I was there.)

I click on the inbox. It is full again, with countless messages telling me how disgusting I am, that I'm a liar, that I'm making everything up. *Slut, liar, skank, bitch, whore.* Maybe I am. I can't remember it anyway.

Ah, yeah baby. You like that, don't you? That's a good girl. That's a good girl.

I can't remember, I said.

I open one email. There's a photo of a pillow, and a link to a Wikipedia page. **Asphyxia** or **asphyxiation** (from Greek α- 'without' and σφύξις sphyxis, 'heartbeat') is a condition of severely deficient supply of oxygen to the body that arises from abnormal breathing. An example of asphyxia is choking. Asphyxia causes generalized hypoxia, which primarily affects the tissues and organs. There are

335

many circumstances that can induce asphyxia, all of which are characterized by an inability of an individual to acquire sufficient oxygen through breathing for an extended period of time. These circumstances can include but are not limited to: the constriction or obstruction of airways, such as from <u>asthma</u>, <u>laryngospasm</u>, or simple blockage from the presence of foreign materials; from being in environments where oxygen is not readily accessible: such as underwater, in a low oxygen atmosphere, or in a vacuum; environments where sufficiently oxygenated air is present, but cannot be adequately breathed because of air contamination such as excessive smoke. Asphyxia can cause coma or death.

Just some helpful advice, the email continues.

I delete it, and all the other emails too, until there's only one left.

Hi Emmie,

I miss you. I know I'm not supposed to say things like that. It's like I'm breaking some pact between us where I'm not allowed to ask you how you're feeling, or tell you how I'm feeling. But I miss you. So there.

I met Bryan this morning when he was leaving for college. He was pretty pissed off, Em. Don't be angry with him, but he told me what you've decided to do. I'm not going to tell you what to do and I'm really trying to understand your reasons for this decision even though every day when I see one of those fucking assholes, all I want to do is drive my fist through their face.

Sorry. I said this wasn't going to be about me. I don't want to make this about me. I just want you to be happy again, Emmie. I know you don't think that's possible at the moment, but it can be. I know it. Have I ever lied to you?

I wanted to tell you something. I don't know if this makes you feel uncomfortable, and I'm sorry if it does, but I've been thinking of that night I called over to your house after we had heard about what happened. And you tried to kiss me, and I wouldn't, and it wasn't because I didn't fancy you – let's face it, I think we both know where I stand on that one – but I just didn't want to take advantage of you. You were crying and everything was so crazy, and I didn't want to make things worse. But I wanted to Emmie. Fuck it, I'm sorry, I'm probably saying all the wrong things – but I need you to know that. I should have kissed you on the trampoline the night of the party. We were nearly going to, weren't we? Do you know what I'm talking about, or am I making a complete fool of myself again? I remember looking at you, and I just couldn't believe how fucking beautiful you were, how it

337

was possible for one person to be that perfect-looking, and
I should have just gone for it, but I didn't want to stop
looking at you. I wish I had kissed you that night. I wish
I had kissed you, and you had kissed me back, and we
had decided to stay at home and watch TV with Jen and
Bryan. You have no idea what I would give to have that
night back again, to change everything that happened. I
should have been there to protect you. I'm so sorry, Em.

    Conor. x

I delete that message too.

I should have kissed him that night, on the trampoline. I should have kissed him, and we should have stayed in while the others went to the party. We could have watched a movie with Bryan and Jen, groaning when they went to bed and Bryan told us not to do anything he wouldn't do. I should have taken my clothes off before him, and watched his face as he looked at me like I was the most beautiful girl in the world. I should have let him love me. We would have fallen in love. We would have decided to apply for college in the same city because we needed to be together, no matter what. We would have ended up getting married at twenty-two, ignoring everyone who said that we were too young, because we would have known the truth. We would have still been holding hands at eighty, telling people how we had grown up together, how we had been best friends, and how that friendship had blossomed into romance. 'He always had a thing for me,' I would tell my grandchildren, 'but I made him wait.' And Conor would wink and say, 'You were worth it.' I would have been happy.

I can never be with him now. I belong to those other boys, as surely as if they have stamped me with a cattle brand. They have seared their names into my heart.

I look at my reflection in the vanity mirror. How is it that two eyes, a nose and a mouth can be positioned in such varying ways that it makes one person beautiful, and another person not? What if my eyes had been a fraction closer together? Or if my nose had been flatter? My lips thinner, or my mouth too wide? How would my life have been different? Would that night have happened?

Candyman, I mouth at the mirror. *Candyman. Candyman.*

I close my eyes, waiting, hoping for a slash of a hook across my skin, scraping away my beauty. Making me new.

I blink, but it's only me. I don't know whether to be disappointed or relieved.

I make eye contact with the girl in the mirror. I stand up, pulling down the leggings, and take the hoodie off, watching that pale body standing there in just a bra and knickers.

I touch the girl's breasts.

Fuck, Emma O'Donovan's tits are tiny though. I thought they'd be way better than that.

I turn around.

Her ass looks good though.

'Emma?' My mother's voice floats up from downstairs. 'Emmie, where are you?'

'In my bedroom.'

'Come down, will you? I want to talk to you.'

I take a deep breath, then another one. In. *One. Two. Three.* Out. *One. Two. Three.*

I get dressed, covering that body up.

I stare at my reflection.

I look normal. I look like a good girl.

'Emmie?' my mother calls again.

'I'm coming,' I say. 'I'll be down now.'

And I walk downstairs, dragging my mouth into a smile so that I can look normal. It's important that I look normal now. It's important that I look like a good girl.

Afterword

In both *Only Ever Yours* and *Asking For It* I decided to end the stories in rather bleak, ambiguous ways. I didn't do this to be sensational or to emotionally manipulate the reader. I did it because I wanted to have an ending that was true to the narrative itself.

Some people who have read *Asking For It* found it frustrating that, ultimately, Emma capitulated. They wanted to see her fight, to demand justice for what had been done to her. I would have preferred to see that happen as well but, sadly, it just didn't feel truthful. Our society may not appear to support sexual violence, but you don't need to look very far past the surface to see how we trivialize rape and sexual assault. Sexual assault (from unwanted touching to rape) is so common that we almost see it as an inevitability for women. We teach our girls how not to get raped with a sense of doom, a sense that we are fighting a losing battle. When I was writing this novel, friend after friend came to me telling me of something that had happened to them. A hand up their skirt, a boy who wouldn't take no for an answer, a night where they were too drunk to give consent but they think it was taken from them anyway. We shared these stories with one another and it was as if we were discussing some essential part of being a woman, like period cramps or contraceptives. Every woman or girl who told me these stories had one thing in common: shame. 'I was drunk . . . I brought him back to my house . . . I fell asleep at that party . . . I froze and I didn't tell him to stop . . .'

My fault. My fault. My fault.

When I asked these women if they had reported what had happened to the police, only one out of twenty women said yes.

The others looked at me and said, 'No. How could I have proved it? Who would have believed me?'

And I didn't have any answer for that.

I don't want to live in that type of world any more. I see young girls playing in my local park and I feel so very afraid for them, for the culture that they're growing up in. They deserve to live in a world where sexual assault is rare, a world where it is taken seriously and the consequences for the perpetrators are swift and severe.

We need to talk about rape. We need to talk about consent. We need to talk about victim-blaming and slut-shaming and the double standards we place upon our young men and women.

We need to talk and talk and talk until the Emmas of this world feel supported and understood. Until they feel like they are believed.

Louise O'Neill

If you have been affected by the issues raised in this book, the following organizations can help. These websites provide information and can direct you to services available in your local area.

Republic of Ireland
Rape Crisis Centre
1800 77 8888
www.drcc.ie

United Kingdom
Rape and Sexual Abuse Support Centre
0808 802 9999
www.rasasc.org.uk

Australia
National Sexual Assault, Domestic and Family Violence Counselling Service for people living in Australia
1800 737 732
www.1800respect.org.au

Acknowledgements

My two main women – Niamh Mulvey, my superb editor, who makes me look a lot more talented than I actually am. I couldn't do this without you. Rachel Conway, my agent, who is endlessly patient and encouraging and always knows how to make me feel better.

Thank you to my mother, for showing me what unconditional love looks like, and to my father, the kindest man I have ever known.

Thank you to my friends and my family for being so supportive. You all know who you are and how much you mean to me.

Thank you to Lauren Woosey and to everyone at Quercus for their hard work on my behalf. I feel very lucky to be working with such inspiring, passionate people.

Thank you to Children's Books Ireland, to the reviewers and journalists who wrote about *Only Ever Yours*, the bloggers who shouted about it online, the booksellers who forced it into people's hands and the readers who emailed me to tell me how much they loved it. You are making my dreams come true.

Thank you to the Arts Council of Ireland for their generous support.

Thank you to Mary Crilly of the Rape Crisis Centre in Cork. The work you do is incredible.

Thank you to Helen-Claire O'Hanlon for reading the manuscript and giving me such incisive notes about the Irish legal system. Thanks also to Sharon Brooks and Eimear O'Regan for their advice on the law and the education system at the early stages of writing this book. Any mistakes are my own.

Thank you to Isabelle Mannix for being so gracious with me and my incessant texts asking about authentic slang used by Cork teenagers.

Finally, and most importantly, I want to thank the rape victims who shared their stories with me. I will never forget your courage and strength of character.